WHEN THE BRONX
BURNED

WHEN THE BRONX BURNED

a novel

John J. Finucane

WHEN THE BRONX BURNED

iUniverse books may be ordered through booksellers or by contacting:

iUniverse
1663 Liberty Drive
Bloomington, IN 47403
www.iuniverse.com
1-800-Authors (1-800-288-4677)

ISBN: 978-0-5954-2830-4 (sc)
ISBN: 978-0-5958-7169-8 (e)

Print information available on the last page.

iUniverse rev. date: 10/16/2019

To my ever so tolerant wife, Margaret; to firefighters everywhere, especially those fearless devils I have had the honor of working with in Engine 85 and Ladder 59 during those years when the Bronx burned; and to the memory of those precious brothers who are no longer with us.

Thank you John Kenny for your valuable assistance in making this novel a reality.

"No fire too tall. No fire too small. We will fight them all."
Fireman John Hickey, Engine 85, 1969

Chapter 1

Knowing he had but a few moments to make his search for trapped victims, Jackie Mulligan plunged into the burning apartment through the fire escape window. Crawling on all fours, he began feeling for victims. Mulligan hurried into the apartment's long hallway, engulfed in thick, hot smoke that wanted to snuff out his life. Just then the ceiling above him exploded with fire.

"Whoa!" he roared. He felt himself burning; like his cheeks were being pricked by a thousand needle heads. In a flash, he spun around and scurried back through the long hallway towards the room he just came through. The light from the fiery ceiling revealed two smoke-filled rooms where he thought there was one. *Which room did I come through?* Picking the right room could mean the difference between life and death. He needed to enter the room with the fire escape. Otherwise, he would have no escape. By now his lungs were ready to explode for the want of fresh air.

Why do I do these things, he asked himself. *One of these days I won't be so lucky.*

He made his choice. After crawling back into the room, he kicked the door shut as far as he could, hoping to slow the fire's advance into that room. He then snaked across the floor, again slashing at the smoke, feeling for victims. Then all he could hear was a loud, rolling thunder. A powerful water stream was being discharged up ahead.

"Oh shit! They're here," he yelled. *Better get out before they blast my ass out the window.* He was desperate for air.

Engine 85 had just begun its attack on the fire with the hose line and was moving in along the hallway, coming from the apartment entrance. Mulligan knew they would be moving fast and that with all the noise of the water stream pounding the walls and ceilings and ripping them apart, his shouts would be drowned out. He did not want to be caught in the path of the water stream. It could be deadly.

Time was running out. The pounding water stream was closing in on him. He rose to his knees and started punching at the wall, feeling for a window. He shoved a table and lamp out of his way, sending them crashing to the floor. *Air! Air! I got to get air.* He got to his feet and began puking. As he puked all over himself, he kept moving, probing. "Where's that fucking window?" he roared. By now the crashing of the water stream sounded like it was on top of him. He said a prayer. That's when his probing fists went through the open window. "Thank you, God," he shouted, then fell out onto the fire escape and began to gasp at the air. His first inhale passed through his wide-open mouth into his hoarse, soot-covered throat, sounding like the howl of a powerful wind storm roaring through the alleys and backyards of the many tenement buildings that lined the streets of the South Bronx. As he lay there, his chest heaving, sucking in that precious fresh air, his body began to rejuvenate, his strength returning. He could also feel his sore throat, and his overwhelming thirst for water. "Water!" he shouted. "I need water now!" He pulled himself up.

As he started down the stairs, a familiar thought ran through his mind: *One day I'll catch one of these bastards starting a fire. Hopefully on a roof. Off he will go, and I won't feel a damned bit guilty.* Jackie Mulligan looked like a madman as he rushed through the hallway with his sweat-drenched face all reddened and his eyes all bloodshot. He couldn't get his soggy, puke-covered turnout coat off fast enough.

"Out of the way," he shouted to his buddies moving about in the narrow hallway. "Water! Water! Cold water," he bellowed hoarsely, one hand holding his throat.

"Jackie, you okay? You look like shit," somebody yelled.

"Yeah! I'm fine."

Mulligan, a five-foot-eleven, 185-pounder, reached the entranceway and, in one giant leap, cleared the five steps at the front of the building. In mid-air he saw Luke White and Juan Martinez heading toward Engine 85, where cold water poured from an open nozzle attached to one of the engine's discharge valves. "Brothers, my ass," he shouted as he hit the sidewalk running. He didn't stop until he reached the flowing water before Luke and Juan did.

"You'll just have to wait … brothers," he barked, while gulping down great gulps of water. He then dipped his head under the water flow. "Beautiful! Simply beautiful," he continued, suddenly calm. The slow-flowing water poured over his head. Closing his eyes, he let the water run through his hair, over his face, and around his neck.

"Hurry up," his buddy Luke White complained good-naturedly, giving him a hipshot to move him out of the way. Luke was fairly new to the ghetto scene, having spent most of his seven years on the Department working in midtown Manhattan. A college graduate, he gave up a career as a CPA to join the FDNY, "just to be able to help people."

"Yeah, my man. Move your ass," said Juan Martinez, bumping him from the other side. Martinez was the first Puerto Rican from his neighborhood to become a firefighter.

"Patience, me boys. What's the big rush? There's plenty of water for everybody," said Mulligan.

"Sure! Then why'd you rush to beat us?" said Luke.

"Oh no, not me," Mulligan teased, stepping away from the water nozzle with a grin. "Not to change the subject," he continued, "but why do all our jobs got to be on the top floor?"

"Yeah!" said Luke, stepping up to the slow-pouring water. "Wouldn't it be nice if all the fires in the South Bronx were on the first floor?"

"That'd be cool, man," said Juan. "And if this job was, my leg wouldn't be hurting so bad."

"It's going to take time for it to heal," said Mulligan.

"Just be grateful you're alive," Luke added.

"Ain't that the truth," said Mulligan, shaking his head in disgust. He was looking up at the burned-out windows of the sixth-floor apartment where he had just risked his life fighting another suspicious fire.

"Yeah, Juan," he continued with conviction. "What happened to you should never have happened!"

"What's that mean?" asked Luke.

"That building where he broke his leg has been vacant since 1970. Here it is 1972 and the brothers are still getting hurt in it. Too many guys. Look at us. Him with his leg. You took a bad feed. I got burned. Don't you think the damned City would take it down? Before one of us gets killed?"

"What do you think, they're going to waste money on us?" asked Juan. "Not likely," he answered himself.

"You know why we have to go through all this shit? Because the Mayor doesn't possess the balls to confront the arson problem," said Mulligan, shaking his head with disgust.

*   *   *   *

Several blocks away on Charlotte Street, a slender young man of medium height, Jose Nieves, hurried along with a junkie named Pepe, each carrying two containers of gasoline concealed in green shopping bags.

Man, I can hear myself walking, it's so quiet, thought Jose. Then, off in the distance, he heard a siren. "Hey, man. Sounds like the muddafucking firemen are coming here already," he muttered to the unresponsive junkie.

Jose, who sported a fake mustache and goatee, was neatly dressed in red pants and a black shirt, and sneakers of course; his well-groomed black hair had a shine to it. In contrast, the junkie was a greasy-haired, dirty-faced derelict dressed in soiled clothes that smelled of gasoline.

They stopped in front of one of the tenements that lined the street, six stories high, with the number 4401 in peeling gold lettering on its transom, the 01 barely visible.

With deliberate calm, Jose looked up and down the block, checking the sidewalks, windows, alley and cellar entryways, doorways, cars; at the same time he was listening hard for people sounds. Nothing. It was safe for him to do his deadly deed. And besides, he thought, nobody would dare call the cops. *Not on me.*

Arching his neck, he scanned the building façade. He saw lights on the fifth floor. "Let's go," he whispered.

*   *   *   *

"Watch out below!" a voice shouted from a badly charred top-floor window, where a fireman appeared, then disappeared. Then a smoldering mattress was shoved out onto the sill, spewing many small sparks down to the street.

"You guys ever get the feeling that the job doesn't give a shit about us up here?" asked Jackie Mulligan. He and the others cleared the area beneath the window from which the mattress was going to be dropped.

"Okay! Let her go," Mulligan shouted up. He watched the burning mattress fall.

"Definitely," said Juan. "When I was laid up in the hospital with my leg, nobody from headquarters visited me. There I was thinking I was some kind of a hero. I mean, like putting my life on the line so often. You dig? Saving lives.

Nobody even called to see how I was doing. They sure know how to make you feel like shit."

"Thank God the non-combatants don't work up here with us," said Mulligan.

✳   ✳   ✳   ✳

Jose Nieves stepped inside the building entrance, glancing quickly at the mailboxes, at apartment 2A with the names Gonzalez and Matos on it. Right above it he saw the building registration plate with the name Arcows Realty, a name that had become very familiar to him.

Without a sound, Jose and Pepe crept into the dirty, dimly-lit hallway, going straight to the stairway at the end.

These lousy thieves, man, thought Jose, noticing a thin electric wire hanging from the top of an apartment doorjamb, crudely connected to a light fixture in the public hallway. *Robbing the landlord.* He jumped up and yanked the wire, disconnecting it.

"Pay your bills, maricon," he muttered.

Looking under the stairwell, where it reeked of urine, he checked for junkies or winos, the likes of whom he despised; looking for anyone who could be a witness. Instead, he found several bags of garbage.

All was clear! They moved quickly up the stairs, two at a time, still in total silence, thanks to their rubber-soled sneakers.

Upon reaching the third floor, Jose, nodding to Pepe, pointed to a partially opened door leading to a vacant apartment. Pepe stepped inside, closing the door behind him.

Jose entered the adjacent apartment, also vacant, where he placed his bag on the floor and removed a smaller, gasoline-filled jar that he left beside the bag. He retrieved one of the containers of gasoline and walked to the last room, where he began pouring the contents on the floor, splashing it on the walls and anything else lying about. He then moved to the next room and did the same. When the can was empty he fetched the other one, using it to soak the remaining rooms.

Now I take care of the firemen, he thought maliciously. He went back for the jar that was wrapped in cloth.

He returned to one of the rooms off the hallway where there was a closet. In it he placed a chair, and on the seat he placed the gasoline-filled jar after soaking the cloth with the gasoline. He left the closet door partly open to assure the delayed burning of the jam jar. He knew that when the firefighters thought the fire was out and the room was safe, the fire still burning in the closet would shatter the jar. This would free the highly volatile fumes and cause the jar of gasoline to explode, sending a ball of fire throughout the room and out into the adjacent hallway where the firefighters would be operating.

With his deadly scheme completed, he tiptoed out onto the public landing, where Pepe joined him.

After signaling Pepe to leave, Jose wedged open the door to each apartment, using wooden chocks.

Crouched on the stairs just below the landing, with matches at the ready, Jose heard a man and woman whispering somewhere above him. Then he heard footsteps descending the stairs. *I wish that was a fireman*, he thought.

Without a second thought, he lit the match and threw it onto the landing, igniting the gasoline. There was a loud thud as flames exploded throughout the two apartments, shaking the building. Large fireballs blew out onto the landing, rushing up the stairs.

Jose recoiled, his arms covering his face, thinking, *Man, it's hot*. He ignored the wild-animal-like screams of the man caught upstairs who was hit by the rising super-heated gases of the fire.

On the face of the building, flames burst through the windows on the third floor, raining glass down onto the street. The rolling tongues of fire lit up the building's façade, making visible the columns of smoke spewing from each window that merged into one massive column, rising high into the night sky.

Stopping briefly on the second floor, Jose pounded several times on the door to apartment 2A, in which lived the object of his affection. Then he ran to the street level, where he met Pepe. They charged from the building, nearly colliding with a burly black man named Coburn who was running to the building, shouting warnings to fellow tenants.

"I saw you! I saw you," Coburn screamed, pointing at Jose. "You set this fire?"

"Take off," Jose ordered Pepe.

"What you doing, man? You can't stay here," replied Pepe. He started down the street.

"You say nothing, if you know what's good for you, man," Jose warned. He ran across the street into a vacant building, hiding in the shadows just inside the doorway, to watch the fire progress.

Another good job. Soon those big shit firemen come and break their asses. He smiled at the thought.

Windows opened and heads appeared as Coburn ran from the burning building shouting over and over, "Fire, fire! Get out! The house is on fire!" When he reached the corner fire alarm he transmitted the fire signal.

Hurrying back to the building, again shouting for the people to get out, he looked across the street for Jose. All he saw was the glow of a cigarette in the doorway. "Hey, you! You start this fire?" he hollered.

"Don't mess with me, mister," growled an intimidating voice from the dark, out of which a cigarette was flipped in Coburn's direction.

∗   ∗   ∗   ∗

"You damn people, you! Y'awl wrecked my apartment with your damn water," shouted an anonymous voice. "Why'd y'awl have to do that? The fire wasn't in my place. It was upstairs! Goddamn you," continued the angry voice.

"Shit! We get blamed for everything," said Mulligan, staring defiantly at the crowd. "Why don't you go after the guy that started the fire," he shouted back, "instead of blaming us for your misery? Hell, we put the fires out."

"Easy, Jackie. You're going to start a situation here," cautioned Luke.

"Who gives a damn? Sometimes I wonder why I work down here."

Mulligan constantly debated with himself about working in the ghetto, his old neighborhood where he had lived for many years. He liked the people, but at the same time he hated them. He resented how they treated the firefighters, who he felt gave their all. "They don't respect us. They don't appreciate us," he often said.

"Let it go. It's not worth the trouble," continued Luke.

"You're right. I don't need the aggravation," said Mulligan, who then shouted, "The sooner we get this hose back on the rig, the sooner I can get back and wash this funky body."

"I hope we're finished for the night," said the mild-mannered Luke.

"Lukie baby, you got your head up your ass again?" Mulligan laughed, shaking his head.

"What?" Luke said with a grin. "Now what'd I do?"

"You're forgetting that hump on Charlotte," said Mulligan.

"Oh heck! How'd I do that?" He slapped his forehead with the palm of his hand.

"Yeah! After we hear from him … then maybe," said Mulligan before turning his attention to the fire truck again. "Let's go, let's go!" Mulligan shouted. "Get that hose back on the—"

He was cut off by the voice of a dispatcher blasting from two tinny speakers mounted on Engine 85's back step. "Engine 85, Ladder 59," the speakers squealed. "Respond to …" Then, in what sounded like a disappointed tone, the dispatcher transmitted, "Disregard, 85 and 59."

"Like I said, get that hose back on. I wanna get to the showers," said Mulligan.

Again the dispatcher called. "Okay, Engine 85, Ladder 59. You're going in first due on a phone alarm for box 2–7–4–3. Charlotte and 1–7–0. We got an address of 4401 Charlotte. We got additional phone calls, reporting a building fire with people trapped."

"There goes my damn shower," said Mulligan.

"Sounds like a worker," said Luke

"You got to be right this time, Luke. It's simple math. What does a phone alarm, plus Charlotte and 1–7–0, plus the wee hours of the morning equal?" asked Mulligan.

"A working fire!" shouted Luke.

"Let's go kick ass," said Juan.

Mulligan looked over at Luke and said wryly, "Lukie baby … this just might be that hump now."

Reluctantly, he put his soaking turnout coat back on: *God, I hate this feeling.* At the same time he rallied the men, "Let's go! This is the big one." Like the other guys, he was getting himself worked up, ready for whatever awaited them.

"Let's go, Irish Tigers! Let's go kick the red devil's ass," shouted Luke.

"What you mean—Irish Tigers? How about me? I'm a Puerto Rican Tiger!"

"All right! And one Puerto Rican Tiger," shouted Luke.

There was excitement in the air as the Tigers piled into the fire trucks.

Engine 85 led the way, its siren and air horn blaring, with Ladder 59 close behind.

Chapter 2

All eyes were fixed straight ahead looking for signs of fire as Engine 85 and Ladder 59 sped north on Boston Road, encountering little traffic. It was almost 2:00 AM.

When they arrived on Charlotte Street, they saw fast-rolling flames and thick, swirling smoke lapping from at least six windows across the front of the building. The sight was enough to start the adrenaline pumping in every one of the firefighters.

Just below the raging fire, shouting tenants were spilling out of the building onto the street that just a few minutes ago had been desolate.

When Engine 85's chauffeur, Frank Healy, saw the situation, he instinctively yelled in his high-pitched voice to alert the men, "Looks like a good one," which the men already knew.

But they faced a more pressing concern: Engine 82 was speeding into the street from the other end of the block, with the intention of *stealing their fire*.

Lt. Rudy Bilcot of Engine 85, who was sitting in the cab next to the chauffeur, keeping a mean eye on Engine 82, studied the worsening fire situation. Not only were many windows on the third floor showing fire, but twice as many windows on the fourth and fifth floors were pushing smoke.

He knew it was going to be bad up there, having seen many fire deaths, most of them attributable to smoke inhalation.

"Hey, Lieu! Don't let them take our fire," shouted Luke.

"No way in hell," Bilcot reassured him in a stern voice. "You heard him, Frank! Faster!"

Ladder 59 pulled into Charlotte right behind Engine 85. Mulligan was hanging out the side window of the firefighter's compartment. "Don't let Eighty-Two take it, Lieu," Mulligan shouted to Bilcot through his Handie-Talkie while sizing up the fire situation. "This is Engine 85's job."

Look at these poor souls. Mulligan watched the fleeing tenants. Some were half dressed, some were in pajamas; some carried children, others carried their belongings in their arms, in boxes, in suitcases, or in bags of all shapes and sizes.

"How many times have we seen these unfortunates put out on the street?" he said. "If I were one of them, I'd kill the bastards who torch these places."

Where'll they sleep tonight, he wondered. *Probably in some roach-infested motel where they'll be placed by the Red Cross.* He shook his head. *Better them than me.*

Lt. Bilcot's eyes were glued to Engine 82 as he called the dispatcher, "Engine 85 to the Bronx."

"Bronx to Engine 85, K."

Bilcot was too busy to respond. "Take that hydrant!" he shouted to Frank. "Don't let them get it."

Luke yelled, "Move it, Frank! Move it!"

"Easy, girls. Frank's got everything under control."

Lt. Bilcot finally responded to the dispatcher, "Engine 85 to the Bronx. Transmit a ten seventy-five for box 2–7–4–3."

Engine 82 accelerated. Frank saw Lt. Lou Andras staring at him through Engine 82's windshield, shaking his head and smiling, with the devil in his eyes.

Frank raced toward the hydrant that was located in front of the burning building, blasting the air horn. People jumped clear. That did not slow Engine 82. Lt. Andras sounded his air horn without letting up, adding to the excitement. But Engine 85 reached the hydrant first.

A smiling Lt. Bilcot jumped from the rig. "Let's go, men. Let's put *our* fire out." Donning his air pack, he nodded toward Lt. Andras and his men, and in jest, shouted, "You can't trust these humps. They'd do anything to steal our fires."

"You don't like it when the shoe's on the other foot, hah Eighty-Five?" somebody from Engine 82 shouted.

Luke grabbed a length of hose and yanked it from the back of engine. *This is going to be a hot one, I just know it,* he thought, while looking up at the fire. Jimbo grabbed the next length of hose. The others followed suit.

People were still rushing from the building.

"Where the heck they all coming from?" Luke muttered.

"What do you expect? A lot of these apartments have two families living in them," somebody replied.

Several tenants helped the men of Engine 85 pull the hose toward the building entrance.

"When are you guys going to learn? You don't beat the big Eighty-Five," Mulligan shouted to Engine 82.

A voice shot back: "Blow it out of your ass, Mulligan," while pointing up at the building. "There's somebody at that fourth-floor window. By the fire escape."

Looking upward, Mulligan replied, "Ah, bullshit."

"Take my word for it, smart-ass."

Luke and Jimbo, dragging their lengths of hose, were on their way to the building when they were joined by Mulligan, Juan, Lt. Bannon, Copper, and Bull.

A hostile voice from a nearby group of young militant types shouted at them, "Kiss my black ass you white muddafuckers."

"Fuck you!" shouted Mulligan, turning toward the voice. "How about kissing my white ass!"

Oh shit! Now what do I do? Throw the first punch! Mulligan thought quickly, as a big black man in his early twenties started toward him, and then began show-boating, dancing around the street, jabbing at the air.

"Let's do it, muddafucker," he shouted, making sure everybody heard him.

Mulligan swallowed. *I can't let him make an ass out of me.* Then he faced him, ready to drop his tools.

"Keep moving, Jackie," ordered Lt. Bannon, just as Juan and Copper each grabbed one of his arms, forcing him toward the building.

"Come on, tough guy. We got a fire to fight," said Juan.

At the same time a stern voice from the crowd cut in: "Cool it, you fool. Leave them firemen alone. They're here to help us."

Whoever the voice belonged to, he must have been somebody important or a real tough dude, because Mulligan's adversary spoke not another word, just blended into the crowd.

"Guys, you saved him a terrible beating," chuckled Jackie.

"You shoudda knocked him on his ass. They're all no good. All they want is welfare. We pay high taxes so these bums don't have to work," said Bull, raising his voice.

"Is that right?" replied Juan.

"You don't agree with me, hah?"

But the sight and sound of a lamp shattering on the sidewalk in front of them brought the men back to their purpose.

Shit! There must be somebody up there. Mulligan stepped up his pace, while looking up at the fourth floor. *What the fug? There's people up there.* "Lieu," he shouted, "there's two people up there. There's one up top."

"Hey, mister firemen," Coburn snapped, glaring at Mulligan and Luke.

Who the hell's he yelling at? "Back up," Mulligan bellowed, waving Coburn off, at the same time releasing the fire escape drop ladder, sending it crashing down on its base platform, the half fire escape adjacent to the building entrance. Immediately, those people waiting to get down to the street began descending the ladder.

"Firemen, don't you ignore me!" Coburn snapped again. Then pointing to a vacant building across the street, he continued angrily, "The man that started this is in there."

"Listen, mister, we can't talk right now. We got people trapped up there. But if you meet us afterwards that would be great," said Luke.

"I'll be here," replied Coburn.

"Come on, come on, Luke! Get that goddamned line in here," Lt. Bilcot was heard shouting from within the building. Standing at the rear of the hallway by the base of the stairwell, he was looking up at the fire. "Come on! Come on! Move it! We got a hell of a job up there," he shouted.

"Frank, give us water right away! Right away!" Bilcot shouted into his Handie-Talkie.

Luke continued into the building, pulling the hose.

Several tenants rushed out onto the stoop, colliding with the firefighters. Behind them, wearing large-lensed dark glasses and acting as if she hadn't a care in the world, was an exceptional beauty: twenty-five-year-old Ester Gonzalez. She wore her dark brown hair in a high, tight ponytail.

"Get off the stoop," Mulligan kept shouting to keep the small stoop landing clear for the people descending the ladder. But the tenants paid him no heed. Then he roared, "Get the fuck off the stoop." That worked.

When Ester Gonzalez stepped out, she brushed firmly against Mulligan without apology, without even acknowledging him. She thought: *Who the hell does he think he is?* For a brief moment she stood there, cocky and proud, eyeing the crowd in the street.

Ignorant bitch! Mulligan glared at the back of her.

Standing in the darkness of the entrance to the vacant building across the street, Jose Nieves' eyes lit up with approval at the sight of Ester. *Beautiful Ester,* he thought. *When you going to be my girl?*

Ester stepped down on the sidewalk out of the way of the firemen, where she became an observer. "You know, Carmen," she said to her friend standing there, "that guy by the ladder? I know his voice. I think I know him, man." She positioned herself for a better look. Carmen Matos, another good-looking woman in her mid-twenties, shared an apartment with her.

Mulligan started up the fire escape, heading to the fourth-floor landing to enter and search the apartment right above the fire, where he would be operating alone. In the background he heard people shouting, "Don't jump! Don't jump!" Someone else shouted, "Wait for the fireman!" *What the hell is going on,* he wondered.

Removing her sunglasses, Ester looked hard at Mulligan. "Holy cow," she muttered. Her face turned pale. "Sonofabitch," she blurted out. She was unable to conceal her surprise.

The pleasure in Jose's eyes turned to a look of puzzlement when he saw Ester checking out Mulligan. *Why was she looking at that bombero?*

"What's wrong?" asked Carmen.

"Nothing," answered Ester, as she realized that the fireman was Jackie Mulligan. "Come on," Ester directed as she pulled at Carmen and hurried across the street, out of Mulligan's sight.

Move, move your ass, Mulligan urged himself on as he rushed up the fire escape. *Oh shit, this is crazy!* He passed blindly through thick, hot smoke on his way to the fourth floor.

Packy dashed recklessly up the aerial ladder, hardly able to see where he was going, shouting, "Wait for me! Wait for me," on his way to a top-floor windowsill.

Over Packy's shouts, Mulligan could hear people on the street yelling, "Wait for the fireman!" They were shouting encouragement to a man standing on the narrow sill outside the top-floor window, half hidden by the smoke.

"Be careful, Packy! Slow down," shouted Mulligan.

Suddenly Packy locked his leg under a rung of the ladder; at the same time he leaned precariously over the side of the ladder. There was hurt and anger in Packy's voice when he shouted, "I told you to wait for me." The man passed within inches of his outstretched arms.

Mulligan heard the dull, ugly thud of the man as he bounced off the outside of the fire escape railing close to where he was.

The people on the street below turned silent, with the exception of the screams of several women.

Ester looked away as the man plunged through the air. Once she heard the sickening thump of his body hitting the cement sidewalk, she refocused her attention on Mulligan, who was now almost buried in smoke. *What's he doing up there?*

Jose was pokerfaced, watching the man fall to his death. Not even the man's horrifying scream moved him. As a matter of fact, he was grateful. It was one less *maricon* for him to get out of the building.

On the fourth-floor fire escape, just about blinded by the smoke, Mulligan forced open the window with a twist of the axe head. He blessed himself, then slipped through the window head first, vanishing in the smoke, coughing and gagging as he crawled forward. With a tool in each hand he began his search.

Chapter   3

One after the other, they pulled their lengths of hose through the main hallway heading to the stairway.

"Frank! Where the hell's that water?" Lt. Bilcot again shouted into his Handie-Talkie, followed by, "Chief, we gonna need a second line up there."

Quickly, Engine 85 started up the stairs, joined by Lt. Bannon, Juan, and Copper from Ladder 59.

"I hope there's nobody up there," said Lt. Bannon, shaking his head.

The sight above was one of sheer horror. The smoke had already banked down to the third floor. Within the fast, twirling smoke whipped large tongues of red-orange fire, blowing violently from the apartments out onto the landing, making loud whooshing sounds.

Luke and Jimbo arrived at the half-landing a few feet below the fire where they paused for a couple of seconds, then continued a few more steps. The nearness of the inferno just above his head, magnified by the intense heat and the noises of the fire, sent a surge of fear through Luke's gut. "Wow," he said breathlessly. "And we have to go in there." He continued, "Jimbo! Make sure there's enough hose to get us upstairs."

"I'm way ahead of you. Got a length and a half hanging out the window, just in case," said Jimbo.

It was sheer frustration for Luke not to be able to do anything, while waiting for the water.

The smoke was now banking down below the landing and would continue to keep banking downwards, until Bull, the roofman, got to the roof, opened the bulkhead door, and broke out the skylight glass, allowing the smoke to begin venting from the building.

"What do you think, Luke? A good challenge for your Irish Tigers?" asked Jimbo.

"Absolutely! With a team like ours, heck, we'll make quick work of it. Right, Jimbo?"

"Right you are, Lukie baby."

"Copper! See if you can close the doors," Lt. Bannon shouted over the roar of the fire.

Copper dropped prone on the stairs, his head just below the top step, but not out of range of the super-heated gases that were torturing his face; that kept him from getting closer to the doors. He hooked each door with his six-foot hook, one then the other, pulling and yanking, but they moved only slightly, being blocked by fallen debris.

Luke knew from experience that this would be a tough fire fight, a torturous ten minutes that would seem like an eternity.

His stomach was a ball of nerves, the jitters firefighters experience just before commencing battle with the red devil inside a building in tight quarters. He also knew that once the fire fight began, the fear would diminish, just like a boxer once the fight begins.

That meant it was time for Luke to light up a cigarette, while he waited for the line to be charged with water: something he always did to help calm his nerves, even if only for a puff or two. On occasion he was seen moving in on a fire, in the thick of the smoke, with a cigarette between his lips. But usually the cigarette was quickly drowned by the water kicking back on him.

"This is going to be a tough one," he muttered.

"Aren't they all, Lukie baby?" replied Jimbo.

They had just gotten into position when they had to back down a step, then another. The unforgiving heat and smoke kept pushing down on them, forcing them back.

"Frank! The water! Where the hell is it?" Lt. Bilcot barked into his Handie-Talkie.

They heard Frank's high-pitched response through the Handie-Talkie, "The hydrant's broke. We're waiting on Engine 45."

"This thing ... where the hell—. Frank," shouted Jimbo, "start that fucking water!"

Luke knew the fire was raging inside the apartment, probably already burned through to the apartment above, where Mulligan was searching. And where he knew Lt. Bannon, Copper, and Juan would soon be.

"Luke, let somebody with a mask take the nozzle," said Jimbo.

"No way! I'm no quitter."

"Just teasing."

Darn it! Maybe he's right, thought Luke. *But then they'll call me a quitter if I do.* He was just a few feet away from what was now a wall of flame. *Besides, with a mask I'd feel all alone, and maybe get hung up on something*, he thought.

Luke just sat there with the nozzle on his lap, puffing on his cigarette. "Where's the damn water?" he snapped. "I wanna get on with this."

Then came the beautiful sounds they had longed to hear: the hissing of air rushing through the hose line as it was forced out of the partially open nozzle by the surging water; the thumping of the hose line that jerked and popped in different directions as the water gushed through it.

Jimbo shouted, "Water's coming."

"Let's go," shouted Luke. Crouched on the steps, he opened the discharge valve, releasing a powerful stream of water, slamming the door open. Once open, a ball of fire shot out onto the landing that was quickly driven back by the water.

He strained from the back pressure of the nozzle discharging such a large volume of water under great force. On his knees, he moved up onto the landing with Jimbo pressing hard against his back, hugging the hose for dear life. He kept the stream directed upward to his front, shooting into the apartment.

Then he began moving into the flat to take on the red devil.

"Go get 'em, Lukie," Copper shouted, as he and the others from Ladder 59 did a fast crawl past Engine 85 to get upstairs.

A thick cloud of scorching steam enveloped Luke. It was so hot, he wanted to scream, to scramble out of there, but wisely discharged the flow of water right over his head, bringing some relief.

"Where the hell is everybody?" he shouted, thinking maybe the others had to bail out on him.

"Right behind you, brother," shouted Jimbo, slapping his back. "You're doing good, Luke. Just keep it moving."

In a matter of seconds, Copper was on his way back down the stairs, shouting, "Out of the way! Out of the way!" He struggled with a body he was dragging down the stairs; the victim's feet thumping on each step.

Luke continued pushing forward, ever so slowly, working the water stream in an upward, circular motion, driving the fire back into the apartment. His face was stinging hot, but he kept moving forward, inches at a time, often without seeing where he was going. That's when he depended on Lt. Bilcot or Jimbo to guide him.

No sooner had Luke shut down the hose line for a split second, to move the line forward, than the hallway again lit up with heavy fire surging right at them. "Over your head! Over your head," Bilcot shouted.

Luke's response was instant. Opening the nozzle, he again put the water right over his head, just in time to stop the rolling flame, darkening down the fire in the hallway. The men disappeared in the smoke.

*   *   *   *

With his arms extended, a tool in each hand, Mulligan poked all around him, feeling for the soft touch of a body. He felt miserable; his eyes burned, he was blinded by the smoke and could not breathe. *What am I doing here?*

"Anybody here?" he shouted. He kept crawling forward.

He banged into what felt like a bed. Ran his right arm under the bed, then between the box spring and the mattress—knowing people sometimes hide there—then across the top of the mattress. Nothing!

A disturbing squeal that gave him a touch of the creeps came from just ahead, where there was a red fire glow concealed for the most part behind thick smoke. "Anybody here?" he again shouted. Still no response. The closer he got to the red flame, the larger the flame became and the more intense was the heat.

Mulligan continued his advance, crawling on the floor. He could hear the water stream below pounding on the ceiling beneath him. He could feel the vibrations; his face was close to the floor where the heat was more tolerable, where he could breathe a little better. Then finally he could see where the fire was coming from: a foyer area.

Oh shit! What's that? He saw lying on the floor what looked like the outline of a small, motionless body. He pushed ahead. *Got to get that child.*

Just then there were two loud booms right to his front. Bracing himself, Mulligan pressed his face against the floor while wrapping his arms protectively around his face. The ceilings in two rooms gave way, pushing a surge of flame and burning debris out into the foyer, right over the small body. *Save me, God.*

*   *   *   *

Luke reached the first room off of the hallway, which was also raging with fire. As hot as it was, and as much as it pained him, he did not let it deter him from moving ahead. In the midst of another fit of coughing and gagging, he shouted, "More line! More line!"

With ample hose under his arm, and gripping it firmly with both hands, he sat on his heels and braced his body against the wall just opposite the doorway. He opened the nozzle and flooded the room, putting out much of the fire in it.

"Keep it moving, Luke! Straight ahead," commanded Lt. Bilcot. "We got a lot of fire to put out."

Luke again directed the water ahead of him, along the hallway ceiling, where the fire was yet again intensifying and rushing toward them. He heard Jimbo and Lt. Bilcot shouting, "Get it up! Get it up!"

Chapter 4

Tenants searched the crowded street looking for loved ones, calling out their names. Others watched with excited eyes as the fire rolled up the face of the building. It looked as though fire and smoke were everywhere.

"Why you worry, Ester? You dig that guy or something?" asked Carmen.

"He's the guy I told you I thought was going to marry me. But instead he went into the army." She snapped her fingers. "Just like that, that sonofabitch ... I took a lotta shit from the people because of him. 'How come you go out with an Irish guy?' they asked me. Some of them were really pissed, man. I could have killed him, he hurt me bad."

She paused, and then turned to Carmen, a slight smile on her face. "When I saw him before, I got angry. Why? I don't know. It's so long ago. But I should be mad. Right, Carmen?"

*   *   *   *

Luckily for Mulligan, the burst of fire from the falling ceilings was short-lived and did not reach him. But the heat penetrated his firefighting gear and scared the hell out of him, and blistered his already singed face and ears.

Again he moved forward along the floor, stretching his right arm, like a plastic man. He could hold his breath no longer, gulping in large gasps of acrid smoke, causing him to retch; he had already vomited his dinner. *Got to get some air.* Again he heard the water stream pounding the ceiling just below him. *Why couldn't they be up here with me?*

Grabbing the child's arm, he drew it to him, at the same time crawling backward, away from the fire. Scooping up the child, he rose to his feet and keeping low, rushed blindly toward the window he came in. He fell onto the bed, rolled off it—the child still in his arms—landing on his feet almost in front of the window. Leaning out the window, he was hit with a blast of heat from the fire below. With the child in his arms, the exhausted firefighter pulled himself out onto the fire escape and rushed down the steps of fire escape to the safety of the second-floor landing. He couldn't get the clean air into his lungs fast enough.

*   *   *   *

"How's it feel, Ester?" asked Carmen.

"What you mean?"

"To see him, I mean."

"Honestly … I don't know." Ester shook her head, her eyes fixed on the window Mulligan had entered. "It's exciting to see him. And it scares me to see him go in there."

"You don't still like him—do you? Hah?"

"Carmen! Why you ask me that?" Ester smiled. "I never said I still like him."

"You can't fool me."

"But, it's good to see him … and besides, I like *bomberos*." Her smile faded. "I wish he'd come out of there. I told you before that I often thought about him."

"After what he did to you, how can you say this?" snapped Carmen.

"Yeah, you're right. What the hell am I thinking?" Ester said, sounding hard-nosed, motioning toward the window. "He should choke in the smoke. Let's get out of here. I don't wanna see any more of this crazy stuff." But in her heart she feared for him.

*   *   *   *

Luke had advanced but another few feet when he was again hit with a burst of scorching heat. "Stop! Stop!" he shouted, again dropping flat on the floor.

Flames whipped across the hall right in front of him, another burning room. Luke rolled his body against the wall alongside the door frame and took aim with the nozzle and let go with the water stream, knocking the fire down. The thunder and pounding of the water was deafening.

Jimbo shouted, "Doing good, Lukie baby! Doing good!"

Then somebody from behind shouted real loud, "Hey, Eighty-Five! Get in there and put that damn fire out. Or get the hell out of the way. If you're afraid of the fire, give me that damn nozzle."

"Fuck you! Nobody'll take the nozzle from me," Luke roared back.

"Luke, you cursed," said Jimbo. "I never heard you curse before."

"Who was that?" he snapped, deeply offended, thinking he was being called a chicken shit.

"Probably the Big Fella from Thirty-One. They're right behind us."

They could hear the Big Fella laughing. "Got you," he shouted.

"He's just messing with you," said Jimbo.

Again they moved ahead, disappearing in the smoke, only to reappear as silhouettes in the glow of the fire that erupted just ahead of them. Sucking in all that smoke was upsetting Luke's stomach. He knew it was only a matter of time before he'd be vomiting.

At the same time a muffled thud came from behind.

"I'm burning! I'm burning," a man screamed as Jimbo shouted, "Fire behind us! There's fire behind us!"

"Get down! Get down," screamed Lt. Bilcot, covering his face with his arms as the fire raced above him, giving off extreme heat.

Jimbo roared, "Get that water back here!"

Without a word and with great calm, Luke rose to his knees and bent the hose line that was like a steel rod, and passed it to Jimbo, who doused the ceiling above them—raining down on them a flood of hot water—and again knocked down the fire in that room.

Luke's quick thinking saved the day. Instead of several men being seriously burned, maybe even killed, only one man was burned, and he was in the path of the fiery explosion that lit up a room in which they had already put out the fire—Jose's booby trap.

"Who screamed like that?" asked Luke.

"Somebody said it was the Big Fella," said Jimbo.

"Keep it moving, Luke. Let's get this damn thing out," said Lt. Bilcot. "And I think it's time you take a break," to which Luke did not respond.

Just in time, Engine 82 arrived on the third floor with another hose line. The fire in the adjoining apartment was rolling unchecked out into the public landing, a real threat to Engine 85 and more so to the men who were operating above.

Chapter 5

Engine 85's fire fight was taking its toll on the men. Especially Luke. Hell, he was the nozzleman, right up front, catching the brunt of the relentless beating; the treacherous steam that wanted to peel the skin from his face; the smoke that tasted like shit and wanted to suffocate the life out of him. But they were undeterred. And Luke continued to push ahead toward the blaze, down the long hallway. And the heat continued to intensify.

Luke simply shook his head from side to side to escape the heat, as if it were going to make a difference. He grunted and groaned and yelled, "Ah, hell! Crap! Shit, piss … and corruption!" He knew if the fire didn't go out soon, he'd have to give up the nozzle. *I can't do that … I won't do that,* he thought doggedly.

But when Lt. Bilcot heard him retching again, he made the decision for him.

"That's enough, Luke. Get out," Bilcot shouted. "Give Jimbo the nozzle."

"That's okay, Lieu," he said, coughing out his words. "I'll finish it."

"That's an order," Bilcot barked. "Get down to the street!" Then Bilcot roared, "Right now!"

$$* \qquad * \qquad * \qquad *$$

Flames still lapped out of the windows on the third and fourth floors, continuing to light up the street.

On the street, Mulligan knelt next to the body of the young girl he had pulled from the fire, who was covered from head to toe with a blanket.

Watching Mulligan from a second-floor window in the building into which he ran, hidden in the dark shadow of the lightless room, was Jose, as stone-faced as ever. He immediately recognized Mulligan as the guy Ester was watching. His thoughts were not on the body of the lifeless child lying on the dirty pavement. Instead, he was consumed by the thought of Ester looking at Mulligan.

"Jackie! That's not your fault," said Juan, standing over Mulligan.

"I don't know. But to lose a kid. If only I got there," he paused, then shouted, "just a fucking minute sooner!"

"Cool it, my man," Juan stopped him. "Stop that second-guessing shit. Listen to me, my main man. You got there as fast as you could." Juan put his arm around Mulligan's back, softly shoving him forward. "Let's go. We got to see that old man about the arsonist."

They headed back to the building, but not without Mulligan looking back one more time. "Why don't they take her away?" he said in a soft voice.

"You look terrific," Juan barked jokingly at Luke, pretending he hadn't heard Mulligan.

Sweat and mucus streaked Luke's soot-blackened face. His eyes were blood-shot, no white to be seen. "Where's the guy who saw the arsonist?" he asked.

"Clear the way! Make room," a voice shouted from inside the hallway. Several men from Engine 82 were being assisted to the street to await an ambulance.

"Hey, Boyle," shouted Mulligan. "What happened?"

"A ceiling came down on us. Jimmy and Nick got some nasty burns. All over their faces, their necks. Some embers went down Nick's back. Drove him crazy. Jumping up and down, yelling and screaming, just about tore his clothes off. We had to put water down his back while he ripped off his gear."

"Who got burned in Thirty-One?"

"Big Guy. Bad burns too. On his face."

✳   ✳   ✳   ✳

From the stoop Luke scanned the faces of the people in the street. "There's our man." He pointed at Coburn. "By Eighty-Five's rig. Let's check him out."

Coburn was taken aback by the sight of them. "You guys don't look too good. What happened?"

Smiling, Mulligan responded, "Let's just say we've been to hell and back."

"Yes, I can see that. You look like hell." Wrinkling his nose, he added, "And smell like hell. You don't even look like the people I was talking to before."

Jose, still secreted at the second-story window, watched them as they eyed the building looking for him. He saw Coburn talking to the firefighters. *Why that maricon talking to the firemen?* he thought. *Maybe I better teach him a lesson.*

Mulligan introduced himself, shaking Coburn's hand. "These are my partners, Luke White and Juan Martinez."

"Gentlemen, I'm Harry Coburn and I am angry as hell at that bastard who started this fire. And why did you all have to use so much water? It flooded my apartment, and brought down just about all the ceilings. Everything is destroyed. And I mean everything: my bed, my furniture, carpets, our clothes, and every damned thing. Now I have to move to my daughter's house."

"Sorry about that, sir, but—"

Throwing up his hand, Coburn cut Luke off. "Oh, it's not your fault. It's just that we can't get fire insurance around here. Nobody will sell it to us."

"Have you seen that guy since?" asked Luke.

"No, sir. The bad man disappeared right away into that building." Coburn nodded toward the vacant building. "And I think he's still in there."

Unnoticed by the four of them, a meticulously dressed, boyish-looking thirty-year-old named Tito, from Jose's gang, walked up to within a foot of where they stood, all the while looking up at the fire. With his back to them, he listened attentively to their every word. In doing so, he heard Mulligan ask Coburn if he would identify the arsonist to the fire marshals, and he heard Coburn agree. He also heard Coburn tell them that he would probably live with his daughter until he found another apartment.

Lt. Bilcot joined them. "What are you up to, guys?" he asked.

"This gentleman saw two guys run from the building as it lit up," said Mulligan.

"Did you see them do it?" Bilcot asked Coburn.

"No, I did not. But I saw them running from the building just after the fire started. One of the bastards threatened me."

"Well, if you didn't see them do it, there's not much the fire marshals will do. Of course he threatened you. But I don't know if that will make a difference."

After Bilcot left, Mulligan pulled a stubby pencil from his shirt pocket. But he had nothing dry to write on. Coburn resolved that with a matchbook cover.

"What's your daughter's address and phone number?" asked Mulligan. "Should the fire marshals want to get back to you?"

"Now what does that mean?" asked the surprised Coburn.

It means they don't come to the South Bronx to investigate fires," said Mulligan. "Just why, we don't know."

"Why, that's terrible. Should I even bother giving you the information?" he asked.

"Please do. You never know what'll happen," said Mulligan.

He dictated her phone number and repeated it, then pointed to her house, a turn-of-the-century, three-story wood frame building. "Number 2416," he said.

A matchbox, Mulligan observed. *I wouldn't wanna be in there when it goes up.*

"Thanks, Mr. Coburn. If we're able to do anything, we'll be in touch. And please bear in mind; we don't have the power to arrest anybody, unless we saw the person start the fire. So you see, if we do the work of the fire marshals, we can get in trouble," said Mulligan.

"You know they'll come after you, even if they just suspect that you're helping us?" Luke warned.

"I know! But I would be willing to take that chance. Somebody has to, or we'll never put an end to these animals."

Chapter 6

"You know you got an admirer here," said Gina. The middle-aged, blond-haired waitress was taking payment from the ever-smiling, ever-cool Jackie Mulligan at the cashier's booth in Mugavin's Diner. Mulligan and his neighborhood friends often went to Mugavin's for breakfast after a night out on the town.

"Yeah. And she's a beautiful Irish girl straight from the other side. Am I right, Gina?"

"Yes, you are." She offered him his change, but he told her to keep it.

"Exactly the girl my mother would have wanted me to marry," he replied as he lit a cigarette. "Am I right?"

Mulligan's Irish-born mother never let up on him about Irish girls. "You should be going out with your own kind," she would say, without fail, whenever she saw him hanging out with Puerto Rican girls.

"Still smoking, hah? Don't you get enough of that stuff?" asked Gina.

"Nope." He blew smoke rings at her.

Gina shook her head. "She's a good girl, Jackie."

"Right you are, Gina. But …" Mulligan hesitated.

"But what?" she asked.

"Ah—you know. My love from the old block."

"Yeah. You left your heart on Caldwell Avenue. I know all about it. That girl's probably long gone. Most likely married. You got to get on with your life. Get married, raise a family."

"Well—as you say, if I get on with my life," smiling, he shook his head, nodding yes, "it might be her … or how about you?"

"Ah, get out of here," she laughed.

Looking confident, the twenty-seven-year-old left the diner. *Man, I feel like a million bucks.*

As he walked his cool strut across Tremont Avenue, he passed several stores where he did business, including Montel's Drug Store and Santore's Fruits and Vegetables. They were part of a one-story commercial building that included nine stores and took up the whole block between Davidson and Jerome Avenues, where the elevated train ran. The train he often took to Yankee Stadium to watch his second-favorite baseball team win and lose, or to go to the Paradise Movie Theatre on the Grand Concourse, just south of Fordham Road.

"Hello, Mr. Santore," said Mulligan with a wave.

Mr. Santore didn't smile. Shaking his head and speaking with an Italian accent, he asked, "When the hell you going to get out of that crazy place? You guys are stupid."

Jackie just smiled and kept walking. This was the west side of the Bronx, his new home turf, and he loved it. He dug the mix of people; much like Caldwell Avenue of the past.

As of 1972, this racially-mixed, working-class neighborhood was still fairly sound, never the scene of rioting, but lately there had been a noticeable increase in suspicious fires.

By the early 1960s, because of the civil rights movement, the area started a slow change along racial lines. But by 1970, people were flooding in from burned-out sections of the South Bronx.

Mulligan moved to the area in the fall of 1966, several months after completing his tour of duty with the 82nd Airborne Division. He hadn't much of a choice. Since he had lost his parents during his military service, he had no home of his own to go to when he got out. He had been living with his Uncle Jack and his family, until they moved out of Caldwell. That was Mulligan's cue to get his own place.

During Mulligan's youth there was a preponderance of neighborhood youth gangs. Belonging to a gang was important for one's ego and safety, and helpful when trying to attract the young ladies. It was all about being tough and cool. The Napoli Boys was his gang. Oddly enough, Juan, whom he did not know at the time, belonged to a close-by Puerto Rican gang called the Commandos.

If you weren't perceived as being cool and tough, you were prone to being picked on. That is, unless you were big or obviously bad.

Being part of a gang was also a sure way to get in trouble with the law. Older gang members sometimes took advantage of younger ones, telling them that to prove themselves they had to steal. On several occasions, as a gang member, Mulligan got in trouble for stealing.

Of the three close friends at the fire station—Mulligan, Luke, and Juan—Luke was the only one not to have a juvenile police record; nor was he ever a gang member. Where Luke lived at the time, in Queens, there were no gangs to speak of.

At thirteen, Mulligan was arrested for the theft of several cases of soda from a delivery truck at the direction of an older gang member. He was taken to the 42nd Precinct and booked. Lucky for him, the judge was a graduate of Cardinal Hayes High School, which Mulligan was attending. The judge dismissed the charges on Mulligan's promise that he would "stay in Hayes and graduate." Mulligan did graduate, for which he was forever grateful. Without that diploma he would not have been able to join the New York City Fire Department.

Juan had earned the GED equivalency diploma while in the military. But not Luke; he was special. He was a graduate of New York University, one of only three college grads in the firehouse.

This time, when he took the soda off the truck, his father did not beat the hell out of him with his belt. Instead, in a tear-jerking manner, he told Mulligan how much hurt his actions caused Jackie's mother and himself, a tactic that had a lasting effect. As an only child, Mulligan was very close to his father. In earlier years, every Sunday, the two of them would stroll to the East River, and he cherished the memories.

To Mulligan's credit, which his Irish immigrant father recognized, he was his own man after that incident. He learned to use the gang to his advantage, especially for making friends.

Unlike most of his friends, many of the cool-dude ways he adopted as a gang member he maintained, especially his swagger, which Ester always dug. He did get rid of his DA hair style, however, but that was thanks to the military.

When he reached Fred's Barber Shop, he tapped on the large plate-glass window and waved to him. Mulligan was very particular about his hair. Only Fred was allowed to cut it. He kept it short, and on the sides he kept it combed toward the back, not crew-cut short. He couldn't stand having long hair, especially when it got wet at fires, which was all the time.

Walking on, he stepped up to the small front window of the Log Cabin Pub. With a grin, he pressed his nose against the glass and looked in. A couple of smiling faces waved to him.

During the sixties he had served in the elite 82nd Airborne Division as an infantry paratrooper, and was proud of it. Although he'd longed to serve in Vietnam, his unit, which was rumored on several occasions to be shipping over, did not go until after he was discharged.

He considered himself a bit on the crazy side, and wanted everybody to know he was a paratrooper. That's why the first thing he did upon completing Jump School at Fort Bragg, North Carolina was to get a pair of Jump Wings tattooed on his right bicep.

As a firefighter too he was a risk taker, sometimes to the extreme, always striving to be one of the best.

Even as a kid he had taken risks. In his youth on Caldwell Avenue, he and his friends devised a dangerous and highly creative playground—the multi-leveled roof of the abandoned Eblings Brewery that fronted on St. Ann's Avenue. If they weren't doing crazy stunts up there, they were being chased by security guards working for companies renting space in the brewery.

The three-foot-high brick parapet wall around the roof was at least sixty feet above the loading docks below. Every time Mulligan and his friends ventured onto Eblings' roof, he ran along the twelve-inch-wide parapet, often causing great distress for the women on the street below, from where he heard many a shriek. He and his friends thought nothing of jumping from roof to roof—sometimes dropping as much as fifteen feet—when being pursued by security.

His parents knew nothing of his antics until one of his friends died from a head injury sustained while *playing* at Eblings.

One of his favorite aerial tricks on the rooftop was to swing from a support cable at the top of the thirty-five-foot-high cooling tower, then work his way down the cable hand-over-hand.

He never got as much as a scratch with all the shenanigans.

Mulligan was the kind of a guy who got along with just about everybody. People liked his *cool demeanor with a smile*. As his coworker Juan would say, "He's cool, man."

When he reached the corner of Tremont and Davidson Avenues, he made a military-style left turn and almost bumped into Clarky Jones, a black friend who also used to live on Caldwell.

When Mulligan and his parents lived on Caldwell Avenue, it was a thriving, mostly white, ethnic neighborhood with many immigrants, where just about everybody was employed at unskilled, low-paying jobs. Even some of the wives and mothers, including his own mom, worked in the evenings cleaning offices in midtown Manhattan.

But by the time Mulligan moved from there, the civil unrest that already dominated in Harlem and parts of Brooklyn was ready to erupt in the South Bronx. It was teeming with young minorities, many of whom were unemployed.

Just about all the white folks, with few exceptions, had moved out to the "better neighborhoods" in the north or east side of the Bronx or had fled to the '*burbs*.

The smiling Mulligan slapped five with Clarky. "What's happening, my man?" he asked.

"Nothing. That's what is happening," Clarky replied. "Why you so happy? You're always smiling."

"I'm happy, that's why. What you been up to?"

"Can't talk right now. You going to be in Dorney's later?" asked Clarky.

"Probably."

"See you there."

Mulligan continued on his way the short distance to where he lived by himself, on the third floor of a six-story tenement; a walk-up, of course. Being a firefighter, he couldn't afford to live in a building with an elevator.

Hanging out on the stoop were a group of his friends, all in their mid to late twenties, all casually dressed, ready for a good night.

"Hello, Smiley," said Lucita Morales, a friend who was sitting with her sister Maria and her sister's husband, Papi. Also on the stoop were Jimmy Mac and Irene Hogan. Jimmy Mac, an Irishman, recently emigrated from Belfast. Rumor had it that he was *on the run* for taking up the gun against British oppression in Ireland. Must have been true because he was often called the Freedom Fighter.

Mulligan was a bit of an entertainer. He strummed the guitar and loved to harmonize. As a youth he had sung in the parish choir, and as a teenager and while in the 82nd, he'd sung with rhythm and blues groups and with the 82nd's glee club. Luke White once said of Mulligan, "That guy transforms sourpusses into smiles."

"What's on the agenda for tonight?" Mulligan asked.

"*Nada mucho.* Probably go to Dorney's for a few *cervasas*. Papi wants to hear his favorite song, 'Black Velvet Band,'" said Lucita.

"Cool." Mulligan started singing the song. Right away Papi joined in harmony, singing in broken English. Lucita and Irene joined them in harmonizing.

They sounded good, prompting Jimmy Mac to say, "Dorney's it is."

"Come on, we'll all go for a cold one," said Mulligan.

"Let's go, man," said Lucita, slapping five with Mulligan.

Off they went, like a bunch of excited kids. When they neared the corner, by chance Mulligan caught a glance of Luke White sitting in his car, not moving, pretending he didn't see them.

Luke was always in a hurry to get home. His wife made sure of that. She did not tolerate him drinking and hanging out in the bars. And Luke knew exactly where they were heading.

"Hey, Lukie baby! Where you going?" shouted Mulligan.

Luke shook his head, like he was caught. "Going home to Mama, where else?" He stepped out of the car.

"Join us for a *cervasa fria,*" Lucita said.

"Can't … got to get home. You know how Mama is." He rushed toward one of the stores.

"Luke! At least say hello," snapped Mulligan.

"Oh, I'm sorry. Hi, everybody." He smiled, waving to them. Then he continued on his way. "Jackie, I'll see you tomorrow at the firehouse."

"Poor Luke," said Jimmy Mac with his northern Irish burr. "I think he be a bit melodramatic with the wee woman. I've never seen her giving out to him."

"She's too smart for that, man," said Mulligan.

As they entered the bar they again started singing "Black Velvet Band." Most patrons turned to listen, smiles breaking across their faces. But they were quickly drowned out by the jukebox when Xavier Cougat's "Mambo Number Five" started playing.

"Shit," shouted Mulligan, teasingly, "turn that shit off 'til we're finished."

The jukebox went dead.

"That's better," he continued.

They resumed singing the popular Irish tune and did a rhythm and blues dance routine, to the delight of the patrons.

Jerry D, the six-foot-five, 250-pound, Irish-born bartender and owner of Dorney's, poured their beers.

When the singing stopped, "Mambo Number Five" resumed. Lucita danced in place. "Let's dance, Jackie."

"Sure thing. I just love getting close to you," he said, grabbing hold of her.

"Oh, you making me excited," she teased.

The bar was a dingy place. Several antiquated light fixtures provided minimal lighting, which served well to hide the filthy, tobacco-stained ceiling tiles that hadn't been painted in years. Smoke hung overhead in the musty air, and the smell of stale beer was strong. But if you were drinking and smoking, you wouldn't give a damn.

Juan Martinez came from the other end of the bar and joined them. *"Hola, mi amigos,"* he said in his normal friendly but cocky tone, welcoming them. "Jackie, my main man Ritchie Molletti, the fire marshal, is with me." He nodded toward the end of the bar. "We should pick his brain. He's got to know something about this arson shit."

"Will he tell us what's happening? Whatever he knows, even if it goes against the City?"

"He's cool. He'll do just that. Besides, he loves telling everybody how great he is at arson investigation."

"Make sure he doesn't leave," said Mulligan.

"No sweat. My man's here for the duration. I'll feed him some booze … that'll get his mouth going. Couple of whiskeys should do it." He added in a gravelly voice, "You know what I mean, my man?"

"Drinks for my friends," Mulligan said to the bartender. Juan declined; he had a beer in his hand. "I won three big ones today, so I'm buying," Mulligan continued.

"And how did ye win, me boyo?" asked the bartender.

"What? Don't even ask, thank you," said Mulligan. "I'll join with you—" Mulligan abruptly ceased what he was saying when he heard another mambo from the jukebox. "Come on, Lucita. Let's dance." He took her by the hand. "Juan, I'll see you in a minute."

Juan, who had three sisters, and whose Puerto Rican-born parents were still alive and living on Bruckner Boulevard in the east side of the Bronx, was born and raised on Forest Avenue, just three blocks from where Mulligan was born. Yet they never knew each other until they met on the Fire Department.

Juan and his sisters attended Catholic elementary school. But unlike most other kids who attended Catholic elementary schools, they went to a public high school, which Juan quit at sixteen. It wasn't cool to go to school as a gang member.

Maria and Papi joined them on the floor. Mulligan danced the mambo as well as any Puerto Rican guy. He'd been dancing it and the merengue ever since he met Ester Gonzalez. She had been his teacher, and he knew he was good. He knew Latin dancing before he learned how to do the Fish, Grind, and Foxtrot.

When the music finished, they walked back to their spot at the bar. Fresh drinks were waiting for them, compliments of Juan.

Into the bar came Clarky and Luis, who were both friends of the group. They took seats next to the others, at the same time exchanging hellos.

"Lucita, you hear what's happening to the neighborhood?" asked Clarky, getting everybody's attention.

"No! What? Tell me," said Lucita. She *shished* everybody, putting her finger to her mouth.

"The neighborhood's getting bad, man. It's going downhill," said Clarky.

"Why? What happened?" asked Lucita.

"Another Irish family moved in up the block from me."

They all laughed.

"God bless the Irish," shouted Mulligan.

Right then Mulligan got the nod from Juan. It was time to pick Molletti's brain. "See you in a few, peoples," said Mulligan, walking off to join Juan and his friend at the end of the bar.

"Jackie Mulligan. Meet my main man, Ritchie Molletti. Me and Ritchie lived in the same building on Forest for many years."

"What's happening, Jackie Mulligan," said Molletti in a loud, raspy, slightly slurred voice, while pumping Mulligan's hand. "You a friend of Juan's, you a friend of mine," he said with a snort.

"And the same for me, man. Juan's number one," responded Mulligan, while wrapping his arm around Juan's shoulder. "He's my main man."

"Ritchie, Juan tells me you're with the marshals."

"Yeah, yeah! The best part of the job." Another snicker.

Mulligan smiled at Juan, happy that the whiskey was doing its job. *Don't think we'll have any trouble getting info out of him.*

"Where you work out of?" asked Mulligan.

"Manhattan," he said with a laugh. "Where the action is."

"You get many torch jobs down there?" asked Mulligan.

"We get enough! But nothing like where you guys work. At least from what Juan tells me. But to be perfectly honest, sometimes I think he's full of shit." He laughed aloud.

"What do you do all day?" asked Juan.

"Between arson investigation and checking out all the beautiful women in those minis, we keep busy," he said with a smirk.

"Why don't you go to the South Bronx? There's a hell of an arson problem there," Mulligan asked, swigging his beer.

Molletti was broad at the shoulders, a brick layer before entering the Fire Department, and a Marine before that. He also had a big gut.

Meanwhile the Irish tune "Wild Rover" played on the jukebox. Instantly Papi's high-pitched singing voice, with his Spanish accent, was heard singing along. Fortunately, he had a good voice.

On the television, coverage of a building fire in lower Manhattan was being reported. Somebody at the bar yelled, "Hey, Jackie! How come they never show the fires you guys catch?"

Molletti snapped his head in the direction of the voice and shouted, "You crazy, pal? They'd never let them cover that stuff. It'd scare the shit out of the public."

Another mambo played on the jukebox, like somebody was making sure the music selections were evenly divided between Irish and Latino.

"Dance with me, Jackie," said Lucita, stepping in front of him. She grabbed his hand and pulled him over by the jukebox. Mulligan and Lucita were not lovers, just good friends who enjoyed dancing together.

"Be jasus, you guys are going to lose me license yet," Jerry D complained in his Irish accent. "Sure, you know you can't be dancing here. I got no license for that. And you know that, don't you?"

"Please, Mr. Jerry! Let us finish just this one." Mulligan faked a sad face as he pleaded with him. Jerry D just shook his head, as he did a hundred times before. "Mulligan, you—you're a ball-breaker."

The dance ended. Mulligan shouted to the bartender, "I love you, Jerry D." He returned to Molletti and Juan.

"Ritchie, what'd you mean, 'They'd never let them cover that stuff'?"

Molletti looked Mulligan in the eye and smiled. "Don't you frontline guys know anything? Don't you know what's going on?"

"Nope. All we hear is shithouse rumors. We don't get the inside scoop like you, Ritchie. You're connected," said Mulligan.

Molletti smiled, shaking his head as though proud of himself. Out of Molletti's view, Juan smiled, knowing Molletti was ready to tell all.

"Well, let me set you guys straight, okay?" Looking them in the eye, making sure he had their attention, Molletti continued, "'Hands off' is the word. The fire marshals and police are not being pushed to investigate arson in the South Bronx."

Mulligan interjected, "That's obvious. I've never see your guys at any of our many suspicious fires. We just had a man offer to be witness for a suspicious fire where two people died. So far, your guys haven't even contacted him. What kind of bullshit is that?"

Juan added his two cents: "It seems the arson investigation ends with the chief filling out the fire report. He takes a mark that the fire was suspicious and that's the end of it. Why? Why don't they want you investigating these fires?"

"Because of the owners. They are very influential people. Political bigwigs and their supporters. And many are financial supporters of the Mayor. In return, City Hall looks the other way. And besides, the Mayor wants the area cleared for redevelopment. Or is it, revitalization?" He laughed. "These people hide behind the bullshit corporations that they set up for that purpose."

"Who are the bastards?" snapped Mulligan.

"I don't know. I never bothered to check."

"So what does that have to do with the fires?"

"Everything, Jackie! The owners hire local gangs to burn them out. Then they collect the fire insurance. Some of the buildings have several policies. And they're allowed to collect on them all. Then they abandon them. Walk away from them."

Mulligan ordered another round of drinks, then bummed a cigarette from Juan, who was lighting up.

Juan asked, "Don't any of them have a conscience? I mean—like people have been killed, you know."

"Well, like I said," Molletti continued, "they want the area cleared for redevelopment. And the destruction underway is doing just that. Gets the people out so they can knock the shit houses down. You know, the ends justify the means."

"Well, they're not knocking them down," said Mulligan.

"Of course not. They don't have no money," said Molletti.

"Yeah, they never have money when it comes to us. Even with all the brothers that got messed up in these damned vacant buildings. Like don't we count?" Mulligan snapped angrily.

"Your man over there asked the right question: 'How come they never show the fires you guys get?' It's a conspiracy, I tell you," said Molletti.

✳   ✳   ✳   ✳

Luke's wife was tough on his drinking with good reason: his father was a little too fond of alcohol for her liking. She didn't want him following in the old man's footsteps. Especially since he was just like him in so many ways. Like his dad, he was an amateur boxer, a college graduate, an accountant, and indeed he liked his beer. And he loved Irish music.

Luke looked up to his father. He'd been born in New York, where he was college educated on the GI Bill—he was a World War II veteran—and had a very good job at General Motors, as a certified public accountant. Luke was so proud of his father's military record; he'd been an Army Ranger during the war.

But, unlike his father, Luke wasn't content to be an accountant. He wanted action, the kind of action that helps people, and his preference was to be a fireman.

As a child, Luke lived with his parents in their own home, a fine one-family house in an affluent, crime-free Queens neighborhood.

Luke's father had pushed him through college, wanting him to be a CPA, and did everything in his power to stop him from becoming a fireman. "You'd never be able to raise a family and give them a good education on a fireman's salary," he warned Luke repeatedly.

But he couldn't change Luke's mind. By nature Luke was a caring person, a trait he had picked up from his mom, a nurse; hence, his decision to join the FDNY was a decision of the heart.

Chapter 7

May 1, 1972 was a beautiful spring evening: sixty-five degrees, humidity thirty percent; perfect weather for fighting a good building fire, as far as a firefighter was concerned.

It was about 6:30 PM when the big red fire truck with the number L 59 in large gold numbers painted on the front of the cab lumbered across 170th Street. The company was returning to the Tin House, as the firehouse was known, from a false alarm at Vyse and 174th. They proceeded down a hill to Southern Boulevard where the elevated train ran, also called "The El." The El's tracks were held up by unforgiving solid iron pillars that didn't budge when hit by a vehicle, regardless of its size. Countless cars had wrapped around these pillars, killing many a poor soul.

Under the elevated train, standing flush against one of the pillars as if trying hard not to be seen, was a man wearing a shirt and tie, with a suit jacket. It appeared to Mulligan that that was all he was wearing. He yelled, "Shit! On the right—check it out."

Everybody moved into position to get a look. The man didn't have anything on from the waist down: no trousers, no underwear, not even shoes and socks. With one hand he covered his tool kit; with the other he hid the crack of his ass.

Juan yelled, "Man, this guy literally got caught with his pants down."

There was a lot of laughter and random comments from the firefighters. Lt. Jim Bannon, yelling over the loud drone of the motor, made a point to the men: "It serves him right, the snake in the grass. Probably screwing around with somebody's wife and had to leave in a hurry. Let that be a lesson to any of you young perverts that might consider an affair with a married woman."

The men laughed, and at the same time they booed him out.

"Listen to the preacher," shouted Mulligan.

The evening was bright and alive. Even the ghetto looked good, at least parts of it, in the late day's sun. A lot of cheerful-looking people hung out: some sat on stoops or stood in front of the tenements. Others ambled along the sidewalk. Kids played in the street.

✳   ✳   ✳   ✳

For the fourth time, the frustrated, nine-year-old Chico Vasquez had missed hanging a pair of sneakers on a utility wire that crossed from one side of Charlotte Street to the other. He kicked and cursed the sneakers.

Watching him was Jose Nieves, a one-time friend of Chico's father, whom he had admired since his heroic death in Vietnam. The army said PFC Miguel Vasquez threw himself on a grenade, saving the lives of several comrades. For that he was awarded a Silver Star. Some said he should have received the Medal of Honor.

That admiration, and the fact that the kid never knew his father, were the reasons Jose had a soft spot in his heart for him, and he sometimes displayed fatherly affection.

"*Mira,* Mr. Jose! You put them up there for me? Please!" young Chico yelled to Jose, who stood on the stoop of a burned-out vacant tenement watching him. Chico's request brought a slight smile to Jose's ever-angry face.

"Okay, Chico! I do that for you, *mi amigo*," said Jose, truly delighted to be able to help the kid.

Chico handed Jose the sneakers that were tied together by the lace ends. The spread between the sneakers was about three feet. Holding one sneaker, Jose allowed the other one to hang free, and then began to gyrate them. When he had them spinning quite fast he let go, rocketing the sneakers toward the utility wire some thirty feet above, where they caught on his first try. This is where the sneakers would hang for God knows how long. Jose's face beamed like a child's, although just for a few seconds.

"Thanks, Jose. You're my friend too," said the happy Chico. Young Chico looked up to Jose, but with mixed emotions. Jose's bad temper scared him.

"Anytime, my friend. You see Ester?" Jose asked.

"No. I no see her."

When Jose heard the Mr. Softee truck entering the block, with its attention-getting musical sounds that he despised, he gave money to Chico. "Buy ice cream for yourself and your amigos. You tell them Jose paid. Okay?"

"What I do with the change?"

"Keep it, man."

"T'anks, Mr. Jose. You're my friend." Young Chico was pleased with himself, thinking he was a big man because Jose, who was considered a cool dude by the neighborhood kids, was his friend and trusted him.

"One more thing, Chico," he yelled after him. "Tell that *maricon* to shut off that stupid music or I kick his ass."

Chico's jaw dropped. "But why, Mr. Jose? He's a nice man."

Jose hesitated, then in a soft voice simply said, "Never mind."

Twenty-eight years old, Jose Nieves was generally better dressed than most people in the neighborhood. Having money seemed to be no problem for him, and his clothes were always freshly cleaned and pressed. At least that's how he appeared when he was seen around the streets.

He genuinely liked children, and would never purposely do anything to corrupt their morals. But of course, his ethics weren't too high. He had a vulgar mouth with children, but always enjoyed their company. And he bought them ice cream or pidagua—syrup-flavored crushed ice. Only when he was with the kids did he crack an occasional smile.

As the kids ordered their ice creams, Jose slipped away unnoticed, replacing his pleasant smile with his trademark look of defiance. He strode back to the vacant building and up the once grand slate steps, carefully bypassing the missing step. He stood on top of the stoop, leaning against the front entrance with his hands in his pockets and his feet crossed.

In 1950, Jose, then five years old, came to New York from Puerto Rico with his parents and two older sisters. One of his sisters was exceptionally good-looking, the other was exceptionally intelligent. Typical of immigrants, his parents had high hopes for good fortune. And like most immigrants, their good fortune was never achieved.

His parents, both uneducated, who had worked on farms and in sugarcane fields and who couldn't speak English, struggled with menial jobs to raise Jose and his sisters.

Jose was a loving son, a happy-go-lucky kid. As a youngster he had loved firemen and wanted to be one. Whenever the fire trucks came by he would be seen chasing them, calling to the firemen.

On his fifteenth birthday his father, in a drunken stupor, had set fire to a row of stores, causing extensive damage. He was identified at the scene of the fire by several firefighters to whom he had bragged that he'd started the fire. Subsequently, they testified at his trial, and their testimony sent him to prison for two years. This embittered Jose against firemen, and a hatred grew in him that equaled the intensity of his former admiration for them.

It wasn't long after his father got out of prison that Jose, then eighteen, left home. His father too was a bitter man. They could no longer tolerate each other.

Heading in Jose's direction was Pepe the derelict. The only consistency about his clothes was that they were always dirty. He wore green pants, a dirty white tee-shirt and red sneakers. He was unsteady on his feet, probably high.

Jose watched Pepe with contempt as he walked back down the steps to the street. Jose then shouted to Chico while beckoning him with his hand, *"Mira, Chico! Ven aqui …* come here. You guys too."

Chico and his friends hurried to Jose. "Yes. What you want?"

"Tell me you never shoot up," Jose said, staring coldly at the kids and scaring Chico.

"What you mean, Mr. Jose?"

"That you won't mess with drugs," Jose challenged him while motioning in Pepe's direction. "Or you'll wind up like him. A no-good, fucking bum."

"Yes, Mr. Jose! I won't take drugs." He tapped his chest while shaking his head, "No, not me."

With more hard looks, Jose pointed to the others, "And you guys too. Don't you ever mess with that shit. Now get out of here."

Jose made an about-face and climbed the stoop back to the entranceway, where he was joined by Pepe. *I got to get rid of this guy,* he thought.

They hardly acknowledged each other. Jose simply pointed inside the vestibule to a green shopping bag that sat behind the entrance door. Pepe picked it up and carried it into the building, where he disappeared.

Jose remained on the stoop watching what was happening on the street.

Oddly enough, Jose had a reputation for being tough on drug dealers operating in his neighborhood. All because of an incident that had occurred about a year earlier.

One evening while in Santana's Bodega chewing on *chicharum* and talking to the store owner, he observed through the store's plate-glass windows a known pusher pulling up across the street. Two youngsters joined him as he remained sitting in the car. Jose saw, clear as day, the guy handing the kids packets of what Jose knew to be heroin, in exchange for cash.

Jose demanded, "Give me your fucking bat," startling the bodega owner, who stared blankly at him.

"Wha … what you mean?" stammered the owner.

By that time Jose had leaned over the counter already and grabbed the hidden baseball bat. "There's a pusher out there messing with the kids, man," he shouted, dashing from the store. When he reached the car—it had started to move—he raised the bat and took a vicious swipe at the man, shouting, "Don't ever come around here again with your shit! Or I will kill you!" The kids took off running.

Lucky for the driver, he saw the bat coming and ducked. The bat hit the post between the driver's side front and rear window, denting it, the crashing sound echoing through the street. In a fast motion Jose swung again, shattering the rear window as the car took off, with the driver shouting, "You crazy muddafucker!"

Calmly, Jose returned to the bodega, handing the still startled owner his bat.

"What happened?" asked the bodega owner.

"Those two kids, man. He just gave them dope. I don't want them junkies messing with our kids."

As the story goes, no pushers were seen in the immediate area after that.

∗   ∗   ∗   ∗

One block away Ladder 59 moved slowly across 170th Street. The truck passed Miniford Place heading toward Charlotte Street. Mulligan sat in the fire-fighters' compartment, daydreaming, staring blankly at Santana's Bodega, when a face from the past appeared, stepping out of the cab of an H & M Plumbing van. "Stop the rig!" he shouted.

The truck came to a sudden stop. In a flash, Mulligan was out on the street, shouting, "Carlos! Carlos Hernandez!"

Carlos' face lit up when he saw Mulligan. In a loud, happy voice he shouted, "Son of a gun! Irish Jackie!"

They hurried toward each other, meeting in the middle of the street, where they shook hands and embraced.

"Unbelievable! When—when's the last time we saw each other?" asked Mulligan.

"You," Carlos pointed at him. "My main man's a fireman? I don't believe it."

"I ain't been called 'Irish Jackie' in years." He faked a left jab at Carlos that was deflected. Then Carlos countered with a left hook that stopped just short of its target: Mulligan's chin.

"Ah, it's good to see you, Carlos."

"And you too." They slapped five. "It's been a long time."

Their families had become good friends over the years. They'd lived as neighbors in adjacent apartments for more than twelve years. Mulligan and Carlos played together as children, hung out together as teenagers, and sometimes liked the same girls, which did cause a little friction. Ester Gonzalez had been one such girl.

"You still live in the old place?" asked Mulligan.

"No! That dump's all burned out," said Carlos.

"I guess I should've known that. How's Maria? You got kids?"

"She's good. Two boys. How about you? You married?" asked Carlos.

Mulligan shook his head no as he asked, "Where you living?"

"Still on Caldwell, man. Eight twenty-three."

"Tell me, you ever see Ester?" asked Mulligan.

"No … but why you asking about her?"

"Just curious," said Mulligan.

"Now you got me curious. You mind if I ask why you dumped her? That always bugged me. She dug you."

"Dumped her! Shit!" Mulligan replied. "She dumped me for that clown, Ricardo."

"Ah, my friend. That's why you went in the army? You ran away." He laughed. "Was it the right thing to do?"

"I don't know. After all these years, I still think about her. I couldn't accept it when she told me she wanted to go with her own kind. So, as you said, I ran away."

✳   ✳   ✳   ✳

Back on Charlotte, Jose, as cocky as ever, reemerged from the darkened hallway of the vacant building and stood at the top of the stoop. He dropped an empty green shopping bag behind the glass-less entrance door. Pepe was not with him.

"Chico, your amigos like the ice cream?"

"Yes! I told them you paid for it. They like you, Jose!"

"How about Ester? You see her? She come out of the house?" asked Jose.

"She went down the corner. With Carmen," said Chico.

Jose nodded his head. "If anybody's looking for me, I'll be around the corner. Okay?" He took off down the block, turning into 170th Street, where he passed right by Mulligan, who was helping Carlos unload a tub from his van.

"Man, what are you doing working around here anyway?" asked Carlos. "This place is crazy."

"Good question," said Mulligan as they lugged the tub to the sidewalk. "At times it seems like everybody down here hates us. How about you, Carlos? I hope that doesn't include you."

"Not at all," said Carlos. "Just like most of my people, I just wanna make money and raise my family. Give the kids a good education."

Being born and raised in the South Bronx, Mulligan still knew people who lived in the area. Some, like Carlos, had been good friends. Unfortunately, a few became hardcore anti-establishment. They shunned Mulligan and the other firemen.

"Who's burning the buildings?" asked Mulligan.

"The gangs or the junkies, depending if people live in them. The landlords pay them to do it so they can collect the insurance. The junkies burn the empty buildings for the junk to sell to the junk dealers."

"I just found out about that shit. Do you know who they are?"

"There's a gang that does it around here. Bad peoples, man," said Carlos. "The people know who they are."

"Gimme their names. We'll put them in jail where they belong."

"You crazy? They'd kill us, man. Nobody'll tell you," said Carlos.

Ladder 59's air horn sounded, followed by a shout from Packy. "Come on, Jackie! We got a phone alarm."

Again they embraced, bidding each other farewell, promising each other to meet again.

"One more thing," shouted Mulligan. "If you should see Ester, give her my best, okay?"

"Sure. And I'll tell her you love her," said Carlos, but Mulligan didn't hear him over the air horn.

*   *   *   *

Ladder 59's rig backed across 170th, then zipped into Miniford with its siren blaring.

Miniford Place was another block with its share of burned-out tenements, potholes and garbage. Right dead center on the east side of the street stood a turn-of-the-century Queen Anne that had all its siding and roofing burned away. All that remained was a skeleton-like frame of charred two-by-fours, two-by-eights, and two-by-tens.

Between the Queen Anne and a vacant six-story tenement stood a three-story, polished red brick, freshly pointed brownstone with a well-maintained little flower garden to the right of the front stoop, surrounded by a freshly painted five-foot-high, black wrought-iron fence, over which a small sign hung reading "PLEASE LET ME BE!"

On the street in front of the brownstone was a new automobile with its hood and trunk door gone. It was sitting on four milk crates, stripped of its wheels, radiator, and battery. The car had been set afire, but was not totally destroyed. It had probably been stolen by drug addicts, who sold the easily removed parts to a local junkyard. The owner of the junkyard most likely knew the parts were stolen, but didn't give a damn. The resultant cash gave these dope fiends enough to buy their next fix.

Before the day was out, the "neighborhood mechanics" would have the car completely stripped of all usable parts, which they used for their own financial gain.

It bugged some of the firefighters that the City classified all these new and almost new cars as abandoned derelict vehicles (ADVs), which gave the illusion, not necessarily the intention of the term ADV, that they were abandoned by their owners. Mulligan often joked: "What are we supposed to believe? That the owners simply drove their new cars to the ghetto and threw them away?"

Observing the increasing amount of destruction in this community he loved dearly, Mulligan shook his head, wondering if he was doing any good working there.

Chapter 8

It was two minutes to seven, just fifty-eight minutes after the night tour had begun, when the rig pulled up across from 609 Miniford Place. Mulligan didn't see any of the usual indications of fire. People weren't running from the building, nor was there any fire or smoke showing. No reason to be alarmed.

All he wanted to do was get back to the firehouse to finish a handball game with Frank Healy, whom he'd been beating soundly when the alarm came in. *I just love kicking that sore loser's fat ass.*

Mulligan had been a better than average athlete as a youngster, and he'd continued to keep himself in good physical condition, considering he liked a few beers and was a smoker. He was an avid handball player.

Right in front of the six-story tenement a group of musicians performed rather loudly, a common occurrence during the spring and summer months in this area. Mulligan knew one of the musicians, Cuba Pedro, from Caldwell Avenue. Cuba had taught Mulligan and his friends rhythm and blues harmony.

A sizeable crowd had gathered to listen, some of whom were dancing.

Jose was in the crowd with one of his associates, Tito, also a well-dressed individual for the neighborhood. Jose grabbed the hand of a young woman and started dancing. He even smiled, like he was enjoying himself. The atmosphere was festive.

So lively was the rhythm that Mulligan, a lover of Latin music, wanted to join them. Maybe dance, or even play the bongos. He'd heard Latin music all his life.

The fire companies were sent to this address because somebody called the Fire Department's Bronx dispatcher and reported an odor of smoke in the building, which often meant somebody had burned food on their kitchen stove. Nothing to be concerned about, especially for experienced firefighters like Mulligan. With just six years on the job, Mulligan had already fought hundreds of building fires.

Mulligan stepped off the fire truck, looking cool as usual, carrying in his left hand a heavy halligan tool and a six-foot hook. With his right hand he checked to make sure his Handie-Talkie was turned on and that the mike was working and properly secured to its webbing.

He was sure this alarm would be just another minor incident, or maybe a false alarm called in by telephone. But he'd still check the rear and sides of the building. That was his job, and besides, his boss, Lt. Jim Bannon, who was a top-notch firefighter, had an unnecessary habit of reminding the Outside Vent Man to check the rear of the building to see if an emergency existed. A less-experienced firefighter might not do this, and the consequences could be disastrous.

Lt. Bannon often reminded them of an experience he'd had when his Outside Vent Man didn't do the proper check, and how they were called back to the scene to find they had a major fire on their hands, at which a life was lost.

*   *   *   *

Ester and Carmen stood at the corner, just outside Santana's Bodega. They looked up the block at the fire trucks, watching the action. From the distance Ester thought she saw Mulligan stepping off the rig. *There he is again*, she told herself. *I'd know that walk anywhere. Look at him thinking he's hot shit.* She chuckled.

"What you laughing at?" asked Carmen.

"That's Mulligan up there. Thinking he's so cool."

"How you know that?"

"I went with him for two years. Don't you think I'd know him? That jackass." Ester watched Mulligan intently. *"Mira!* Now he's dancing the mambo. I taught him that too. Come on! I got to make sure it's him."

"Why you looking for trouble?" asked Carmen.

"I got to know."

*   *   *   *

Mulligan walked into the narrow alleyway, his eyes darting all around up and down checking windows. Right away his nose began quivering like a cat's. *Shit, that's burning paint I smell.*

He saw smoke pushing from around the doorjamb. *We got a job!*

With the back of his ungloved hand, Mulligan felt the door surface. It was hot. Cautiously, he started opening the door, but the bottom of the door hardly budged. *What the fug? That a dog?* He pushed hard on the door. *It must be a big one.*

Down on his knees he pushed steadily on the door, getting it to open ever so slightly. Just enough for him to see the inferno inside. The blaze started to push out of the door lapping over his head, forcing him to get down on his stomach. From that position he reached behind the door with his gloved hand, where he felt a body. It felt like a human. *Sheeeit! That's not a dog.* Because of the heat, it was a struggle for Mulligan to pull the smoldering corpse out through the doorway.

"Get a line down here," he yelled into his Handie-Talkie. "We got a job. And a roast."

At this point he heard the sound of glass shattering, another indication of a good job. Without hesitation he ran toward the rear yard, where he was greeted by fire and smoke blowing out of a basement window.

Over his Handie-Talkie he heard Lt. Bannon acknowledge him.

Shit! We got a good job here! Mulligan was sizing up the adjoining window through which he would enter the apartment to search for other possible victims. But when he reached the window, ready to force it open, he saw on the inside, engulfed in greenish-gray smoke, the striking face of a terrified, young girl.

"Oh fug!" he said aloud. The sight of the girl disturbed him.

She's going to dive right through the glass. Gotta stop her. He saw panic etched all over her face. She couldn't breathe. Her eyes were bulging.

"Wait! Wait!" he screamed. "Don't break the glass. I'll open it." But he knew his shouts would be in vain. She was suffocating and would pay him no heed.

Joining her two little fists together, she punched through the windowpane, knocking out some of the glass. Then she pushed her arms through the glass, spreading them as if doing a breast stroke, followed by her head and upper torso, ripping her arms and body against the unforgiving shards of glass that remained in the window.

Blood immediately splattered everywhere, including on Mulligan; her sleeveless white blouse turned crimson. He grabbed her to keep her from doing further damage to herself. *Oh God! This poor child!*

Out on the street, the self-confident Jose dazzled the crowd with his footwork, dancing the mambo. They cheered him on. While enjoying the accolades, he saw Ester approaching. Only she wasn't looking at him, she was moving toward the firefighters. Before she reached them, Jose intercepted her, pushing his dancing partner aside.

"Dance with me, beautiful Ester," he insisted, grabbing her hand, pulling her to him.

She yanked her arm back. "One dance only," she said rather abruptly. But when she danced, she took her dancing seriously. They both did and they danced superbly. They were the main attraction, but Ester the more so. And why not? Everything about her seemed to be special. She was as beautiful as she was self-confident.

While dancing she kept looking toward the firefighters, who suddenly dashed into the alleyway. *Now where they going?*

Jose watched her with great interest. He asked, "Why you looking at the firemen for? Those Irishers ... they're no good. Not for you. I'm for you. Why don't you be my girl, Ester?"

"No, no. You're not for me. Let's just finish dancing," she said.

"What you talking about? Who you like? One of them fucks? They're not one of us."

"I didn't say that," she snapped. She made an about face and walked away, toward the alley entrance. She didn't know it yet, but the man she wanted to check out was in the middle of a firefighter's nightmare.

Oh God! She's all torn to pieces. Mulligan couldn't take the time to call Lt. Bannon and advise him that others might be trapped inside. It was all happening so fast.

His first obligation was to prevent her from further disfiguring herself. He reached through the window with his left arm and stopped her forward movement. At the same time with his right hand and arm, he quickly and carefully cleared the remaining shards of glass from the windowpane.

"Stop! You're safe now. I got you," he reassured her with feigned calm, making sure he did not appear excited. The last thing he wanted to do was to terrorize her even more than she already was.

Her eyes were locked on his. She had put her complete trust in him.

What horrible wounds. He slowly lifted her trembling body out through the window, careful that she not do herself further harm. Some of the wounds were severe: long, deep gashes that pulled the flesh apart.

It was experiences like this that brought home to Mulligan why he continued working in the South Bronx. Why he tolerated the abuse from some of the residents and their lack of appreciation for them and their total disregard for their neighbors.

Thank you, God, for getting me here on time.

He had a hard time understanding why such horrible things happened to innocent children. Incidents like this always brought to mind for him what a senior firefighter once told him: "Tragedy doesn't discriminate."

"Mommy, Mommy! Where's my mommy?" the little girl continued to scream in her broken English as she clung tightly to Mulligan and he to her.

Mulligan encouraged her, saying, "We'll find your mommy. Don't you worry. We're going to take good care of you."

When she cried out in pain, "Oh, I'm so sore," in her child's voice, Mulligan cringed. It hurt him so to see her suffer.

"Let's go, young lady. We'll get you to the hospital. Real fast. And everything will be okay," he reassured her, trying to keep her calm, not wanting her to go into shock.

He rushed with her, heading to the street, hoping to find a waiting ambulance. She never took her eyes off his.

"What's your name?" he asked.

"Lucita … Lucita Lopez," she cried.

"What a nice name for such a beautiful girl. My name is Jackie Mulligan. You're going to be all right, Lucita."

"Mommy, Mommy. It hurts so much," she screamed.

If only the dumb shit that called us waited out front, I'd have got to her in time. That dumb ass.

He moved as fast as he could through the garbage-strewn alleyway.

Lt. Bannon, Luke, and Juan ran into the alley.

"There might be more people in there," Mulligan shouted to them.

"You, you need a hand, Jackie?" Bannon withdrew slightly at the sight of all the blood. "That poor kid."

"No! I can handle it. Just got to get her to the hospital real quick like. Take care of my tools, okay?"

"No prob. An ambulance just pulled up across the street. Make sure they take her."

Just let them try and not take her. At the moment he didn't care that maybe somebody else, perhaps in worse shape, needed the ambulance. No! His mind was made up. The ambulance will take little Lucita.

Again she screamed. "Ooh! It hurts so much. Where's my mommy?"

Again her cries cut right through him.

All he saw upon reaching the street was a white ambulance attendant and a black driver, loading someone into the ambulance. *Good! She won't have to wait.*

He rushed past Ester, who stood in front of the entrance to the alleyway, wearing her sunglasses, where others were beginning to gather. Mulligan did not notice anybody, nor did he pay attention to the fire trucks pulling up in front of the building, one of which almost hit him.

Ester saw his face, but was distracted by the sight of the girl. *Oh my God. Look at that poor little girl.*

Ester followed Mulligan to the ambulance to see what was going on, but trailed behind to stay out of sight.

The attendant put his hands up and shook his head when he saw him coming. "Sorry! We're not here for you guys. We already got somebody."

Mulligan, his face reddening, the girl resting in his arms, stepped up face-to-face with the attendant, forcing him to look at her. "Look at her! You're going to leave this kid here?" Mulligan shook his head and snapped, "Over my dead body."

By now people were gathering at the ambulance, listening to the developing argument.

"There's already somebody in there," the attendant yelled. "There's no room for her. Besides another ambulance is coming."

"Then put her on the bench," Mulligan shouted, still standing face-to-face with the man. He then threatened, "You're going to take her!"

Other people started voicing their support for Mulligan, which made the attendant nervous. One person asked, "Why you don't wanna take her? Because she Spanish?"

The ashen-faced ambulance assistant did not respond. He kept busy securing his charge in the ambulance.

Ester, too, was angry with the man, enough to voice her concern even if it meant being seen by Mulligan. With her head cocked, she shouted to the attendant in her cool, deliberate way, pointing her finger at him: "Hey mister! You better take her, man!"

Hearing her voice, Mulligan turned. *Oh fug! Ester. Is that Ester Gonzalez?*

While she stood proud and defiant as ever, staring down the attendant, Mulligan watched in amazement. *That's got to be her. Ready to rumble. If she'd only take off those damn shades.*

Indeed Mulligan remembered that stance, her ready-to-rumble pose. That was Ester Gonzalez to the tee. Oh, how he loved that look on her face.

When she was a kid she'd had many an argument, even a few fistfights with some "white kids" who'd called her a *spic* or *puta*.

When the name-calling started, she would become ultra erect. One could see her body stiffening. With her head held cocked, she would turn and face the culprits, then stare in such a way as to be challenging. Often she stared them down.

Then Jose got into the act, wanting to impress her. Looking real mean, he approached the man. With the cocky-looking Tito at his side, he calmly looked at the girl, who again screamed out in pain. His face showed no emotion.

Staring coldly into the man's eyes, Jose threatened, "Man, you going to take her to the hospital right now. If you don't, I'm going to put *you* in the hospital. You dig?"

"Don't you threaten me," the rattled attendant fired back.

"That's no threat, man. That's a promise." Jose glanced at Ester, hoping she was watching. She wasn't.

The attendant feared for his safety. Wisely he gave in, but would not deal with Jose. He turned to Mulligan, and speaking gruffly, said, "Okay! Okay! Who's going with her?"

"I'll go," Mulligan replied.

"Jose, you were supposed to make sure nobody was home. You gonna get us in big trouble, man," said Tito. Jose responded to Tito with a hard look.

"Lucita! Mi Lucita," a small-framed woman cried repeatedly in Spanish as she ran toward the ambulance, her hands flailing in the air, then crossing her breasts.

"Mommy, Mommy!" wailed Lucita. "Where were you?"

Meanwhile Mulligan stood there watching the girl, waving to her, as the attendant assisted her mother getting into the ambulance. "You'll be better the next time I see you," he shouted.

Lucita stared back at him: her eyes filled with tears, her body racked with pain. Yet she managed a smile for him. Mulligan was teary-eyed. The child continued looking at him while talking to her mother. Then the attendant closed the door and the ambulance pulled away.

"Mira, Carmen!" Ester was surprised. "There's a tear in his eye. After what he did to me, I didn't think he had feelings. Let's go before I scratch his eyes out." She chuckled.

"You got me confused. Was he bad or what?" said Carmen.

"Truthfully, he was okay. When I first met him, he was so bashful. Couldn't even look me in the eye, man … I'll tell you something about him real funny. You know how we went steady? He had his friend ask me to go steady with him."

"Well. He was shy. What's so special about that?" asked Carmen.

"Let me tell you the rest. For the first two weeks he never spoke to me. Never even approached me in the street," she laughed. "He would wave to me from across the street. So I went to him and asked him what was wrong. He turned all red, got all nervous. He couldn't even speak."

"So what did you do?" asked Carmen.

"I had to do the talking. So I told him I liked him and since we're going steady, we should hang out together. Go to the movies together. I told him, 'You're supposed to put your arm around me. We're supposed to hold hands.'"

"What did he do?" asked Carmen.

"He was fine after that. But it took another week before he kissed me. He wasn't a bad guy at all," she said.

Mulligan watched Ester walking away. He was certain it was her. He was anxious to talk to her, but there was a fire to be put out. Turning, he started back to the alleyway, only to be blocked by Jose. "Hey, mister! What happened to that girl?"

"Why're you blocking me?" snapped Mulligan.

"Answer my question, man," challenged Jose.

Mulligan shook his head. "She climbed through a broken windowpane to escape the fire. Now if you don't mind."

Jose moved aside and Mulligan headed back to the alleyway, once again assuming his cool dude stature, but not without one more glance toward Ester. As he disappeared into the yard, the music started up again. At the same time, two firefighters exited the alleyway carrying a body in a partially open body bag out of which one of the victim's feet protruded, wearing a red sneaker.

"Whoa! That's Pepe," cried the stunned Tito. "Jose! That's Pepe's sneakers, man. What the fuck happened to him?"

"I don't know, man. What can I tell you?" said Jose, shrugging his shoulders.

"What you mean? You were with him," said Tito.

"He got trapped inside," replied Jose.

"And you were out here dancing? How could you do that? He was one of us," continued Tito.

"Stoned, man. He was stoned. He was all the time stoned. I couldn't help him—that's all," said Jose. "I'll see you later." Jose took off back toward 170th on his way to Charlotte Street. Tito stood there watching him, shaking his head in disbelief.

For Mulligan, the experience with Lucita would stay with him for a long time. And although he cleaned most of the blood from his coat, the blotches of blood that remained would from time to time remind him of her. But he would never let his feelings be known to his comrades. As always, he would put forward his cool dude image.

When Mulligan got back to the yard he met the rest of his company. They were finished, on their way back to the street.

"Take up, men. We're relieved. Going back to quarters," said Lt. Bannon.

"Jackie, we found a gasoline can just inside the entrance," said Juan as he and the others got on the rig.

"That makes sense. That's where I found the body," said Mulligan, shaking his head. "I wonder, did the guy torch himself?" Mulligan continued.

"Or maybe he had a partner who accidentally, or intentionally, lit the place up with him inside," said Juan.

"Why was the door shut when I got there?" asked Mulligan. "Would you think somebody closed it on him? Wanted him dead?"

"I get the feeling he was the arsonist, or one of them. At least I hope he was," said Juan.

Chapter 9

From just inside an alleyway on the corner of 170th, Ester watched Mulligan's fire truck leaving the scene of the fire, moving slowly in her direction. *He's still a good-looking guy*, she thought. *But why did he leave me? Was it Ricardo? I wasn't serious about him.*

She wanted to get his attention, but didn't know how. At that moment, a water balloon burst right in front of the alleyway. *Oh yeah! That's it!*

"Hey, kid! Gimme one of them. Hurry!" she said.

The kid tossed her a water-filled balloon. *"Gracias,"* she said, excited, just like a kid.

"Uh-oh … you gonna do what I think you're gonna do?" the kid asked.

"Exactly," she said with a smile.

"The fireman's going to be mad at you."

✳   ✳   ✳   ✳

It was on Caldwell Avenue that Ester and Mulligan first met and fell in love, where they first ran into the preferences of their parents, who did not want them dating. Ester's father and Mulligan's mother did everything they could to keep them apart.

And they had more to worry about than just parental objection. Puerto Ricans, newcomers to the United States, were generally looked down upon. So when boys and girls mixed they were also ridiculed by their peers, causing many a fight for both of them.

Jackie had been fascinated with how well Ester could play ball. "She's just as good as any of us," he told his buddies who would try to put her down. He even asked her to be his stoop-ball partner. They remained partners year after year, even though his friends broke his chops. "Only sissies have girls for partners," they would argue.

Where the heck did she learn to play so well? Mulligan wondered, as did many of his friends. "From my father," she told him when he finally asked. "In Puerto Rico he always played baseball. And since I was the only kid in the family, he had to play ball with me."

✳   ✳   ✳   ✳

Ester knew exactly where Mulligan was sitting on the rig, where to throw the water balloon. And she cared less if it hit him in the face. She felt she owed him that much.

When the rig slowed at the corner to turn onto 170th, she stepped out from the alleyway, crouched between two cars, and threw the balloon, hitting Mulligan flush in the mouth.

When she saw the stunned look on his face, she instantly regretted what she had done.

"Stop! Stop the rig! Some shithead ..." Mulligan yelled, pushing the door open.

Ester took off running, feeling like a jackass.

From the rig Mulligan could only see the backside of the culprit, who looked like a girl. She ran toward a nearby vacant building.

He shouted to Packy, "I just got hit with a water balloon. I'll get the bastard."

Ester was first attracted to Mulligan because he always maintained a cool demeanor and was quick to smile. What she didn't like was the flirtatious ways he later acquired. To counter that, she fueled his jealousy. Every now and then she would bring up the issue of mixed relationships and her father's threats. "Should we go with our own kind?" she often asked him. She had a Puerto Rican suitor named Ricardo, whom she used for this purpose, maybe once too often. Ester had loved Mulligan dearly and had no intention of splitting on him.

When Mulligan jumped from the rig, he saw her bolt into the vacant building. He took chase, taking the stoop two steps at a time. Once inside the darkened hallway, there was no trace of her. "Hey! Where are you?" he shouted. "Come out here, you chicken shit!" he taunted as he approached an apartment doorway with its door ripped away.

As he stepped just inside the entryway, he shouted, "Where are you, you chicken shit?" His challenge was met with silence. He searched the dark room with his flashlight beam—its windows were boarded up—but found nobody. Moving through the next apartment, he again found nobody.

Soon after, Luke and Juan appeared in the hallway.

"What's up, Jackie?" hollered Luke when he saw Mulligan at the far end of the hallway. "You okay?"

"I'll handle this, if you don't mind. Be right out," he said confidently, maintaining his cool demeanor despite a huge watermark covering the front of his shirt. *Why did I say that? What if I'm walking into a drug den?*

"You sure, Jackie?" asked Juan.

Mulligan nodded yes. "Please, fellas."

"Forget it, man. Let the bitch go," urged Juan.

"Don't worry about it. I'm a bad dude, man. You know that," said Mulligan.

"Well, if you're not out in a couple of minutes, we're coming back." They shrugged their shoulders and left.

Still cautious, Mulligan walked to the next apartment. He took his time entering it, looking it over from the doorway. He saw no one, but heard the sound of breathing coming from another room. Stepping carefully, he proceeded to the room where he saw standing in the dark the image of a young woman.

"Hey you!" he barked. "Why'd you throw that at me?"

She responded slowly and deliberately, "You're lucky I didn't throw a brick at you … you sonofabitch, Jackie Mulligan."

For a brief moment Mulligan stood dumbfounded. His lips moved, but no words came forth. Then speaking haltingly, he asked, "Ester! Ester Gonzalez … is that you?"

She kept her back to him and did not answer. Slowly he approached her, gently placing his hand on her shoulder. "Ester?"

Then in a flash she was facing him, throwing a half-hearted slap, which he deflected. Grabbing both of her hands and forcing them behind her back, he pushed her against the wall.

"What the hell is that all about!" he snapped.

"Let go of me," she growled. She tried freeing her arms.

"I'll let you go. But don't try that again," he warned her. "Now tell me what's with the slap? Hell, I'm thrilled to see you and you're pissed off at seeing me. Why?"

"You did me wrong. That's why," she said, then sidestepped him and took off. *Why did I do that?* she wondered. *I should have talked to him.*

Mulligan started to run after her, but thought better of it. He just moseyed on out to the stoop where Luke and Juan were waiting for him.

"What's up?" asked Luke.

Mulligan's eyes followed Ester. "You see that sweet little thing?"

"Yeah, what about her?" asked Juan.

"She tried to slap my face," he said, while pretending to block a slap with his hand.

"What's this girl have against you? You know her?" asked Luke.

"Your guess is as good as mine." He said no more.

On the way back to quarters, the usually happy-go-lucky Mulligan wasn't so happy. He was the picture of dejection, staring out the window. All he thought about was Ester, the last person in the world he had expected to see. The woman he still loved. *Why's she pissed at me?*

After returning to quarters, the rest of the men stayed with the rig to check and clean the equipment they had used, but not Mulligan. Luke and Juan watched him as he went straight to the locker room.

"I got to find out what's bugging him," said Juan. He took off after him.

The gloomy-faced Mulligan stood facing his locker. Taped on the inside of the locker door was a picture of himself and Ester when they were teenagers. Next to the picture was an 82nd Airborne Division patch. And to the right of the patch was a photo of Mulligan, Luke and Juan, taken right after they fought a tough blaze.

"What's happening, my man?" said Juan cheerfully as he entered the locker room.

"Same old shit." He never took his eyes off the picture.

"That's all you got to say, same old shit? Come on, man, get off the pity pot. Cheer up!" Juan's liveliness irked Mulligan.

"What's the problem, my man?" asked Juan, now standing beside Mulligan.

"Listen to me, okay? Don't worry about me!"

"What do you mean, don't worry about you? That's no way to talk to your main man. Is it? And besides—who's the broad?"

"Just some broad," Mulligan snapped.

"Hold up, my man. Don't get your balls all in an uproar," said Juan in a soft voice.

As hard as he tried to look cool, Mulligan just couldn't hide the anger and upset he was feeling. "That broad in the vacant. She's the problem."

Juan saw the picture of the girl in Mulligan's locker, and asked, "You mind if I look at that picture?"

"Go 'head." Mulligan stepped aside.

"Who's that? She looks like the broad with the water balloon."

"That's her. And she told me the sight of me pisses her off." Then looking up at the ceiling with raised fists, he shouted, "Ester Gonzalez, will I ever forget you?" He shook his head. "She brought back so many horrible memories. I could see images of my folks lying in bed just before they got killed."

"Ooh! I didn't know. I'm sorry, Jackie. If you don't mind, what happened to them?"

"Another time, Juan. I have other things on my mind. Like that broad." Mulligan smiled faintly. "But I don't know where she lives."

"No problem, my man. I know where she lives," said Juan. He slapped his chest.

Mulligan's face beamed. "Where?" he asked.

"In the building where we had the jumper."

"How do you know that?" asked Mulligan.

"Don't you know I know everything?" Juan smiled. "Nah, all bullshitting aside, I saw her face. How could I forget it, man? A tough-looking broad like that. I saw her when we were going into the building that night. Funny thing, I thought she was looking at me."

Mulligan smiled. *I know where I'm going tomorrow.*

Chapter 10

At 2:30 AM the following morning, Engine 85 left the scene of another arson fire on Charlotte Street. The men were anxious to get back to the firehouse, hoping they were finished for the night. It had been a bad night with several building fires, starting with the fire at 609 Miniford Place, where young Lucita got cut up.

In the cab Frank the chauffeur rambled on about the fire while watching the road ahead. Lt. Bilcot, who Frank thought was listening, didn't hear a word he had said. It wasn't until Bilcot started snoring that Frank realized he was talking to himself.

"Lieu!" shouted Frank. "You see what I see?" As intended, he startled Lt. Bilcot.

"What? What's up?" asked Bilcot, straightening up in his seat.

"Straight ahead," said Frank.

"Ah shit. Now what do we got?" Bilcot focused in on the roadway ahead.

About fifty feet on, a man stood in the street slowly waving his hands over his head.

"Pull over. See what he wants," said Bilcot. At the same time, to alert the men, he tapped on the Plexiglas divider that separated the cab from the firefighters' compartment. Luke and the guys had already seen the man and were aware something was up. Frank stopped the rig.

"I hope it's not another fire. I've had it," Luke said to the others.

"What are you, a candy-ass?" joked Jimbo, who himself was yawning.

Bilcot shouted into the firefighters' compartment, "Luke! Jimbo! Check this guy out."

They stepped from the rig. "How can we help you, sir?" asked Luke.

In a cool, calm voice, the neatly-dressed young man responded, "You can't help me, mister." Looking at Luke while pointing back over his shoulder, he continued icily, "There's a body up there on the corner. Maybe you can help him."

Luke asked, "Will you show us where it's at?"

"No! I know nothing. You know what I mean?"

"I mean, did you see anything that would be helpful to the police?" asked Luke.

"Don't you understand English, man? I know nuttin'," the man answered, raising his voice, then turned and walked away.

Luke shook his head in disgust. "Nobody knows anything around here. People get away with murder." He then shouted to Lt. Bilcot, "Lieu, the guy says there's a body up the block."

"Jump on! We'll check it out," said Bilcot.

Luke and Jimbo stood on the back step as Frank raced the rig to the corner.

"Never ends, does it?" said Jimbo.

"No. Life's so cheap around here," replied Luke. "I hope my neighborhood never gets like this."

"Stop bullshitting yourself. It's already happening. Where you think the people from here go after they're burned out?"

"What do you mean?" asked Luke.

"They go to the west Bronx. Where you live … And didn't Jackie tell you the number of fires over there have more than doubled since last year? That they're torch jobs?"

Luke gave Jimbo a surprised look. "I never really thought about that."

With a puzzled look, Jimbo asked, "Why'd you move there from lily-white Middle Village? I'll never understand that."

Luke shrugged his shoulders. "To be close to work."

Except for Frank, who remained in the cab to monitor the radio, everybody else dismounted the rig in front of the alarm box. There they found the stiff body of a good-looking Hispanic man in his late twenties, lying on his back.

There was a large, still-wet bloodstain surrounding a butcher's knife that protruded from the man's solar plexus. The blood had drained to the sidewalk, where it pooled. A startled look was fixed on the victim's face. His open eyes bulged.

"Looks like he knew it was coming," said Luke.

"You got that right," said Jimbo.

Luke knelt by the man, pulling a sweat-stained bandana from his back pocket with which he gently wiped blood from the man's neck. He pressed two fingers against his neck, feeling for a pulsating carotid artery. Shaking his head, he said, "Nothing. I'd say he's dead." Then he felt his cheeks. "He's cold. Cold dead."

"What a pity," said Lt. Bilcot. "Some poor mother will be devastated."

"Maybe we should take him to the hospital," said Luke.

"Give it a break, Luke," said Jimbo. "Stop that bleeding-heart shit. The guy's dead. There'll be an ambulance here shortly. Let them handle it."

"Jimbo—shame on you!" Luke was surprised by Jimbo's reaction. "That's so disrespectful."

"Come on! We're not a meat wagon. We fight fires. We don't deliver dead bodies to hospitals or morgues."

"No, no, mister! He no good." A young kid, speaking in a whisper, came from behind them.

"What do you mean?" asked Lt. Bilcot.

"I heard people talking today. They said they were going to kill him."

"Frank! Call the dispatcher," shouted Bilcot. "Tell him we got a possible 10–45. Request an ambulance and a police response."

"Ten-four, Lieu," Frank acknowledged.

"Why'd they want to kill him?" Luke asked the kid.

"They said he makes fires in buildings. They said he made the fire in there," he pointed to a building, "that burned a little boy. That's why they kill him."

"What people said this?"

"I don't know. Just people," he said.

Jimbo covered the body with a blanket.

"Hey, mister," the kid called to Luke.

"Yeah, kid."

Pointing, he said, "That's his bottle behind that car."

"Thanks, kid," said Luke. While going to retrieve the bottle that turned out to be filled with gasoline, Luke began questioning himself, wondering why he'd volunteered to work here. Why hadn't he chosen Queens, where it was much more peaceful? He told himself when he got promoted maybe he'd clear out. But he wouldn't dare tell his brother firefighters about those thoughts. A group of them had pledged to each other, as a result of the brainchild of Mulligan and Juan, never to leave the Tin House of their own accord.

When Luke returned, the kid was gone. "Where's the kid?"

Nobody noticed him leave.

"What do you got there, Luke?" Bilcot asked.

"Gasoline. Looks like this guy might have been a torch. If we can believe what the kid said. And this gasoline is supposed to be his," said Luke, raising the bottle of gasoline for Lt. Bilcot to see.

"And you wanted to bring this scumbag to the hospital," Jimbo chuckled, shaking his head.

"I guess you're right, I don't know," replied Luke, shaking his head in disgust. He continued, "Before I got on this job I saw a few dead bodies. They were in coffins, clean and neat. Since I got to this godforsaken place, I've seen too damn many bodies. Three tonight and most of them were messy. Like a dead body means nothing anymore … I don't know if I like that."

A patrol car from the 41st Precinct arrived, followed close behind by an ambulance.

They gave the cops the container of petrol and what little info they had.

Engine 85's services were no longer required; they were free to leave. Once again they were making haste to get back to the firehouse, to get that well-deserved break. Once again they were in for another surprise.

Straight ahead they saw a patrol car parked in the middle of the street. Both front doors were open. What looked like a body was lying beside the driver's door, but that was hard to tell because the closest street light was out. It was like something out of *Twilight Zone*. An eerie feeling overtook the firefighters.

"What the hell is this?" muttered Luke, a sense of anxiety churning in his gut. Then he shouted, "That's a cop! That's a cop!"

Suddenly, a blond-headed man appeared out of the dark from behind the car—his back to the firefighters—who was punching it out toe-to-toe with a much larger man. They could see the policeman was on the losing end of the brawl.

"Frank! Call the dispatcher. Get the PD here right away. A cop down, tell them," ordered Lt. Bilcot.

"Lieu, we better stop this guy before he gets one of their guns," shouted Luke.

"Let's go," shouted Lt. Bilcot as the rig came to a stop.

"Lieu!" Frank shouted. "Take this with you. You might need it." Frank handed Bilcot the hydrant wrench. Bilcot jumped to the street. Then, with the others, he charged to the assist.

They tackled the big man from all directions, high and low, immediately dropping him on his gut. Jimbo jumped spread-eagle across his legs. The other men grabbed his arms, placing the weight of their bodies across them. Together, in one fast swoop, they immobilized the man, who had the strength of a bull.

"What the hell's he on?" shouted Jimbo.

Frothing at the mouth, he fought them all, heaving, shoving, pulling; but the cops cuffed his wrists and then his ankles, totally restraining him, to the relief of them all. But that didn't stop him from spitting at them.

"I was never so glad to see firemen," said one of the cops as his partner called for backup.

"Glad we could be of assistance," Jimbo replied. "We brothers in blue gotta watch out for each other."

"Hey, before you guys go, would you give us a hand putting him in the car?" asked one of the cops.

At that moment patrol cars swarmed the area, appearing out of nowhere. It took six of them to pick up the perpetrator, who was still jerking and kicking even with his legs cuffed, and place him stomach-down on the back seat. In his stupor he rolled off the seat, jamming himself in the footwell behind the front seat.

"That's even better," said one of the cops.

"Hey, pal?" Lt. Bilcot called to the cop who was knocked out when they first arrived, a big black man. "If you got everything under control we'll take up, okay?"

"Yeah, go ahead. If you guys ever need us, just stop over at the Four-One. Ask for Billy Jones or P. J. Murphy."

"Thanks, gents," said the other cop. He was checking his front teeth with his fingers, from where blood oozed. "Damn! These two are loose."

"Try some Crazy Glue," joked Jimbo.

The cop smiled, "I don't think so."

They were now only one block from the firehouse, less than a minute away if there were no more surprises.

∗   ∗   ∗   ∗

Mulligan pulled from his locker two shirts on their hangers, eyeing them closely, trying to decide which one to wear when he got off.

"Jackie," Luke called to Mulligan while on his way to his locker.

"What did you guys have?" asked Mulligan.

"An action-packed hour while returning to quarters from that fire. First we had a DOA with a big blade sticking out of his chest. Then we had to assist two cops trying to arrest a crazy son-of-a-gun. It took all of us to bring him down."

"What a waste," was all Mulligan had to say.

"What are you doing checking out shirts at three-thirty in morning? You must have something important planned?"

Mulligan smiled, but said not a word.

"Oh, I get it. That girl. You're going to hunt her down, aren't you?"

"Exactly. This morning," said Mulligan.

"Good luck. But be careful. We're not always welcome around here."

Chapter 11

That morning Mulligan doused himself with Old Spice. He wore black penny loafers, black slacks and a black pullover that highlighted his biceps and shoulders. He was looking good.

At 9:00 AM sharp, he left the firehouse bound for 4401 Charlotte to find Ester. His mission was to renew the relationship they once had.

Reckless was the best way to describe his driving. He thought he hit a cat—heard a thump in his wheel well—and just missed a dog. When he arrived on Charlotte he found the street deserted; normal for a Saturday morning.

Just to the right of the entrance to 4401, where Ester lived, was a large pile of charred debris from recent fires there. The scorched remains of a couch sat impaled on the spikes of its once decorative wrought-iron protective railing.

After parking his car just short of her building, he turned off the engine but kept the radio on. It announced, "It's fourteen-ten on your dial," followed by the song "We Got to Get Out Of This Place."

Sitting in the car holding the steering wheel, then cracking his knuckles, then bringing his joined fists to his mouth and blowing on them, he watched the building entrance, waiting for Ester to appear. He closed his eyes as if praying. Then, for a moment, fear of rejection overcame him, diminishing the beauty of the blue sky and bright sun above. *What am I doing here?*

Unnoticed by Mulligan, Jose was sitting directly across the street on the stoop of his hangout, the vacant building. Frowning, he watched Mulligan closely. Jose knew he was a fireman. He began to fester at the thought of him waiting for Ester.

Time dragged. Mulligan had been waiting more than thirty-five minutes, getting restless, doubtful she would appear. And Jose was getting more agitated, waiting to see what was going to happen.

Maybe I should get out of here before I make an ass of myself. Mulligan lit up a cigarette, then turned the ignition key and started the car, but immediately turned it off. There she was, standing in the entranceway. The air rushed from his lungs; his stomach dropped.

Look at her, as proud as ever. She stood erect with her head held high and her legs apart. She had her hands on her hips and wore tight dungarees that revealed her fine figure. *And as beautiful as ever.*

Ah shit. The sight of Jose sitting across the street annoyed her—he waved to her. She thought about going back upstairs to avoid him. But then she spotted Mulligan sitting in his car looking right at her, wearing a big smile. *Oh shit. Now what do I do? Jose will kill him.*

Mulligan saw the fear in her eyes. *Something's wrong,* he was certain.

She turned and rushed back into the building, hoping that Mulligan would leave. But instead, sensing there was trouble, he charged into the building after her, bringing with him a tire iron. "Ester, Ester," he shouted.

Jose's mouth pursed, his eyes narrowed; the sight of Mulligan running into the building after her was too much. From behind the entrance door, he snatched up his always-ready weapon, an eighteen-inch-long piece of one-inch black pipe, and ran across the street, following Mulligan into the building.

Mulligan darted to the end of the hallway looking for her. When he did not see her, he started up the stairs. There he saw Ester fidgeting with her keys at her door.

"Come in here," she shouted, but it was too late. Jose was right on his tail

"What the fuck you doing around here, mister?" barked Jose.

"Who the fuck wants to know?" Mulligan yelled back with great machismo.

Jose stood with his weapon at the ready. "You want me to take care of this muddafucker?" he asked her.

Who's this guy talking about? Mulligan turned to Jose. "Who the fuck are you? Going to take care of me. Bullshit!" he shouted, flaunting the tire iron.

Ester screamed. The ashen-faced beauty did not want bloodshed. She dreaded Mulligan getting hurt. "Jose! I don't want your help. You go away … Stay out of my business."

Right then, memories of the abuse she took from her people when she went out with Mulligan flashed through her mind. When one of the girls called her "*la puta Irish,*" and how she put an end to that label with her fists.

"*Maricon,*" shouted Jose, while glaring at Mulligan and looking like a madman. He slammed the pipe against the wall, then stormed off down the stairs.

Mulligan tried, but couldn't hide the fact that he was trembling. "What the hell is going on?" he asked, trying to sound unaffected by it all. "All I want to do is talk to you. And this wacko wants to kill me."

"Why did you come here?" she asked.

"'Cause I wanted to see you; to talk to you. Find out why you're angry at me after all these years," he said.

"I think you better go. That guy, Jose, he thinks he owns me. Wants me to be his girl. If he thinks you stayed too long, he will go crazy."

"Well, can I meet you? Maybe go for a drink or something?" he asked.

"I'd like to, but not now. Okay?" she said. "Now go."

Mulligan's face dropped. "Why ... Why not?" He was miffed.

"Please go. You got me in enough trouble already," she said.

Mulligan wasn't looking for Jose when he reached the street. He was preoccupied with thoughts of Ester. But Jose was watching him and thinking about him from his hangout across the street, promising himself, *I'll get that muddafucking fireman and get him good.*

*   *   *   *

Mulligan wasn't a happy camper when he pulled up in front of Dorney's, his favorite watering hole and a favorite drinking place for many South Bronx firefighters.

The way Ester treated him did not sit well. He projected the worst: that she wanted nothing to do with him. He was hurt, but not ready to give up. Of course he didn't let his vulnerability show, and when he entered the pub he was looking cool as usual.

"Well, well! Where have you been, Jackie me boy?" asked Luke. "We've been waiting for you."

"Don't get your balls in an uproar there, Lukie baby," said Mulligan as he joined him and Juan at the bar. "Give me a beer, Jerry D," he called to the bartender. "And besides, what are you guys doing here?"

"Jackie, my man, you didn't hear. Tell him the good news, Luke," said Juan.

"I'm your new boss. From now on you got to call me 'Lt. Lukie baby.'"

Mulligan's radiant smile returned. He gave Luke a hug and a handshake. "Congrats, Luke, and good luck. Couldn't happen to a better guy. This calls for a cel-e-bra-tion. Jerry D! Give us three cold ones here," Mulligan called to the bartender. "And a shot for my new boss."

Patriot Game was playing on the jukebox, Luke's favorite Irish rebel song. On the wall behind them hung a poster, *Support our Troops.* Next to that was an *England Get Out of Ireland* poster.

"When did you find out?" asked Mulligan.

"Right after you rushed out the door this morning. I've never seen you in such a hurry," said Luke.

"Where were you?" asked Juan.

"Had to make a stop on Charlotte," he said, sipping his beer.

"You crazy, my man? By yourself? Shit! You know some of the people around there don't like us, especially you white guys," he said with a laugh. "You're lucky you didn't get your ass cut. Next time take me with you. Let me protect your lily-white ass." Again he laughed.

"Probably looking for some broad," said Luke.

"Ah, now I know where you were. That broad, the one that hit you with the balloon … Am I right, Jackie?" asked Juan.

Mulligan nodded yes. "I was prepared, Juan. And I almost had to punch it out with that scumbag, Jose. But let's talk about our new boss, Lt. Luke White. All right?"

"You're right, Juan. It was that broad. And things didn't go his way." Luke laughed and called to the bartender, "Give us another round here."

"Let's just say she blew a golden opportunity, and leave it at that," said Mulligan.

Suddenly Juan's focus was on the television: a news report about an anti-war protest. On the tube, a couple of protestors burned an American flag, while others burned their draft cards.

Juan despised anti-war demonstrators. He had lost a brother in Vietnam. He supported the fighting men and had regularly turned out at rallies to show his support for the troops. He was quick to throw punches at the anti's, whom he often referred to as "Commie-sympathizing, liberal candy-asses." Sometimes when Juan was having a few beers he got to reminiscing about his brother, and he would tell the others, "My brother would have made one hell of a firefighter."

"Look at those fuckers," said Juan, himself a Vietnam vet who had seen considerable combat. "Scumbags, one and all. Civil unrest everywhere. If it's not the war they're protesting, it's for civil rights. And when they decide to riot, who catches the brunt? We do. The bottles and the bricks, and everything else thrown by those lousy pricks."

While still watching the television, he tapped a scar on the right side of his forehead with his right index finger and said, "I got this from one of those scumbags."

"Where'd you get that?" asked Luke.

"Right down the corner from quarters. A Coke bottle came through the open window."

"It's not all about civil rights," said Mulligan. "Some scumbags are making money on it. Like that dude, Jose. I'm sure he gets a decent buck for every building he torches. And once again it's us that pays the price. We get our jocks knocked off."

"Well, let's finish our drinks and get out of here. Don't wanna get the wife pissed, you know," said Luke.

"Man, Luke! Like who wears the pants in your house?"

"My wife." His response was immediate.

Juan just smiled and shook his head.

Mulligan put his arm around Luke's shoulder. "Now that you're a boss, will you still be one of the boys, Lukie baby? Or will you become a—"

"Wait a minute. Don't give me that baloney," Luke interrupted. "Of course! You guys are my brothers." He picked up his drink, held it in front of him and toasted, "To the best damn firefighters, Engine 85 and Ladder 59; my Irish Tigers." He put his arm around Juan's shoulder, "And one Puerto Rican Tiger."

They raised their glasses and saluted Luke. "Good man, Luke! You're the best. That's why we love you," said Mulligan.

"Hey, Jackie," shouted Jerry D. "I understand you got my Puerto Rican customers singing Irish songs?"

"Oh yeah? What'd you hear?"

"You had Papi and Lucita down here singing 'Black Velvet Band.'"

"And Irene Hogan. And it was good," Mulligan said, "I don't vocalize with just anybody. They got to be good."

*   *   *   *

When Mayor Nicholas Dunlap took over the reins of New York City, there was turmoil in the streets. Civil rights demonstrations and anti-war protests were the norm. That meant civil disorder: rioting, looting, and fires, fires, and more fires. Whole blocks of commercial and residential properties were burned. "Burn, baby, burn" became the rule of the day for many in the ghettos, the most affected areas being the South Bronx (which prior to the troubles was home to hundreds of thousands of people), parts of Brooklyn, and Manhattan's Harlem and Lower East Side.

Most of the destruction occurred in the ghettos during the spring and summer months; hence, the long, hot summers. They were the nightmare months for the Mayor and the emergency services.

Most hard hit was the Fire Department, its resources often stretched beyond its limits. Normal FDNY responses could not handle the ever-increasing number of conflagrations, even with the creation of more than a dozen new firefighting units. To fill the void, units from stable neighborhoods were often relocated to the ghettos, leaving their own communities at risk.

A most extreme case was that of La Casa Grande (The Big House), where newly created Engine 85 was quartered with Engine 82, Ladder 31 and Battalion 3.

In 1968 the four units, working out of the one firehouse, responded to over 35,000 alarms between them, the busiest firehouse in New York history. And in their response area was box 2–7–4–3, Charlotte and 170th, the busiest fire alarm box in the City. In the early 1970s, people from around the world visited Charlotte Street to witness the devastation, as did Presidents Jimmy Carter and Ronald Reagan.

The situation was out of control! There were many times when the fire and police forces were not able to cover all the emergencies. The saving grace for the Mayor was his slush fund (money he used as he saw fit, to keep the peace—or to buy the peace) and federal money that became available to New York and other cities to create summer jobs for the youth of the ghettos. The jobs lessened the disturbances, which in turn dramatically reduced the rioting.

But the destruction by fire and the number of fires in the poorer areas continued to soar, and most of the burning had nothing to do with civil rights. It was about arson for profit, with the profits going to the slumlords. Very few people were ever convicted of related crimes during this period, which saw the loss by fire of many thousands of sound buildings. The destruction of whole communities resulted in the forced relocations of hundreds of thousands of people. This amount of devastation was unprecedented in America.

To some in the ghettos, firefighters and cops were the enemy. They were the establishment. Firefighters reacted by showing their undaunted support for the establishment by wearing American flags on their fire gear and affixing flags to the fire trucks. Local leaders in the ghetto complained to the Mayor that such flaunting of the flag provoked the citizenry.

Consequently, Mayor Nicholas Dunlap directed that the American flag could not be displayed on Fire Department apparatus (including all City vehicles) nor could the men display the flags on themselves while working. Even the tradition of displaying the flag on all firehouses during daylight hours ceased for many years.

Mayor Dunlap went all-out to keep the lid on the long, hot summers. "God forbid the strife would spread outside the ghettos," he would say. Certainly that was one of the reasons he went overboard with his slush fund handouts. Some people thought the handouts were designed to win him votes, but many of the people in the affected areas didn't vote. They weren't even registered to vote.

The Mayor was betting on the goodwill of the voters in the stable, middle-class neighborhoods. Most of all, he didn't want any surprises; no more destructive riots.

The man who watched the Mayor's back, which included the arson-for-profit situation in the South Bronx, was Terrence Rubin, a thirty-four-year-old so-called whiz kid, the son of a real estate baron.

It was rumored that Rubin's father had made a large monetary contribution to the Mayor's campaign fund. In gratitude to Rubin senior, the son was appointed to the powerful position of special assistant to the Mayor.

One of Rubin's functions was to keep in touch with the different communities that made up the City, especially those people in the more volatile ghettos. He was to seek out and establish good relationships with their leaders, which he did. Through these contacts and the Mayor's slush fund, he, with the Mayor's approval, was able to cool many a situation that in the past would have led to rioting or other disturbances. Rubin's work was especially important during the summers. His job was to know the communities' pet peeves, their perceived injustices and other problems, and if possible resolve them quietly, so as not to cause the Mayor any humiliation. It was also his function to impress upon the people in the ghettos that the Mayor was their friend, that he was fighting to better their lot. This was true, and the Mayor did this in all earnestness, usually at the expense of the white middle class.

He liked the Mayor's fast-fix approach to the problems of the different minorities; make a lot of promises and hand out money, and hopefully the problems would go away, much like the federal government. There were many handouts, just to keep a lid on the troubles.

The long-term future of the City, for which everybody would one day have to pay, was not one of his concerns, which could explain why he refused to act against the arson.

Another reason could be that Terry Rubin didn't like the firefighters and their unions. Likewise, they despised and degraded him, labeling him as a: "Candy-ass who wouldn't make a pimple on a firefighter's ass." Rubin used his position to hurt the firefighters whenever possible. It was said that he went so far as to delay for a long time the demolition of many, many hundreds of vacant buildings that were a constant source of injury, often serious, to firefighters. According to union leaders, he urged the Mayor not to spend "badly needed funds" for that purpose, but rather to use the money for job creation projects.

The fire commissioner had frequently advised Dunlap of the serious threat the vacant buildings posed for his men; the two most common causes of injuries being missing steps (and flights of steps) from the interior stairwells, and missing bathroom floors. The Mayor was quite surprised to learn that the bathroom floors were removed by junkies so they could quickly lower and remove from the buildings items to be sold at the junkyard.

A battalion chief doing research on vacant building fires told the Mayor that junkies also started fires in buildings because they knew the firefighters would pull down the walls and ceilings, which gave the junkies access to all kinds of sellable junk.

Supposedly, the Mayor responded, "Nothing goes to waste with those efficient bastards."

Rubin's job was a full-time one. Generally he would be the first person the Mayor met with each morning to exchange information. Every Thursday they discussed the arson-for-profit crisis.

Rubin waited in the Mayor's office, as he did every Monday through Friday, under a plain wall clock that read 7:05. Fresh coffee was brewing, the pleasant aroma filling the large room. A pet peeve of Mayor Dunlap's was to arrive at his office and not find fresh coffee ready for him. Making sure that happened was Rubin's responsibility.

The office door opened and in walked the handsome six-foot-three Nicholas Dunlap, an upper-class Yankee who had spent much of his adult life in politics. To his credit, he had also served in the U.S. Navy during World War II.

Most of what he knew about New York City's poor and middle-class constituents he had learned while serving in the U.S. House of Representatives, during which time he often promoted the demands of the black and Puerto Rican communities. He'd also made their plight a big part of his rhetoric during his campaign for Mayor. He was inaugurated in January 1965. He was a pleasant person, at least in public.

Politically speaking, the Mayor was a liberal, which made him unpopular with the firefighters. But he was very popular with the people in the ghettos. Oddly enough, these same people never made a big issue of the arson that plagued their communities.

Dunlap left that issue to Terrence Rubin, to whom he once said, "It's obvious to me that nobody cares about the South Bronx or any of the ghettos. Nobody! Because nobody's complaining, other than a few members of the City Council and the firemen and their unions."

And it was so obvious that nobody cared about the poor souls crammed into the ghettos. With all the politicians and religious leaders *shouting* out against the war and calling for quick solutions to the civil rights crisis, rarely did any of them call attention to the burning of the ghettos that was affecting the minorities directly. Not even the news media made a big deal out of it. As long as it didn't affect them.

Rubin poured the coffee, black with no sugar, and handed it to the Mayor, who was looking out the window behind his desk.

"Good morning, Terry. At least I hope it's a good morning." Mayor Dunlap did not look at Rubin. He continued looking out the window.

"Good morning, Your Honor."

"Terry, Commissioner Steele told me there was another arson-related death in the South Bronx last night. And at another suspected arson fire a young girl got terribly disfigured." The Mayor clasped his hands together, then turned to Rubin and gave him a look that made clear his annoyance. "There's been too much of this up there. Much too much! It scares me. This young girl … That should never have happened."

"But still no one is complaining, sir. Other than the commissioner and his men. He's too sensitive. And as far as his request for more fire marshals to investigate the fires, if you don't mind me saying, Your Honor, say no. We don't need the attention. Let the firemen up there cover the extra workload. Those fools love it, sir."

The Mayor cocked his head, locking eyes with Rubin. "Why would I want more fire marshals? By the way, what have you got against the firemen? I've never heard a kind word from you about them. You're ungrateful, young Rubin. They're the people you can depend on. They always show up, don't they?"

Rubin shrugged his shoulders. "They don't vote for you, sir."

"That doesn't make them bad people." Dunlap again looked out the window. "You've been to the South Bronx a lot more than I. Tell me. What's it really like up there? Not just the Charlotte Street area, but the whole of it, I mean."

"As a visitor from England once said, sir: 'It's like bombed-out London during the War.'"

The area Rubin was talking about was saturated with burned-out vacant buildings and partial burn-outs, in which people still lived. Every block was lined with stolen cars that were stripped and burned. Sidewalks were littered with debris from fires. Alleyways were piled with garbage. It was crime-ridden and drug-infested. Its outlook was bleak.

"How long now has this 'arson for profit' been going on?" asked Dunlap.

"It began in earnest in '66. So that makes it six years, sir. In parts of Brooklyn, a little longer."

"As long as we keep the public in the dark, they'll think it stems from the civil rights disturbances. Right, Terry?" He was coaxing Rubin.

"Yes, sir."

"And Terry, why the hell wasn't I kept more up to date on it?"

Rubin was startled. He kept the Mayor fully updated on that situation. As a matter of fact, it was the Mayor who coined it "New York's best-kept secret." Rubin kept a neutral expression.

Mayor Dunlap again looked Rubin in the eye. "How extensive is the destruction?"

"Unbelievable," said Rubin. "Thank God the media has kept the lid on it. I hate to think what would happen if the public suddenly became fully aware."

"Is it really that bad?" asked Dunlap.

"Sir, hardly a block's not affected."

The blighted area was very large and getting larger. It affected great numbers of people. One high-placed religious leader in the Bronx estimated that between 1966 and the current year, 1972, as many as 200,000 people had fled the South Bronx, which was expected. An enormous number of previously occupied buildings were now totally vacant. Many of them extensively burned.

"Would you agree, Terry, that most of the buildings the people are fleeing are dilapidated rather than burned out? Isn't that right, Terry?" asked the Mayor, who was again coaxing Rubin.

"I'm afraid not, sir. Arson. It's arson."

People wanted out, not just because they feared being burned alive, but also the damage it did to the overall building and to their apartment, if it was close to the fire. Not to mention the destruction of their personal belongings. And experience had taught them that once the burnings began, there were usually more fires to follow. *Coincidentally*, enough of the owners of these properties, the very people who gave the orders to burn the buildings, were financial backers of the Mayor.

"Where are the people going?" asked Mayor Dunlap, shaking his head.

Rubin replied, "Mostly to the west Bronx, taking the apartments abandoned by the whites who are running to the suburbs."

"There goes our tax base," said Dunlap.

The west side of the Bronx had many large five, six and seven story apartment buildings. And every time a white family moved out, a minority family from the South Bronx moved in. The landlords didn't waste any time. In 1972 there was a dramatic increase in suspicious fires reported there.

"If I may continue, sir, Miss Johnson from Planning told me that not too long ago the Bronx's population was well over one million. Her early research shows it's now just over seven hundred thousand."

"Oh God! If the public ever found out, we'd lose every taxpayer," said Mayor Dunlap.

Suddenly Dunlap's disposition brightened. "Well then, as we both know, it serves the common good. We are getting rid of the slums of the Bronx. But I don't want to see it repeated throughout the Bronx. God no!"

Mayor Dunlap had earmarked the South Bronx for redevelopment. The sooner it was cleared of people, the sooner *Mayor Dunlap's South Bronx Revitalization* could be started. No doubt that when this project was underway, it would be the talk of the nation. It certainly would enhance the Mayor's bid for reelection. And maybe a bid for the Presidency.

"I worry about the west Bronx," Rubin shook his head. "That's not part of the plan."

"Don't remind me," said the Mayor, raising his hand to stop Rubin. "If it gets bad there, then we'll have to put a stop to it."

Again the Mayor looked out the window. But this time he wasn't looking at anything. He was in deep thought, beginning to regret that he had ignored the arson problem; that he had not taken action to rectify such a serious situation that had already devastated so many neighborhoods and caused many injuries and deaths, not to mention a major loss of taxable properties.

"I assume that most of the people up there are on welfare?" said the Mayor.

"Yes, a high percentage of them," Rubin replied.

Most of the people were poorly educated and without any skills to speak of, nothing to offer an employer. Most of the unemployed were between the ages of sixteen and thirty. From their ranks came the culprits that formed the arson-for-profit gangs. An easy way to make a few bucks. Too many of them quit school the first chance they got. Many came from broken homes and had no guidance. Many couldn't speak English. On top of it all, there was a devastating drug problem.

Steps were being taken to improve the education of the young people. But even that didn't make sense. New schools were under construction in the heart of the areas being burned out. The children the schools were intended for were being forced out of their neighborhoods, leaving very few kids to attend the new schools.

"Terry, arrange for me for this Tuesday morning, a meeting with the fire commissioner. And include someone from Planning. Preferably Miss Johnson. She'd be a pleasant addition. And tell them to have some stats with them concerning deaths and injuries. And how many people displaced."

"I'll get right on that, Your Honor."

Chapter 12

It had been a long three weeks for Mulligan since he last saw Ester. She had dropped out of sight. *Where did she go? Did she move? Will I ever see her again?*

Every day, either on his own time or while working, he showed up in her neighborhood looking for her, sometimes twice a day, but without any luck. She and her friend Carmen were gone.

On Tuesday, May 17, 1972 at 3:30 PM, the two companies got called to 170th and Miniford. Mulligan sat in the rig, looking out the open window. This time he was more interested in finding Ester than in finding a fire.

"Looks like another false alarm," he said to Juan, who was sitting opposite him puffing on a cigarette. *Where the hell is she? Can't stand this not knowing.*

When the rig pulled up in front of the fire alarm box, Ester's friend Carmen stepped out of Santana's. She stopped momentarily to see what was happening. She watched the firefighters as they visually checked the area for a fire or emergency. But to Mulligan's annoyance, she never looked at him. She then continued on to Charlotte Street.

Mulligan hurried after her, shouting, "Miss! Young lady ..."

She faced him, showing no reaction, waiting for him to reach her. "Yes, fireman, can I help you?"

Ah, get this shit. Like she doesn't know me.

"Hi! You're Ester Gonzalez's friend, yes?"

"Yes. And who are you?" Carmen replied coolly.

"Her fireman friend, Jackie Mulligan."

"What you want?" she asked.

"Where is she? I haven't seen her lately."

"I don't know. Your guess is as good as mine. She just disappeared, gone like that." She snapped her fingers. Carmen felt a little guilty toying with Mulligan's feelings, but that's what Ester wanted her to do. And she agreed with Ester that she must not appear to be overly eager to go out with him. After all, he did run out on her.

Mulligan couldn't hide his dejection. He stood open-mouthed with drooped shoulders. All he could do was stare at her.

"Is that it? I have to go," she said.

"No, no. Please! How—how long has it been since you saw her?"

"I don't know, three weeks, maybe." Again Carmen misled him while monitoring his reaction.

"Thank you, miss," he said.

"If I should see her, should I tell her you were asking for her?" Carmen asked.

"Yes. Please do."

On her way she went, but didn't get too far before she heard Mulligan shouting after her. She turned to find him running towards her. "Please tell her I … I would like to talk to her. Tell her … Never mind."

✳   ✳   ✳   ✳

The next day, hundreds of miles away in Puerto Rico, a pensive-looking Ester Gonzalez sat in a hot, stuffy telephone booth with beads of perspiration forming on her forehead. She was in conversation with her roommate, Carmen, as previously planned. She listened attentively.

"That fireman's been looking for you. I think he's desperate to see you. I mean, I could see it all over his face."

Ester's solemn look did not change. "How many times did he come looking for me?"

"Many times I saw him. Twice he was parked in front of the house."

"When did you talk to him?" Ester asked.

"Yesterday. He was with the fire truck at the corner. He called to me when I came out of Santana's."

"What did he ask about me?"

"He wanted to know where you were. And when I told him I didn't see you—that you disappeared, he became very upset."

Ester finally smiled. "Maybe it's time to cut him some slack." She laughed, then sobered. "But I must remember he did me wrong. Treated me like shit."

"Ester, that's a long time ago. You got to think about today, you know. Talk to the guy. See what he has to say. He's really hurting for you."

"Thank you, Carmen. You're a good friend. I'll see you tomorrow."

"Ester, you do dig him, don't you?"

"Since I came here, all I thought about was him. But he's got to be punished for what he did."

"Then if you like him, don't make the mistake of not talking to him. Don't chase him away … Goodbye, my friend."

As she hung up and exited the telephone booth, she thought to herself, *God help me. What am I going to do with this guy?* Her feelings for Mulligan were again surfacing after years of dormancy. Strong feelings that had been suppressed by anger and hopelessness. She never thought she'd see him again.

Chapter 13

Juan was standing at the counter in the firehouse kitchen pouring cups of coffee for the newly promoted Lt. Luke White, himself, and Jimbo, when Mulligan walked in.

"Put my name on a cup of that shit!" Mulligan barked.

"You got it, my man," said Juan.

"Throw me another cup," Juan shouted to Jimbo, who was cleaning up at the kitchen sink.

No sooner had Jimbo, a superb athlete who had tried out for the Los Angeles Dodgers farm team, said yes, than he had a cup in the air on its way to Juan, who had only his left hand free. But somehow he snatched the cup out of the air as it flew just over Luke's head—Luke didn't see it—and had it down on the table pouring the coffee for Mulligan, while Mulligan took a seat at the table.

Mulligan, Juan, and Frank Healy, 85's chauffeur, were the only guys in the firehouse who were raised in the South Bronx. Brought up near the firehouse on Caldwell Avenue, Mulligan was proud to work in the Tin House. This was the home of two of the busiest firefighting companies ever, something that would make these guys forever proud.

Just like many of his gung-ho comrades who worked in New York's busy fire companies, Mulligan considered himself one of the best of firefighters—not the best, but one of the best. As he would often brag, in jest of course, "I'm sure there has to be at least one or even two firefighters around who are better than I am."

For the most part, Mulligan and most proud ghetto firefighters didn't blow their own horns. That is, not until they were drinking alcohol and mixing with members of other fire companies at a firefighters' social event.

On occasion somebody would become obnoxious and make a provocative remark or two about one company or another. The firefighter who made the remark sometimes got knocked on his ass. That is, if he didn't get the first punch in. Fortunately, the drunken brawls would be forgotten soon afterward.

"I just love this place," said Mulligan. "This kitchen. Everything's brand spanking new."

"That makes sense," Jimbo cut in. "It's a new firehouse. What do you expect to find, an old kitchen? Hah, dummy?"

"You know what I mean," said Mulligan.

These guys were a close-knit group. They worked together, hung out together, and risked their lives together. At fires they were a perfect team and were good at covering each other's back. To a firefighter it is critical to know his back is covered by men he can trust. Such knowledge enables him to go above and beyond the call of duty when attempting to save a life, which happens often enough.

And when they stopped for a few drinks on the way home together, it was not unusual for them to have more than a few, causing them to get home late to their darling wives, who just didn't understand their needs. All except for Mulligan, the instigator; he wasn't married. At the end of the night, without fail, he'd start laughing, and remind them: "Pretty soon, boys, you'll have to face Mama. Yeah, you'll be sneaking in the door, tiptoeing through the house, thinking you're not making noise. Then you'll knock something over, and when you do the greeting will come from the bedroom: 'Is that you, you sonofabitch?'"

Then just like that, the humor left Mulligan. "What're we going to do about this arson bullshit? That job where the kid Lucita got all cut up. That haunts me, man. I keep thinking of something like that happening to my niece. And you know what really bugs me?" Mulligan continued, slamming his fist on the counter. "It was a torch job. Right, Juan?"

"That's right. I found that can. Just outside the cellar where the roast was found. It still had some gasoline in it."

"What'd you do with the can?" asked Mulligan.

Juan answered, "I gave it to Bilcot. He informed the chief, who's holding it for the fire marshals, who so far have not even called about it. And they certainly didn't contact me."

"We got to do something about this shit," insisted Mulligan.

"Lighten up, Jackie," said Jimbo. "It's not your fault. Besides, there's nothing we can do. We're not trained to catch arsonists. And don't forget, there aren't any witnesses."

"Whoa!" said Mulligan. "How about Coburn? Hell, he's as good a witness as anybody. He saw the guy run from the building and he was threatened by him."

"But he did not see him in the act," said Jimbo. "Did he? Cause that's what counts."

"No, he didn't. Sometimes I feel like if we want something done about it, we got to do it ourselves. And I just know if we do it, we'll probably wind up in trouble," said Mulligan.

"Listen to me," said Jimbo. "I'll tell you what we do. Probably the only thing we can do. Keep the pressure on the unions. They're the ones who got to get City Hall off their asses. That's why we elected them. What we pay them for."

"What can the unions do?" asked Mulligan, swigging his coffee and dragging on a cigarette.

"Reach out to the public while pointing the finger of blame at the Mayor. Where the buck stops," said Jimbo as he stomped the life out of a roach. "Look at that little shit," he said, referring to the roach, then continued, "The Mayor's been stalling for years on his promise to hire more fire marshals. Rather than hire them to go after the landlords and their torch men, he protects them. You know why he stalls?"

"Yeah, I know why," replied Mulligan. "Because the landlords are part of the political system and probably support his reelection kitty. And I'm sure many of the landlords themselves are politicians or friends of pols."

"Say no more. You got it right, brother," said Jimbo.

"Jackie, how's that young girl anyway?" asked Luke.

"I've got good news. I spoke to her mother at the hospital. She said Lucita was healing well, but there'd be mucho scar tissue. But there's further good news. The doctor told her a plastic surgeon would fix her up gratis. Ain't that terrific? Her mother is so grateful for what we've done. And you know what? She told me she prays for us to be safe."

"Well, isn't that nice," said Luke, who was moved. "To think somebody down here is praying for us."

"That is a shocker, isn't it? Next thing you know, somebody will say thank you," said Juan.

"That'll be the day," said Jimbo. "In the five years I've been here, I never heard anybody say thank you. Not even when I pulled somebody out."

"I don't know about that. I mean somebody's got to appreciate us. Probably they're so shook up they just don't think to say thank you. I don't know," said Mulligan.

"As a matter of fact, they'd rather throw something at us—a brick, a bottle, whatever. Won't you agree with that?" continued Jimbo.

Sometimes when the area was under siege during riots and other disturbances, firefighters needed a police escort when responding to and operating at fires. That was the price they paid for working in the ghettos.

"Who the hell owns all these buildings anyhow?" asked Mulligan, to which Jimbo replied, "The Jews. Who do you think? Some of them own a lot of buildings, my friend. One of the big ones around is Arco, or Arcows. Something like that."

"Where the hell you see that?" asked Mulligan.

"It's right on the building inspection cards and those registration plates over the mailboxes. We should check that Arcows out. They're up on the Concourse, near Fordham."

"Yeah. We can pretend we're looking for an apartment," said Luke.

"That'll be a good start for us. Let's go check out front and see what's happening on the street," said Mulligan.

"Sounds good to me," replied Luke.

When they reached the street a patrol car sped by with its siren blaring. No sooner had the patrol car disappeared than the Fire Department's Rescue 3 raced by in the opposite direction, its siren and air horn blasting. The chauffeur waved out the window to the men.

"Man! Like it never stops," said Juan, melodiously. "One thing the South Bronx has that you won't find in the rest of the Bronx."

"What's that?" asked Luke.

"Constant excitement, man. There's always somebody, or something, getting fucked up down here."

"Tell you the truth," said Mulligan, "I'd rather be working here than in a quiet place. I think I'd go bananas in a slow house."

At that moment another siren squealed. An ambulance sped by.

"You'd have enjoyed it last night when we had a surprise guest," said Luke.

"Tell me about it, my man?" said Juan.

"It was just about dusk. The apparatus floor door was open. In runs this guy wearing not a stitch of clothes. A whacko. He stood right next to Packy at the Housewatch Desk. The guy stood almost on top of Packy with sweat dripping from him. Packy was all embarrassed. Then he started shouting in broken English, 'They're after me. They're coming to get me. Get the police.'

"He's jumping up and down. His dick flopping around right in front of Packy's face. Needless to say, Packy was uptight. Then the guy bent over, almost sticking his ass in Packy's face. Too much for Packy. He planted his foot on the guy's rear and shoved real hard, sending him about ten feet out into the apparatus floor, where he almost fell."

They laughed hard, just picturing Packy, a modest, easily embarrassed person.

"Who was after him?" asked Juan.

"Nobody. It was all up here," said Luke, tapping his temple.

"What'd you do?" asked Mulligan.

Luke continued, "We waited for an ambulance. As far as the guy was concerned, he did no harm. Just ran around the apparatus floor. In a few minutes the PD and an ambulance showed up and took him away."

Luke and Juan sat on a crude handmade bench out in front of the firehouse.

"Jackie! I hope you don't mind me asking, but what did happen to your parents?"

"No, I don't mind. I told you I'd tell you." Looking out on the street as if watching the traffic, he leaned his back against the wall of the firehouse, crossed his arms and legs. "Besides, I got to talk to somebody about it. Get it off my chest. It's all coming back to me now. Not that I'll ever forget them. You know who that girl was I met the other day?" he asked Luke.

"Yes, Juan told me," said Luke.

"This is between us, right, guys?" Mulligan insisted. They nodded their agreement. "Right after she dumped me, I went into the service. Several months later, right after I finished parachute training, I got the telegram notifying me that my mom and dad were dead. To come home. There was no explanation as to what happened. As distraught as I was, I thought when I got home that the broad would've been there. If not for me, at least for my folks. I never saw her. Didn't even hear from her. My parents were killed in a fire. It started in the apartment below that was occupied by two drunken Limeys. Smashed all the time. I'll never forget the old fuck's name—Thatcher Churchill!"

"Man, what a handle," said Juan.

"Almost every night they'd have one of their drunken arguments. All you'd hear was his snobby English accent: 'How dare you,' and 'bloody hell,' he'd yell all night long. He hated the Irish with a passion. That sonofabitch."

Mulligan got angrier as he talked. "If I had run into him at the time," he raised his fists, "I think I'd have caved his ugly fucking skull in."

"Easy, Jackie," said Luke.

"Yeah. The thought of him still pisses me off. One night in their drunken stupor they started a good job, four rooms of fire. Probably a cigarette. The smoke killed my folks. They died in bed. And the two Limey bastards got out unharmed, except for hangovers the next day."

He looked at them apologetically. "I hope I'm not making an ass of myself."

"Shit no. This is heavy stuff, my man," said Juan.

"I got to get it all out. The girl, too. I never spoke to anybody about this stuff. And the broad's brought it all back to me."

Mulligan struggled to control his anger. "She dumped me for another guy. And instead of me hating her guts for that … hell, I still dig her. After all this time. And the way she treated me the other day, you'd think I dumped her. Fucking broads. They'd drive you crazy. That morning I met you guys in Dorney's, when you got promoted, I stopped by her place to see her. She hardly even talked to me. And one of her friends came after me with a pipe. Luckily, I had my tire iron at the ready. I would have busted his head open. Fortunately, she chased him off."

In an instant his look of despair changed to one of great expectation. Ester's friend Carmen had just come around the corner and was heading right for him.

"Be right back." He stepped off to meet her. "Hi," he said.

"Hi, Mister Jackie." This time she was smiling.

"Just call me Jackie. What brings you around here?" he asked.

She replied, "I think I have good news for you."

"Oh yeah? Talk to me," he said.

"Ester is coming back from Puerto Rico tomorrow," she said.

"Whoa, that *is* good news." His face lit up like a light bulb.

"Why don't you surprise her? Pick her up at LaGuardia tomorrow?" she asked.

"I'd love to," he shouted.

"She won't be expecting you," she said with a note of caution.

Chapter   14

With his car windows wide open and the radio blaring, Mulligan was harmonizing at the top of his lungs with Van Morrison, who was singing "Brown-Eyed Girl." He was in a great mood, keeping time with the music, pounding on the steering wheel while rocking in the seat. He got the attention of many drivers. Perhaps they thought he was high, but he wasn't. Just a happy man on his way to pick up the love of his life.

A few minutes later he pulled up in front of American Airlines' arrivals. That's when his nerves began to act up; little butterflies moving around in his gut. *I mean if she told her friend to tell me she was coming back, she must want to see me*, he told himself. *And if she wants to see me, she wouldn't mind me picking her up. Or would she?*

He got out and before he could make himself comfortable leaning against his car, the sliding door directly to his front opened and there she was, struggling with a brown suitcase that was bursting at its seams. The big old thing was much too heavy for her.

"Can I take that?" he shouted. He strutted real cool like towards her, with his arm out ready to take the bag.

She turned to him like a woman being accosted by a man on the street. And when she was about to tell him where to go, he was at her side looking her in the eye.

"Jackie! What are you doing here?" She gave him a welcoming smile.

"Let me take that," he said, gently removing her hand from the suitcase. The touch of each other's hand caused an instant resurgence of the warm feelings they once enjoyed together. He lifted the bag and carried it back to the car, then placed it in the trunk. Then, like the gentleman he was, he opened the door for her and she got in. All along, he was welcoming her back and telling her how glad he was to see her. And likewise, she was delighted to see him and grateful that he came for her.

"I would never have been able to handle the bag," she told him as the car drove away.

"I hope I am more important than a bag carrier," he said with a chuckle.

"Oh, I didn't mean it that way," she said. "I am happy to see you. I mean that."

That made his day. "Then why don't we go for dinner?"

"That sounds good. I am starving. On the plane all I got was a bag of peanuts and a soda," she said. "But where can we go?"

"Over to my neighborhood. You don't mind a diner, I hope?"

"Nope."

To Mugavin's they went.

*   *   *   *

"You're ordering corned beef and cabbage? That's for us Irish," he said.

"No. I've always liked corned beef. Don't you remember that St. Patrick's Day when you took me out for a corned beef dinner? I enjoyed that. And when I saw it on the Specials," she pointed to a small blackboard on the wall, "I just couldn't say no to it." She licked her lips.

"Then I'll take the same," he said.

"I am glad to be back," she said.

"And I'm glad you're back."

"You know, I thought about you and your job while I was over there. Your job is crazy," she said.

"It's not half as bad as it looks," he said. He turned off the radio.

"Their wives must worry about them all the time when they're working," she said.

"Oh no, it's not like that at all." He was playing down the dangers of firefighting, but he was talking to the wrong person. She was an eyewitness to many fires.

"I see the crazy things you guys do. I saw what you did at the fire in my building the other day. You scared the hell out of me. I know if I was married, I wouldn't want my husband to be a fireman."

*   *   *   *

It was Friday evening, not even 7:00 PM and the El Tico Bar on the corner of 170th and Intervale was already jumping. Several couples danced to a merengue. The music from the jukebox could be heard out on the street. The well-dressed, self-confident Jose, wearing red patent-leather shoes, was one of the dancers. He flaunted his dancing prowess.

Several young women smiled approvingly at him, making some of the young men envious. One guy looked like he was jealous.

The El Tico had a reputation as a hangout for the local bad boys. So naturally not only the bad boys flocked there, but so did the wannabes.

Two good-looking young ladies were dancing with Jose; one was his sister, Linda.

When he waved to his fellow gang members sitting at a booth, he noticed they returned unfriendly looks.

The gang leader, Miguel Rodriquez, old-looking for his thirty years, was sitting with Tito Lopez and George Garcia. He said to them, "Look at this muddafucker. Really thinks he's cool. Why'd we put him in the gang?" He looked at Tito. "Wasn't it your idea?"

"What can I tell you, man? I fucked up," said Tito, looking at the floor.

Without a word, Jose left the women standing on the dance floor and walked over to the booth. "What's happening, amigos?" he asked stiffly.

"Why you didn't make sure there was nobody in that place you burned? You got that little girl all messed up, man … What is your problem? Hah, Jose?" asked Miguel, struggling to control his anger. Miguel reiterated the group's policy to Jose: "Neither Tito, George, or I want anybody hurt at these fires. I told you this many times, man. It's strictly business. Burn out the buildings, get the people out, and collect our money. No questions asked. And that's the way I want it."

"I got no fucking problems, man." Jose was his cocky self. He didn't give a damn about what they thought.

Miguel continued, "Then why didn't you check to make sure nobody was in there?"

"I rang the bell. A bunch of times. Nobody answered," he said, in such a manner as to provoke Miguel.

"I guess you can say anything you want to, hah? Now that your partner's dead."

"What can I tell you, man?" said Jose.

"I just don't fucking understand how Pepe, with all the places he torched, why he got himself killed like that." Miguel paused, staring coldly at Jose, and then said in a calm, deliberate voice, "You know, man, your story sounds like bullshit."

"You bullshit, man," Jose shouted back.

Miguel just shook his head. "What you going to do about that black *maricon* who saw you on Charlotte?"

"When I leave here I take care of his ass."

"Make sure you don't kill anybody. You hurt too many people. You understand?" demanded his cousin Tito.

"Why you guys messing with me?" asked Jose.

"Because you don't listen. When I fix it so you could get into the gang and make some real fucking money," continued Tito, "you told me you'll do whatever we tell you to do. So don't make any more fucking problems for us. You understand, man?"

Miguel cut in: "Our business is not to fuck up people. It's to burn buildings. To make fucking money, man … You understand that?"

"Yes, yes. I go now and take care of business," said Jose.

"One more question," said Miguel. "Why you start the fire in the basement for? Why you not go to that empty apartment on the top floor?"

Jose nonchalantly shrugged his shoulders. "Oh, I forgot." He grinned and Miguel seethed.

Concerning collecting the maximum on fire insurance, landlords and their arsonists learned that the most effective location in an apartment building to start a fire, to obtain maximum damage and therefore a maximum payout, is an apartment on the top floor.

Top-floor fires quickly burn through the ceiling into the cockloft, the wide open space about thirty-six inches in height between the top-floor ceiling and the underside of the roof surface, allowing the fire to spread rapidly throughout the cockloft, then burn down into other top-floor apartments.

Fighting these fires calls for a lot of hose lines, a lot of water that eventually works its way down through the building destroying ceilings, floors, and walls, doing extensive damage. The holes in the roof assure that rain water will continue to run through the building.

Without answering him, Jose started to leave, but was temporarily detoured when "Mambo Number Five" started playing on the jukebox.

"Dance with me, Linda," he shouted to his sister, who quickly obliged. Once again his footwork excelled, and she too was good. He even smiled, making sure Miguel, Tito, and George saw him.

Miguel's closed mouth tightened, his eyes narrowed. "Look at that muddafucker. He gives a shit about what we told him … I don't like him, Tito."

Meanwhile, on the dance floor, Linda asked Jose, "Why do you chase after Ester all the time?"

"Because I dig her. That's why. Why you ask me that?"

"She's not interested in you. She asked me to tell you to leave her alone. She likes another guy."

"Who?" he snapped. "The fucking *bombero*?"

"I don't know," said Linda. She shook her head. She was afraid of her own brother.

"I got to go." He turned and left the bar, again leaving his sister standing on the dance floor.

It was seven-fifteen.

✳   ✳   ✳   ✳

Mr. Coburn, who was recently burned out of 4401 Charlotte, now lived with his daughter Loretta in her three-story house, diagonally across the street from 4401. He was standing on the porch of the well-kept house, taking in what was happening on the street. And something was happening indeed. No sooner had he came outside than he heard what sounded like somebody pounding on a car windshield, followed immediately by a car burning rubber as it sped down the block.

But he didn't have time to investigate. The well-disguised Jose approached, wearing sunglasses that covered an eye patch, a false mustache-goatee combination, a wide-brimmed hat, and dark blue coveralls with the collar up. He even limped.

From the base of the stairs he shouted, "Hey, you! *Maricon!* I don't want you talking to the firemen anymore. You understand, mister?" Jose spoke coolly, his voice well disguised.

"Who are you?" asked the visibly shaken Coburn. He did not recognize the voice, but sensed he knew the man.

Ester was fast approaching Coburn's house on her way to investigate the commotion in front of her house, two men throwing punches at each other, when she overheard the confrontation between Jose and Coburn. Stopping just out of view of Jose, she watched and listened.

"Let me tell you, mister," said Jose, as he threateningly pointed his right index finger at Coburn. "You stop talking to the firemen, or we will take care of you ... And your fucking family."

Coburn was alarmed, not knowing who this man was. "Who are you? What do you want?"

"Don't talk to the firemen anymore about the fire up there," Jose pointed to 4401. "That's my last warning, mister."

"Oh, I know who you are," Coburn shouted, sounding confident, but he wasn't sure at all. Jose did not look like the man he saw the other night. "Don't you dare threaten me, you evil bastard," he continued in his stern way of talking. "I'll tell the firemen you threatened me."

"Fuck the firemen, *maricon*," shouted Jose. That's when he spotted Ester. He kept his back to her.

Do I know this guy, Ester asked herself. *Jose?*

Jose glanced at her as he rubbed down his fake mustache-goatee combination, then made one more threat to Coburn, in the disguised voice: "I'll fix you, you sonofabitch." He scurried away; his limp very prominent.

Coburn nodded in appreciation to Ester. She saw his hands trembling, with good reason. One doesn't take such threats lightly.

"Are you okay?" she asked.

"Yes. Thanks for your concern. Something tells me he's the man that started the fire the other night. But I just could not recognize his face." He went back inside the house.

Is that Jose? What the hell is he up to? thought Ester as she hurried across the street toward her building, where the fight was still in progress. She wondered where the hell the police were when you needed them, and then with relief she heard the police siren in the background.

Peace soon returned to Charlotte Street. It didn't take much for the cops to break up the fight. Fortunately there was little resistance from the combatants. By the time she reached her building, everything was peaceful, at least for the time being.

Jose exited the alleyway of his hangout, the vacant building across from Ester's, carrying a green shopping bag. He hurried unnoticed to Coburn's daughter's house. He climbed the steps and slowly opened the door and stepped inside, then closed it behind him.

✳   ✳   ✳   ✳

Frank Healy, the cook for the day tour, was preparing a special lunch, this being his birthday: Cornish hen, fried brown rice, turnips, and stuffing. He even brought in a large chocolate cake for the occasion.

He kept everybody out of the food preparation area, except his "assistants."

Mulligan and the others watched a live TV report on an anti-war rally. As usual, Juan was perturbed. "Those 'commie' fucks," he barked.

"Hey, old-timer! When'll that shit you call food be ready for consumption?" asked Mulligan in a loud, raspy voice, to the pleasure of all.

"I beg your pardon," responded Frank, also in a loud voice. "If you continue to: one," he raised one finger, "refer to me as an old-timer, and two," he raised two fingers, "refer to my cooking as shit," he tapped his chest with the two fingers, "you'll not," he raised his voice another notch, then pointed the two fingers at Mulligan, "I repeat, you'll not be eating. Do you read me loud and clear, young man?"

"Yes, yes, Frank," said Mulligan, feigning timidity, looking like a man who was about to cry. "But I'm starving and in need of substantial quantities of your superb cooking."

"What a line of shit," said Frank. "If you and your gentlemen friends give me a hand right now, we'll be eating momentarily. Jimbo, put out the plates, then get this stuff out," yelled Frank.

"You got it, Frankie baby," said Jimbo.

"It won't be long now, guys," Frank called out. He placed the tray of hens on the table.

With paper towels in one hand and a restaurant-style spatula in the other, Mulligan removed the hens from the tray, placing one on each dish. Juan served the rice, followed by Jimbo serving the stuffing.

The rest of the men eyed the plates, deciding which one they would grab, if they got to it first.

"Help yourself to the turnips," hollered Frank.

"We should be ashamed of ourselves," said Luke, sounding like a preacher as he looked up at the ceiling with his hands spread apart as if asking the good Lord for forgiveness. He then bowed his head as if weeping. "Our wives and children are home eating franks and beans, while we're here eating only the finest of foods … Oh, I feel so terrible."

Juan added, "What they don't know won't sicken them."

They stood around the table like a pack of starving animals, waiting to pounce on their preferred plate once Frank yelled, "Chow's on." And he was about to yell just that, when the alarm bell tapped out box 2–7–4–3.

Instantly, the men let go with a chorus of nasty remarks: "scumbags," "prophylactics," "fucking whores!"

"Seems like this shit happens every time we're going to eat," said Frank with disgust.

The alarm was followed by a call over the voice alarm from the dispatcher, which was delivered through several speakers placed strategically throughout the firehouse—to make certain everybody heard the messages.

"In the Bronx, stand by the following units. Engine 85, Ladder 59, Engine 82, Ladder 31, and the 2–7 Battalion. Respond to box 2–7–4–3, Charlotte and 1–7–0. We are also receiving phone calls reporting a building fire."

Frank grabbed two rolls of paper towels from the cabinet and placed them on the dining tables. "Gentlemen, cover your plates. Hopefully the mice and roach populations will leave us something to eat."

The men reached for the towels; some covered their plates more securely than did others. Two men shoved handfuls of food into their mouths before covering their plates. They knew that if they caught a job it would be a long time before they would get to eat.

"Shit, my man," said Juan. "Another meal destroyed."

They scurried out to the apparatus floor, took their places on the rigs and responded.

Nightfall had begun, which made the flashing emergency lights on the rigs more visible. Everybody knew when the fire trucks were coming, especially down here. The chauffeurs and officers kept the sirens and the air horns blaring.

Mulligan, Juan, Bull, and Copper rode in the firefighters' compartment. In the cab were Lt. Luke White and Packy.

Outside, the temperature was ninety-two degrees. The humidity was ninety-four percent. It was even hotter inside the firemen's compartment, considering their seats abutted the large diesel engine that generated considerable heat. Worse yet, the men were wearing their heavy turnout coats.

Up ahead near the Boston Road/Wilkins Avenue intersection, Mulligan saw a group of young men stepping out onto the street aiming hard, nasty looks at their fast approaching fire truck. Defiantly, they stood there holding missiles at the ready.

"Close the windows. Looks like the little fucks are going to bombard us," yelled Mulligan.

"Oh, shit man. Now we'll really feel the heat," shouted Juan.

With the windows closed there was no longer the little breeze that helped cool them. "Yeah, but you do what you got to do, when you got to do it. Not when you want to do it," said Mulligan. "Nobody wants a bottle in the face."

"Who's it this time? Nigs or spics?" shouted Bull.

"You mind knocking off that shit?" shouted Juan. "I'm tired of you knocking my people."

"Oh, we're getting sensitive. Oh, I'm so sorry," said Bull, who grinned as he spoke.

"Oh fug! Here they come," warned Mulligan.

No sooner said than done. *Kplunk! Kplunk! Kplunk!*

The bricks and bottles started hitting the rig: front, side, and center. Luke's windshield spider-webbed, causing him and Packy to draw back, as if expecting the glass to fall in on them. Outside, one of the young punks yelled, "Fuck you, whitey."

"Black bastards," shouted Packy.

Luke grabbed the radio handset. More missiles slammed against the rig. One of them bounced harmlessly off of Mulligan's window.

Luke shouted into the handset, "This is the third time this week we've been hit." He paused, then continued, "Same place, Boston and Wilkins. Can't the damn PD do something?"

The dispatcher responded, "Ten-four, Ladder 59. All we can do is give them the message."

"We put their fires out. We save their asses. Why do they attack us, the dummies?" asked Bull.

But their attention was quickly diverted on reaching the intersection, when they saw Ladder 31 racing to the crossroads from the other direction, with one thing in mind: beat Luke and his crew to the fire.

But Luke wasn't about to let that happen. "Step on it, Packy," the men in the firefighters' compartment heard Luke shout. "They're not gonna take this fire from us," he continued.

Thirty-One's chauffeur had the pedal to the metal. At the speed they were going, they would broadside Ladder 59 if they didn't slow down.

Mulligan stared right through Ladder 31's windshield. He could see the excitement in Captain Ferrell's bulging eyes. He swore he saw Ferrell mouthing, "Don't stop. Don't stop."

That's when Mulligan roared, "Beat those humps, Packy. Don't you dare slow down." He braced himself, ready for anything.

Packy roared back: "No sweat! This is our job. No way am I letting them take it." He was not going to back off.

Finally, when Ladder 31 realized they would not slow down, they applied their brakes, but almost too late. They swerved around two other vehicles, coming close to hitting Ladder 59. Bull and Luke rolled down their windows and grinned at them. They could hear the obscenities and grumbling the men of Ladder 31 hurled at them. In jest of course.

$$* \quad * \quad * \quad *$$

At the El Tico Bar, the Latino music continued to boom. The patrons chatted away, a few mimicked the music, and others danced. Thick cigarette smoke whirled in the air.

Upon hearing the sirens of the fast-approaching fire trucks, Miguel and the others hustled to the front door. There they stood and watched as Ladder 59 and Engine 85 turned into 170th Street, driving into a cloud of smoke. Miguel thought with nervous satisfaction, *I guess he took care of that old man.*

Chapter   15

"We got a good one," shouted Luke, as soon as they turned into Charlotte Street.

Midway down the street a large volume of smoke was shooting skyward from a wood frame building. All kinds of people lined the street to watch the fiery show.

Luke's young friend, Chico, and several of his buddies ran close to the rig, waving to Luke and Mulligan. Too close for Luke's comfort, causing him to yell, "Get back, Chico. You're too close," waving him off. Once Chico was safe, Luke called out, "One day you'll be one of us. Right, Chico?"

Chico smiled with pride. "You're my best friend, Mr. Luke."

Chico's father was one of the 173rd Airborne Brigade's first combat fatalities in Nam. His mother worked and was not always at home for him. Luke was attached to the kid and cared about his well-being and did not like many of the influences he was exposed to. He strove to be a role model for the kid. On several occasions over the past year, he brought him to his home for a day's outing.

A sight that would instill fear in the heart of any firefighter was unfolding as the rig pulled up opposite the burning building. Right in the middle of all the smoke and flame that obscured the building frontage, was a hysterical woman climbing from a window three floors above the ground.

"Oh fug! That's Coburn's daughter's house," shouted Mulligan, watching the woman hanging from the windowsill. She hung by her two hands, looking down over her left shoulder, then her right shoulder, and back again. She was looking for someone to save her, but she tired and let go. She bounced off the small entrance overhang and passed through the roaring flames, screaming horribly, landing on a flowerbed.

At that moment Mulligan saw the face of another woman pressed against the windowpane of an adjacent window, staring at him with a look of hopelessness. Suddenly she vanished.

"Stop, Packy!" Mulligan shouted. "Get me to the roof. There's somebody up there."

"I'll be right up there, Jackie," shouted Bull.

As soon as the rig stopped, the men jumped off and ran toward the building. Packy and Mulligan began setting up the aerial ladder.

A frantic woman ran up behind Mulligan and tugged on his arm. "They're up there! They're up there," she screamed.

"Who's up where?" asked Mulligan.

"My daughter. Her baby." Tears poured from her terror-filled eyes.

"Where, ma'am? Where?" asked Mulligan.

"Up there! Up there," she shouted, pointing to the window where he'd seen the woman's face vanish.

"We'll get them, lady. We'll get them. Don't worry," he said reassuringly. *Oh fug! What am I getting into now?*

Mulligan was scared. He doubted whether he could get to these people. Experience had taught him that these wood-frame buildings were like matchboxes. Fire spread rapidly throughout the entire structure. A firefighter must get in, make his search, and get out very quickly. Such a search, and hopefully a rescue, was way above and beyond the call of duty.

Mulligan pulled himself up on the aerial ladder platform, where Packy stood operating the ladder controls.

Just behind the police line, in the crowd of spectators, stood Ester Gonzalez. She heard every word the woman said to Mulligan.

Engine 85 was busy pulling hose off its hose bed, laying it out in front of the building, getting ready to attack the fire. The blaze was making headway inside and out: tongues of fire, surrounded by thick, black, swirling smoke, spewed from the entranceway and adjoining window, up the front of the structure.

In a matter of seconds, the flames from the doorway and window started spreading across the front and right side of the building, reaching up over the roof. The conflagration gave off an immense volume of smoke that swiftly blackened the sky above.

The men of Engine 85 kept looking back to Frank, anxious that he charge the hose line so they could move in on the fire that threatened to extend to an adjoining building.

"Hurry up with that fucking water, Frank!" one of them yelled.

Working from the aerial ladder platform, Packy jockeyed the ladder into position at the roof. He kept a cautious eye on the not-always-visible Mulligan, who was performing a strictly prohibited maneuver. In a hurry to get to the victims, he was scaling the ladder as its sections were shifting. One wrong step could cost him a foot.

"Yo, Jimbo! Cover my ass," shouted Mulligan from midway up the ladder, moving through thick smoke. "I'll be on the top floor."

"Got you, Jackie," Jimbo replied, shaking his head. He could hear Mulligan, but not see him. "Jackie, you're crazy," he shouted.

Mulligan was anxious to get on with his search for the woman and her child. In a matter of minutes conditions on the top floor would be much worse. Deadly, in fact!

Luke, Juan, and Copper ran to assist the woman who had fallen from the top floor.

"Shit, man! Look at her legs," said Juan.

Both of them were broken. Her left shin bone protruded through the flesh several inches below the knee, and the leg was bleeding profusely. Her right leg, below the knee, was bent awkwardly at a ninety-degree angle.

"Where's her hair?" asked Luke. Her hair on the right side of her head had been singed back almost to her scalp when she passed through the flames. Also burned were her face and exposed arms. The flesh was puffed and peeling. Her severely swollen eyes had closed to mere slits and were oozing liquids that were already crusting. She moaned, in a semi-conscious state.

"I'm going to the rear, Lieu," Bull yelled while vaulting over a fence that led to the side yard.

Luke shouted back, "Let me know what you got back there. And don't forget Jackie on the roof."

Flames continued roaring out of the front entrance and the adjoining window. Fire and smoke had also begun lapping out of the first-floor windows on the right side of the building, scorching the adjacent structure.

Many noises filled the background: spectators yelling, firefighters barking commands back and forth, the groans and drones of the engines of the fire trucks, with sirens blaring and air horns blasting. But Mulligan was oblivious to the noise, fully concentrating on the safety of Coburn's daughter and her child. *If anything happens to them, it will be my fault. And the god-damned fire marshals!*

When he reached the top of the aerial ladder and stepped off onto the roof, he got a quick glance of the scuttle door he had to enter, just before the smoke rising from all sides of the building banked down on the roof, completely obscuring his vision, but not before he pointed his six-foot hook that he would use as his guide in the direction of the scuttle.

He moved forward surprisingly fast, shoving the tip of his hook along the roof surface in front of him. It quickly found its target, the scuttle cover where he knew there would be a ladder that led to the top floor. Once he reached the scuttle, he easily popped it open with his halligan tool, allowing the hot smoke and gases from inside the building to start escaping.

"Anybody there?" he shouted down the opening while dropping to his knees. Listening attentively, he heard a faint female voice crying, "Help us. Please help us."

Thick, hot smoke poured out of the scuttle opening. *Now what do I do? That's hell down there.*

He faced a firefighter's worst nightmare: operating alone, he was the only person who knew of these people's life-threatening predicament and who was in a position to save them if they could be saved. And to go down the scuttle, putting his life in grave danger, was not his job. But his conscience would not allow him a choice.

"Urgent! Urgent! It's me—Mulligan. I got people on the top floor. I'm going down to get them," Mulligan called to Luke over his Handie-Talkie, while stepping onto the scuttle ladder. "I need help here." He knew he would have to descend the ladder real fast, to prevent himself from getting burned by the hot smoke gushing up all around him. Already his face and ears were stinging.

"Be careful, Jackie," Luke responded on his Handie-Talkie, speaking in a slow and firm tone. "If it's bad, get right out. That's an order. No ifs, ands, or buts!"

The top floor was getting dangerously hot. It wouldn't be long before it would be ready to light up, roasting everything in its path. And Jackie knew it. His stomach was in knots, yet he started down the scuttle ladder. "Oh, I'll be okay. It's not as bad as it seems," he muttered, trying to calm himself.

Then he blessed himself, and in a flash he was down the scuttle ladder, dropping prone to the floor in the thick of the smoke. He began his search by feeling with his hands and listening intently for human sounds. This was difficult because of the crackling and roaring noises from the blaze.

Still he heard whimpering. He moved toward the sound and found the woman and an infant.

"Thank you! Thank you," he muttered. Finding them right away was a blessing. It only took a few minutes in these conditions to become physically spent; unable to rescue anyone, let alone to save one's self.

Rising to his knees, he rolled the semi-conscious woman over onto her stomach, allowing her nose and mouth to rest on the floor where there was still a couple of inches of breathable air. He then picked up the child.

Crawling on all fours back to the scuttle, with the infant tucked under one arm; he saw a flickering red glow along the ceiling. *Shit! There's fire in the cockloft.*

The cockloft is the area between the top-floor ceiling and the underside of the roofing, through which his escape route, the scuttle, passes. The fire could burst through the scuttle panels at any moment, catching him and the child in the inferno.

His lungs wanted to explode. He was desperate to inhale fully. And that's exactly what he did when he got to the top of the ladder, freeing his head of the smoke.

A quick look at the child told him it wasn't breathing.

Oh God. Let me get this kid breathing again, he prayed, as he stood at the top of the scuttle ladder. Most of his body was still submerged in the billowing smoke. Leaning over the scuttle opening, he gently held in his hand the back of the child's head and blew a couple of puffs of air into its mouth. Again the heat penetrated his turnout gear. The child revived and began squealing, its hands clawing at the air around him. *Thank you, Jesus.* He placed the child on the roof.

Although finding the child and getting it to the roof took less than two minutes, operating in an environment where one can hardly breathe was rapidly draining him of his strength.

He shouted into his Handie-Talkie, "Get somebody to the roof!" Then he paused, sucking in the air. "Got a baby up here in bad shape. I need help." Again he gasped. Couldn't get enough fresh air. "I'm going back down for the mother."

Bull completed a quick search of the second floor. His sweaty, soot-blackened face looked strange as he emerged through a smoke-filled window back out onto the rear fire escape. Smoke was everywhere.

"Bull, you get Jackie's message?" Luke was worried.

"Yeah, I got it."

"Go to him right now," said Luke.

"I'm on my way," he replied, his massive chest heaving as he gasped for air.

In the meantime, Mulligan took a deep breath and again went down the scuttle to the top floor. The fire on the second floor had intensified, with flames rolling throughout that landing and beginning to lap up the stairs to where Mulligan was.

No sooner had he disappeared down the smoky scuttle than flame shot up through the scuttle opening. At the same time Bull reached the smoke-covered roof. All he saw was the fire venting up through the scuttle. The thought of Mulligan being trapped down below scared the hell out of him.

Upon reaching the burning scuttle, Bull knelt by the child and moved it further away; at the same time he yelled down the scuttle, "Jackie! Where the hell are you?" There was no response. Again he called in a worried tone, "Jackie baby! Talk to me, talk to me." He then roared, "Where are you?"

Mulligan, now nearly motionless, lying face down on the floor, responded in a faint, hoarse voice into his Handie-Talkie, "I'm in trouble!"

Then finally, after what Bull considered an agonizing pause, Mulligan added, "I'm on," he gagged, "I'm right down here. The cockloft," he gagged again, "lit up on me."

He's in big trouble, Bull concluded. "Can you get to the front? Packy's putting a ladder up."

"Don't know. I have an unconscious—" With that Mulligan went silent.

"Shit, shit, shit! I better move my ass," shouted Bull. He picked up the child and ran to the aerial ladder at the front of the roof.

They were readying to set up a thirty-five-foot extension ladder. "Yo, Packy," Bull shouted.

Packy looked up and before he could say a word, Bull began shouting: "Get that fucking ladder up here. Jackie's in trouble." Bull pointed to the window below him. "He's in on the landing … I don't know why the fuck he went down there."

The fire on the first floor was burning unchecked. Engine 85's hose line still was not charged with water.

The second-floor window over the front entrance shattered; exploding with fire, and then the shooting flames merged with the flames from below. The hydrant Frank had hooked up to was not working. So Engine 45, the second engine to arrive, hooked up to a hydrant further up the block. A hose line was being stretched from that pumper to Engine 85 to supply it with water.

Damn it, Bull thought, *and I can't even help him! Because of this damn kid. What the fuck do I do?* With the child under his arm, he started down the aerial ladder.

Ester heard every word of what Bull had said. He scared her to her core, bringing tears to her eyes. *Why did he have to come back into my life?*

Like the pros they were, very efficiently, Packy and Copper raised the heavy thirty-five-foot extension ladder to a straight-up position, extended it, then placed it into position at the window. While Copper butted the ladder, Packy began climbing it.

It was all too much for Ester. She found herself trembling. *Enough! I'm getting out of here.* She turned to leave, but just couldn't walk away.

Jose was infuriated watching her. He wanted to shake some sense into her. *Why she worry so much about this guy? She should be worrying about me, the Puerto Rican. Just like her, man!* Meanwhile, he tucked the green shopping bag under his shirt to keep it out of sight.

Jose soon lost himself in the excitement of watching the burning building, with flames reaching well over the roof. *This will stop that sonofabitch. He won't be talking anymore to the fucking bomberos. Not if he wants to keep his family safe*, Jose assured himself.

"Let's go," shouted Jimbo, when they got water in their hose line. He opened the nozzle and directed the stream of water at the window next to the entrance and then straight into the entranceway where the fire was raging. Then they moved up the steps and started moving into the house, where they were met by a wall of fire and were quickly engulfed in super-heated steam.

If they were to improve conditions for Mulligan on the top floor, just in case Packy and Copper couldn't get to him, Jimbo had to move fast to knock down the main body of fire.

Packy pulled himself through the window into the smoke-filled room. Copper crawled in right behind him.

The child Bull carried stopped crying midway down the ladder, falling limp in his arms. "Oh my God!" Reaching the street, Bull fell to his knees and began checking the child's vital signs; there weren't any. After giving the child several two-finger-over-the-heart depressions, he began puffing into the child's mouth.

Once inside the window and on the floor, Packy and Copper crawled on their stomachs toward the center of the building where the hall landing would be. They could see the fire that had burned through from the cockloft rolling across the ceiling. They also spied tongues of fire licking up the stairs.

"Where are you, Jackie?" shouted Packy.

Mulligan was hardly conscious, lying next to the woman.

"Get me out of here," he mumbled like a drunk.

They reached him and the woman.

"Copper, you take the woman," said Packy.

Copper got to his feet, still keeping low. He grabbed the woman's arms and pulled her along the floor. Packy had a real struggle dragging Mulligan toward the window. It was hard work for the two men, especially when they had great difficulty breathing. As soon as Copper reached the window, he climbed out onto the ladder. Then he leaned his upper body back inside into the billowing smoke and took the woman from Packy, placing her over his shoulder. He then took her down to the street.

Packy helped Mulligan straddle the sill. From just below they heard Juan shouting, "I'm coming, Jackie. I'm coming." At that very moment Mulligan vomited, spraying the liquids down the ladder, splashing Juan, who was on his way up. "Ahh, shit!" was Juan's reaction.

Juan and Packy had to help guide Mulligan's feet onto the rungs of the ladder, he was so disoriented. That's why Juan stayed one rung below Mulligan, absorbing his weight, just in case the exhausted firefighter lost his balance.

Chapter 16

Ester stood frozen in place, weeping uncontrollably. The sight of Mulligan being pulled from the inferno by his comrades was just too much for her.

Juan and Packy assisted the rubber-legged Mulligan over to their rig. They sat him down and propped him up against one of its tires, near where three other firemen waited to be transported to the hospital. Copper arrived with the oxygen bottle, quickly placing the face piece over Mulligan's face. Soon afterwards Mulligan began regaining his senses, but his voice was still hardly audible.

Ester wanted to go to him, but she felt she had no right to. They were just friends. And besides, she could not cross the fire line. But her thinking changed when she heard somebody say, "He almost bought it." She bolted to the police line, ducked under the tape and ran towards Mulligan, only to be intercepted by Packy. He raised his arms and yelled, "Whoa! Where you going?"

"Please, fireman!" she said. "I'm his friend, Ester."

"Oh! Okay," said Packy.

Then she heard somebody shouting, "The scumbag left his calling card." *Kplunk!* A container that was used to carry gasoline landed nearby. She turned to see a battered-looking, angry-faced fireman standing at the doorway.

She knelt beside Mulligan, trying in vain to hide the tears. The sight of him struggling to breathe was so upsetting to her. "Jackie. *Mira,* Jackie," she spoke softly.

Mulligan's eyes opened at the sound of her voice. He grabbed her hand and felt it shaking. *This is no good*, he thought. *I don't want her worrying.*

As bad as he felt, he managed to crack a smile on his soot-blackened, sweat-streaked face. "It's okay, Packy. Give me a few moments with this beautiful woman." It hurt for him to talk.

Copper handed her the oxygen mask. "Here, lady. Keep this over his mouth and nose. Just like this." He showed her how. "Now you're his nurse." He smiled.

"Why are you looking so serious?" he muttered. He did not like to see her cry.

"Why? You got to be kidding. You're a friend and you almost got killed. What do you expect me to do, laugh? Now you understand why I wouldn't want a fireman for a husband?" She managed a weak laugh.

"I'm fine. Just need a little time and fresh air," he said, his voice sounding raspy.

"Why'd you go in there?" she asked. There was anger in her voice.

"People were in there." He started rubbing his throat with his fingers. "I just couldn't leave them."

"But you could have got killed. Is that your job? Do you have to do that?"

"No. That's not my job. But when you know somebody's in there … when you hear them calling you. How can you not try to save them?" He started coughing.

"That's crazy!" She shook her head. "You people are all crazy."

"Let's go, Jackie. We got to get you checked out," shouted Luke. He and Packy approached. "The ambulance is full. You're going to the hospital in the chief's car."

Luke knelt beside Mulligan. "You're a lucky man, I'm told."

Mulligan smiled at Ester as he responded to Luke, "In more ways than one. I think."

Ester found it difficult to return his smile, but she did.

"Come on. We'll give you a hand," said Luke.

"Give me a moment, okay?" said Mulligan.

"Ester, I got to go to the hospital for a quick check-up. I'll be out before the morning. Can I—can I see you then?"

"At my place." She nodded in the direction of her building. "Tomorrow, in the morning. About ten, okay?"

"Hey, Mr. Luke," Chico shouted from behind the police line. "I'm all ready for tomorrow."

"Chico," acknowledged Luke. He and Packy joined the youngster. "Don't run out in the street and chase the fire trucks. You scared the crap out of me. That's how you get run over."

"Oh, okay, Mr. Luke. I'm sorry," said Chico.

"Just don't scare me like that anymore." They slapped five. "You're all set for tomorrow then, hah?"

"Yes. I'm so happy! I'll be at the firehouse. Nine o'clock, right?" said Chico.

"You got it. See you then," said Luke. Again they slapped five.

On the way back to the rig, Packy asked, "What's that all about?"

"Mean with the kid?"

"Yeah."

"Ah, every now and then I bring him to my place. We have a big breakfast, then with my boys we go to a movie. Sometimes we play ball."

"You're shitting me."

"No, I'm not. His father gave his life in Nam. It's the least I can do. Besides, he's a good kid. And hopefully by my doing this, I'll give him some good guidance that'll help keep him straight."

"You're a better man than me," said Packy.

"Well, I gain too, you see. He got my two little guys interested in playing ball. I couldn't do it for beans."

"Doesn't he feel out of place out there in whitey country?" asked Packy.

"Nah. He's used to it now."

As soon as Ester returned back behind the fire line, Jose rushed her and grabbed her arm. "What the fuck you doing with that Irish muddafucker?"

"That's not your business, mister!" she snapped. "And let go of my arm!"

He tightened his grip.

"Ouch! You're hurting me." She tried to free herself, even attempted to kick him in the groin but he was ready for that.

"Look at that jerk. He's roughing up Jackie's friend. Come on, Packy," said Luke. "Hey, you," he shouted, running to Ester's aide.

Several people in the crowd also saw Jose abusing her. Although they gave him nasty looks, they did nothing; didn't even tell him to leave her alone. They feared him because of his reputation.

"You fucking *puta*," Jose shouted at Ester.

That's when Luke and Packy arrived by her side.

"Hey! Why you bothering our friend?" snapped Luke.

Jose glared at him, pointing his right index finger at Luke's face, almost touching it. "Fuck you, mister," he said, then sauntered off, strutting cool. He even looked back at Luke and gave him the birdie.

"You okay, miss?" asked Packy.

"I'm all right, thanks. I won't let that sonofabitch scare me."

"You know him?" asked Luke.

"Yes, I know him." She nodded. "Why you ask?"

"We think he starts the fires around here. Lots of them," continued Luke.

Ester had known Jose for many years and had spent much of that time dodging him. When he tried to date her, she always refused. She would tell him, "You're not my kind."

"I think it was him I saw just before the fire. He was arguing with the man in that house," she pointed to Coburn's house, still smoldering from the fire.

"But you're not certain?" asked Packy.

"Well, no. He had to be wearing a disguise. Even his voice was different. But I don't know. Like I just know it was him. You know what I mean?" She grimaced.

Luke turned to leave, but was stopped by Mrs. Coburn, who was sobbing almost uncontrollably. She grasped his hand and shook it vigorously. "I'm happy you're okay, Mr. Fireman. When I saw y'awl putting my daughter out the window—and the fireman too, I thought deys dead."

Then she wrapped her arms around Luke and gave him a hug. "Thank you, mister. Thank you … For saving my daughter and our baby. Lordy, lordy, thank you firemens."

"Yes, yes!" agreed Mr. Coburn. "I don't know what we'd do without them."

"How's that fireman that saved my daughter?" she continued.

"He'll be okay. But if he'd been there a little longer, he'd—they'd not have made it," Luke informed her.

"Thank you, sweet Jesus!" she screeched prayerfully, while fluttering her raised hands.

"And how about you, Mr. Coburn? You okay?" asked Luke.

"I know who started the fire." He pointed to Jose. "That bastard. Right over there."

Jose knew Coburn was talking about him, but did not look at him. Instead, he took a knife from his pocket, opened it while raising his head to fully expose his neck, then slowly slid the knife across his throat.

"Look at the bastard. Who does he think he is? Threatening me like that," said Coburn.

Jose was getting to Luke. His reddening complexion gave him away. He was generally a soft-spoken, quick-to-smile individual who rarely cursed. But behind the good-guy image was a scrapper and ex-amateur pug with a record of thirty-one wins and three losses. Yes, under normal conditions he'd be quick to throw punches and that's exactly what he would do if challenged by Jose.

Mulligan, on the other hand, preferred to talk, even with Jose. A fistfight would be his last resort, unless he was drinking.

Now's the time to act, thought Luke. *Coburn knows it was him. And the girl Ester would swear it was him.*

"Mr. Coburn. How about we turn him in to the police? Let's get this guy off the streets." Luke considered Coburn the perfect witness. Just before the fire he was threatened by Jose.

"No. No, I'm sorry. I can't—I can't do that," insisted Coburn.

"What do you mean?" asked Luke, shocked by Coburn's change of heart.

"You saw him threaten me. Said he'd kill me and my family."

"What? You going to let this bum get away with this? Burning your house—I mean? Almost killing your daughter and her baby?" Luke asked, raising his voice.

"Mr. Fireman, I'm going to be very blunt with you. I know I'm letting you down. But you must understand, my family must come first," said Coburn, speaking in his stern way. "And besides, those fire marshals you spoke about, heck, they never came around to ask any questions. Perhaps if they investigated the fire in my place, this would never have happened. They might have arrested the bad man."

"I can't believe this," said Luke. "I would think you and your neighbors would want to stop him."

"It's just too risky for us, as you can see. Besides, it's a job for those so-called fire marshals you spoke of," Coburn challenged.

"Oh, I'm so sorry. Of course it's their job. I'm just so used to them doing nothing," said Luke apologetically.

"As far as around here is concerned, there aren't any fire marshals. The City won't hire any more and they won't send the few they have up here. The truth be, Mr. Coburn, the City doesn't give a damn about what happens around here," said Packy.

"Please, fireman. I feel bad enough without you making it worse … but I got to think of my family." Coburn walked away.

"Now what do we do?" asked Packy.

"Maybe it's time to get Juan's friend to help. What's his name … Molletti?"

"Good idea! Maybe he'll catch the whore," said Packy.

✳   ✳   ✳   ✳

While en route to the hospital, Mulligan thought hard about Ester, about how she had reacted to his close call. How she didn't like him going into the burning building. Suddenly he became conscious too of Luke and the other married guys, about how their wives must feel. *Was she right? Of course if I hadn't taken the risks, the woman and her baby would be dead.*

Several months back, he and Packy had the gruesome experience of having to put the charred remains of an infant and its mother into a body bag. They were in terrible shape, like a burned pot roast. The mother's breasts were burned away. Her remains were frozen in place as though she were reaching for the sky.

The infant was found in what remained of a crib, lying on its back with its arms and legs outstretched like sticks, mostly burned away. All that was left was charred bone.

Damn Ester. You're wrong. I had to go get that baby. Or it would have perished.

A firefighter's worst job-related experience, besides losing a brother firefighter, is to lose a civilian at a fire, especially a child. A fireman would often second-guess himself: "If I got there sooner?' or "Did I try hard enough?" But unfortunately, at torch jobs, where highly inflammable liquids are used, the heat is so intense and the spread of the fire so quick that death usually occurs before the firefighters arrive.

*   *   *   *

Not long after the fire, when Charlotte Street was back to normal, whatever that meant, Ester was on her way to Santana's bodega. She was not the confident-looking person she usually was, thinking about Mulligan and how he was doing.

"Hey, Ester! Ester Gonzalez from Caldwell Avenue," somebody shouted from inside a slow-moving van driving alongside her. The van, with H & M Plumbing stenciled on its side panels, slowed to a stop, and out jumped a smiling man.

"Carlos!" she shouted. "Carlos Hernandez." She stepped towards him.

"What's it? Six, seven years since we last saw each other?" Carlos asked as they embraced.

"I don't know. But it's good to see you," said Ester.

"You too, my friend … you look so good," he said.

"I hope you have more than that to say," said Ester, smiling.

"Yes. Yes, I do. But not now. My boss is waiting for me." Getting back into the van, he asked, "Can I meet you here about five when I get off?"

"Yes, of course. We have a lot to talk about."

"Listen! Guess who I saw the other day?" he teased.

"Don't tell me!" She raised her hand to silence him. "Jackie Mulligan! Right?"

"Yeah! How you know that?" he asked.

"I saw him too, just a little while ago." She pointed to the Coburn house. "He was carried," she choked up, "from that place. They said he almost died."

"Oh my God, man. Was he okay? No wonder you don't look so happy," he said.

She forced a smile, wondering why he asked her that. She answered him, "They said he'd be okay."

"When I saw him he asked about you, Ester … As a matter of fact, all he talked about was you. Wanted to know if you had a boyfriend … If you don't mind me asking, why did you dump him?"

"Dump him! Shit," she snapped. "He dumped me!" She cocked her head, giving him a puzzled look.

"That's not what he says. But before you get too angry, I better go … See you later."

"I'll be here," she said.

He wasn't finished yet. He called out, "Oh, wait a minute! … Did you know that the day you dumped him, he was going to ask you to marry him?"

"What?" She stood flabbergasted. Her eyes riveted to his, trying to speak, thinking, *Shit, I would've married him.*

∗   ∗   ∗   ∗

It was almost 10:00 AM when Luke and Chico pulled up in front of his garage. Chico rocked in his seat, anxious to see the family.

"I like coming here, Mr. Luke," he said, his eyes beaming with excitement.

"We like having you, Chico. Shane and Sean think you're the coolest. Like you're one of the family. They want to play ball after the movie. They want you to show them how to play. They won't let me show them," said Luke. "Here, you can open the garage." Luke handed him the remote.

"Cool, man!" he replied, squeezing the remote, watching the garage door open.

Already Chico could smell the bacon. He closed his eyes and inhaled deeply. "Oh, Mr. Luke. That smells so good."

"You bring the rolls, my little friend. That shirt looks good on you. You look like a fireman."

Chico sported a Ladder 59 tee-shirt, new dungarees, and new white sneakers.

With an arm around Chico's shoulder, Luke escorted him through the door into the living room.

"We're home," announced Luke for all to hear.

Shane and Sean, smiling from ear-to-ear, charged into the living room, running to Chico's side.

Chico shook their hands. "Hey, my friends. It's good to see you again," he said.

Chico hugged Shane, and then cuddled up to Dorothy White's bosom when she hugged him.

"Me too! Me too!" shouted Sean as he extended his arms to be embraced by Chico.

"I wouldn't forget you, Sean," said Chico, embracing him.

"Are you going to play ball with us?" Shane asked.

"Yes. I want to. I brought my glove." He turned to Luke. "Can we play ball, Mr. Luke?" he asked.

"Sure, after the movie. I got everything we need in the car," said Luke.

"Are we gonna hit the ball too?" asked Chico.

"Of course. That's what we do when we play ball," answered Luke with a wink. "By the way, Mama, Chico tells me he's going to stay in school so he can become a fireman when he grows up. Ain't that right, Chico?"

"Yes, Mr. Luke. So I can be just like you."

"Well, thank you, my young friend," said Luke, cracking a broad smile.

"Okay. Let's eat breakfast," said Dorothy, placing a dish of bacon and eggs with home-fried potatoes in front of the smiling Chico. She served the same to Shane and Sean as Luke filled his own plate and poured himself a cup of fresh-brewed coffee.

Thirty minutes later Luke and the three boys were walking side-by-side, holding hands, along Queens Boulevard. Luke was on the outside, Chico on the inside. The kids were excited about the movie they were going to see, *Hang 'Em High,* a Clint Eastwood spaghetti Western.

On arriving at the Elwood movie house, Chico ran to the ticket booth, money in hand; ready to pay for the tickets, as instructed by his mother.

"What are you doing?" asked Luke, pulling him back from the ticket booth. "No way. You're my guest."

But Chico persisted, saying his mother would be mad.

"I'll tell you what, son," said Luke—Chico's eyes lit up when Luke called him son—"You can buy the candy."

They enjoyed the movie very much, but to their dismay, when they left the theater, they were deluged with a heavy downpour accompanied by thunder and lightning.

"Sorry, kids. Looks like there won't be any ball playing today. The grass will be all wet," said Luke. "We'll go home. Find some kind of a game to play."

That night, on their way back to the South Bronx to bring Chico home, the youngster almost brought Luke to tears. In a plaintive, innocent voice that only a child could muster, he said, "I wish you were my father."

✳   ✳   ✳   ✳

"Jake, my boy. This is a wonderful thing we got going here," said Izzy Katzshoe. "I don't know how long it will last. But it's good and we're making a lot of money. And all we have to do is shuffle papers around." Katzshoe roared with laughter and so did his nephew, Jacob "Jake" Lipper. Jake always laughed when seventy-two-year-old Katzshoe laughed. Funny or not, Izzy was his boss and paid him well.

Although Katzshoe was one of the most politically influential people in the Bronx, he kept himself out of the political limelight. He was prominent in the real estate industry, however, and that was a prominence he enjoyed flaunting. As a partner with his relatives in a multitude of corporations, he was part owner of hundreds of apartment buildings throughout the city, mostly in the Bronx and Brooklyn.

"In the ghetto, our rental properties are no longer big profit makers. But the money we collect on the insurance makes up for that," said Katzshoe. "Jake, you understand what I'm saying?"

"No, not quite," said Jake.

"It's simple, you schmuck," said Katzshoe, making Jake cringe. "Through our corporations," he tapped his chest with his ten fingers, "we keep buying and selling our buildings. To ourselves, of course, till we get their values where we want them—good and high. Then, you know what?"

"What?" asked Jake, scratching the back of his head.

"We insure them to the hilt. Then, when your boys burn them, we get our money back, plus a generous profit."

Jake Lipper really didn't want to know the details of their operation. He was happy being ignorant of the minutiae. Getting the job done and collecting his excellent salary was all he was concerned with.

"And there's no end to it in sight," said Katzshoe. "We know exactly what to expect and how to handle it. This is exactly what happened to us in the Brooklyn ghettos. You know—Brownsville, East New York, Bedford Stuyvesant—but on a smaller scale. With the working Irish and Italians in the west Bronx fleeing to the suburbs, and our own people leaving the Grand Concourse for Coop City, the people from the ghettos are moving in as fast as they can. Do you know what that means, Jake?"

"No. Tell me, Uncle Izzy."

"It means this place too will be a slum, a ghetto," said Katzshoe.

"What do you want me to do?" asked Lipper.

Katzshoe handed him a #10 envelope that bulged with cash. "This is for your friends. And can you get them to take care of business over here too?"

"I am sure they'd want to," said Lipper.

Katzshoe continued: "And remind them about starting the fires on top floor when possible."

"They're well aware of that, boss," said Jake.

Many a career started and ended with Izzy Katzshoe. Much of his power came through none other than State Senator Joseph Blackburn, his associate, who was very close with the Senate president, Tucker Walden.

The influence of Senator Blackburn reached everywhere, not just within state government but throughout every borough of the City. He had the power brokers in the palms of his hands. He had the clout to stop hearings and manipulate investigations, and he was good friends with some of the most influential people in the news media. His close friends included Mayor Nicholas Dunlap and Terrence Rubin. With the help of Izzy Katzshoe, Blackburn raised huge sums of money for Dunlap's political campaigns.

Chapter 17

The first thing Mulligan saw when he pulled into 170th Street was his favorite local brownstone building. But it was different. The top two floors were burned out. "Shit! When did this go?" he asked, gesturing toward the building with his thumb.

"Yesterday, my man," answered Juan. "The box came in after we sent your butt to the hospital. You were lucky. Lying on your ass while we got our jocks knocked off."

"I don't know why we told them we were available. We were on R and R," said Luke.

Mulligan just smiled, checking Juan through his rearview mirror.

"It was a tough one," Juan continued.

"Seems like there's always something else burned out every time we come around here. Or at least another burned-out apartment," said Mulligan.

"Right you are," said Luke. "And it seems like there are fewer and fewer people about anymore in the neighborhood."

"Yeah, man. Remember how crowded these streets used to be?" Juan chimed in.

On the face of most of the apartment buildings, whether they were occupied or vacant, were many scorch marks and fire-blackened windows. Some of them had black power symbols painted by the entrances.

A peace sign, with a dried egg stain on it, was painted on one of the buildings. A step was missing from the stoop; garbage and fire debris were sloppily piled on the sidewalk.

Garbage cans in front of one of the buildings were afire, but nobody gave it any heed.

Mulligan showed his uneasiness when he turned the corner into Charlotte Street. And no wonder; the first thing he saw was Jose standing on the stoop of his hangout, appearing to be staring at Ester's place. But to Mulligan's relief, Jose disappeared into the building. At that very moment, Ester and Carmen stepped out onto the stoop of 4401. His unease continued. *Why am I so fucking nervous?*

She was dressed in much the same way she dressed when they were going steady: in a tight-fitting top and dungarees that clung to her curves.

Mulligan parked the car in front of the tenement adjacent to hers. He saw her looking at him. She wasn't wearing the sunglasses, and that was almost too much for him. By then his knees were knocking.

"Wait here for me. I don't know what to expect." He stepped out of the car.

"I don't think she's going to bite you," said Luke, who couldn't help laughing.

"Hopefully this will clear your head, my man," said Juan. "You know what I mean? You've been all screwed up lately."

"It's clearing already. My hammer's getting hard," said Mulligan, trying to sound macho. He took a deep breath, whispered to the guys, "Wish me luck," and walked off.

At the same time Ester started walking toward him, her sunglasses in hand, her dark brown hair in his favorite tight ponytail style. She swayed her hips and upper body in a sexually provocative manner, without taking her eyes off his. She did everything just like she'd done when they were an item.

Mulligan was aroused. *Oh God! This is going to be embarrassing. I should have worn a jockstrap.*

"Thanks for meeting me," he said, clasping his trembling hands behind his back.

"Hello, Jackie. Let me look at you." She moved close to him. "Except for your eyes, you look much better today … What is it you want to talk about?"

Mulligan was taken aback by her cordiality. There was relief in his voice as he answered her question with one of his own. "Can we talk in private?"

✳   ✳   ✳   ✳

On the second floor of the vacant tenement across the street from where Ester lived, Jose's arson-for-profit gang maintained a *clubhouse*. The clubhouse was an apartment with most of its ceilings down and its hardwood flooring all warped. Most of the damage was caused by the thousands of gallons of water that flowed through the apartment every time firefighters fought a fire in the building, and more than a year's worth of rainwater that poured in through the holes cut in the roof.

In the living room there was a kitchen table surrounded by four unmatched chairs. Milk crates served as end tables for the couch. There was a coffee table. Even a print of a pair of horses hung on the wall right behind the couch.

For illumination at night the gang used candles, but only on rare occasions did they utilize the apartment after dark. The fire escape window and the adjoining window were rigidly secured with heavy metal doors that were bolted right through the brickwork. The apartment door was equally secure.

Miguel studied the street through a window, observing Jose entering the building. Tito and George sat at the table. They would shortly be conducting a business meeting to discuss the next buildings to be burned, the locations of the buildings, and who would handle which neighborhoods. But first and foremost, they would divvy up the money Miguel had received from Jake Lipper.

After Jose left, they would also discuss the vacant lots and burned-out buildings being auctioned off by the City. Jose didn't know that Miguel, Tito, and George had formed a corporation and already had purchased several burned-out tenements at rock-bottom prices. They had used some of the money from a very generous grant from the federal government to start the reconstruction of the three buildings. The federal grants were issued for the purpose of rebuilding the South Bronx.

The first thing they had done was get the buildings insured to the maximum value through one of Jake Lipper's friends. One by one, the buildings, in which reconstruction had already begun, were torched and destroyed. They collected the maximum on the insurance, and did not have to return the balance of the federal grant. Why? Because they reported having invested it all on the reconstruction and didn't have to prove different. Thanks to their mentors, Katzshoe and Lipper, they had no problems producing fraudulent receipts for the phony expenditures. They then abandoned the buildings. They were again in the market for burned-out vacants. Their attorney had a new corporation already formed for them and the application for more federal grant money was all ready to go, once they made the purchases.

"He's on the way up," said Miguel, opening the apartment door just as Jose reached it.

Jose went straight to a front window to observe all the recently blackened windows in Ester's building. "I see 4401's almost empty," he boasted. Turning to his partners, he uttered in total confidence, "Jose does good work, hah?"

"You not good! You fucking crazy, man," barked Miguel.

Jose ignored him. Instead he again looked out the window while the others started discussing business. They did not know that he saw Ester in genial conversation with Mulligan, but they knew something had pissed him off. He went into a rage. He picked up a baseball bat and commenced battering the wall, pulverizing it.

"What are you doing?" Miguel roared.

"*Puta,*" Jose screamed in a high-pitched voice that carried out into the street.

"You crazy, man?" asked Tito.

"Fucking *puta!*" growled Jose. He threw the bat on the floor.

"Calm down, man. We got business to take care of. We not here to listen to you yelling and screaming like a crazy man," said Miguel.

Jose glared at him, but said nothing.

"We got a lot of buildings to burn. Lipper's got more addresses for us," Miguel continued.

Tito and George were delighted. They got paid well for doing the devil's work.

"Get me the addresses," snapped Jose. "The sooner we burn these places, the sooner we get our money." He paused. "How many landlords we working for?"

"I don't know for sure, man. Lipper handles all that. One *maricon* owns over a hundred of these places by himself, man."

Jose tapped his chest. "Next time you meet Lipper, I wanna be there."

"Why? Why you have to be there?" asked Miguel.

"Because I wanna know every fucking thing that's going on, man. That's why." Jose returned to the window. He was stone-faced, glaring at Ester and Mulligan, who were smiling at each other.

"I don't think so. You too much of a risk, man," continued Miguel.

"What you mean?" Jose shot back, still staring out the window, asking himself, *What she doing with that Irisher?*

"Man, like why do you have to hang around at the fires? You make trouble for us. We don't need that shit. You know what I mean?" said Miguel.

"I enjoy the fires, and I like to see those *donkeys* breaking their fat asses. I hate them *maricons.*"

"That's bullshit, man," snapped Miguel.

"If you get caught, you'll screw us all," barked Tito. He tapped his chest with his finger as he continued, "And that means me too. You going to get us in big trouble. And don't forget, man. You killed people."

"And if you bring us down—you'll pay dearly! *Comprendo ... amigo,* cousin?" warned Tito.

"And I still don't dig what you say happened to Pepe," said Miguel.

"I heard enough of that shit, man! I wanna know when we meet Lipper," said Jose.

"I'll let you know … and remember," Miguel shouted, tapping his chest with his fingertips, "I'm the boss." He handed Jose his share of the money, which he didn't bother to count.

Jose shot back, "Fuck you guys, man!" He grabbed his money and stormed out of the apartment, failing to shut the door behind him, quickly descending the stairless stairwell.

When Jose stepped out onto the stoop, he could not handle the sight of Ester leading Mulligan by the hand into the building. *Puta!* Digging his fingers into his face, he groaned under his breath while stomping back and forth across the stoop. The hate in his eyes would scare the baddest of the bad.

"That bitch, *maricon*," he mumbled while reaching behind the entrance door to retrieve his old reliable weapon, the piece of pipe. Venting some of his anger, he pounded over and over the last intact piece of marble on the lobby wall, shattering it completely. The pounding was heard throughout the street.

I will kill him, he thought angrily. Holding the pipe with one hand at each end like a cop sometimes holds his nightstick when readying for action, he started after Mulligan, only to freeze in place at the sight of his young friend, Chico, who was running in his direction.

Luke was delighted to see Chico. "Chico, come here, come here," he called out, while stepping out of the car.

"Hey, Mr. Luke," he shouted, running to Luke's side, bobbing and weaving as he did, ready for the left jab he knew Luke would feign at him, which he deflected with his right hand, as he shot two quick jabs at Luke. As the exchange continued, Luke commented: "He's getting good. He's getting better all the time."

Luke then embraced him like he did his own sons. "How's my favorite South Bronx kid?"

"Good! Good! How's my friends Shane and Sean? And Mrs. Luke?" Chico had charisma.

"They're all fine. They always tell me to 'say hello to Chico,'" said Luke. "What's your big hurry?"

"My mother needs something right away from the store," said Chico.

"Listen, Chico. Every Labor Day I have a barbeque at my house. For all my good friends. This year I want you and your mother to come. What do you think?"

"Yes! Yes! I'd be so happy. I'll tell my mother she'll have to go."

"And tell your mother I'll pick you guys up and bring you home. Right to your front stoop." They slapped five. "Go take care of your mom. And what else must you do?" Luke gave him a quizzical look.

"Stay out of trouble," he answered. He resumed his sprint to Santana's.

The sight of Chico being friendly with the firemen added to Jose's fury. *Not Chico too*, he thought as he headed to 4401 to get Mulligan, paying little heed to Luke and Juan.

"There's that Jose," warned Luke. "He must be going after Jackie and the girl." Luke grabbed a tire iron; Juan snatched up Mulligan's Louisville Slugger from behind the front seats. They bounded from the car, taking positions in front of Ester's stoop.

Unaware of events on the street, Mulligan followed Ester, like an obedient child, through the hallway to the outside landing of the basement stairway. When she faced him, he liked what he saw—a warm congenial face. *Wow! What a change.*

Since they met again, they had been thinking a lot about their past together. It was an emotional time for them, revisiting such a happy yet painful part of their young lives, both of them realizing for the first time they never fell out of love with each other; rather they just had accepted that their romance was finished.

Yesterday was a day Ester wanted to forget; there had been much too much emotion. She was still disturbed by Mulligan's close call, and on top of that, learning that he had planned to ask her to marry him … it shook her to her core and kept her awake most of the night thinking, thinking, and more thinking. It made her doubt herself and question what kind of a person she was. Was she selfish? Maybe he'd been right to dump her? Then she got angry at herself for feeling this way.

"Talk to me, Jackie," she said.

"Ever since I saw you again, I've been thinking of nothing but you … I can't think straight," he said. "You treated me like a stranger. Like you were mad at me. Why?"

She raised her hand, cutting him off. "I'm sorry about that. But the sight of you made me so mad."

"But why? What did I ever do to you to make you hate me so? All I ever did … was love you."

She gave him a hard look. "You forgetting? You dumped me! And went into the army."

"I never dumped you. I loved you too much. Don't you remember?" He grasped her wrist. "You chose Ricardo. How many times did you tell me you'd be better off with your own kind? And then the last time you told me you didn't want to see me anymore. That's why I joined the army."

"You stupid, Jackie. You believed that? All this time. I didn't love Ricardo. I wanted to make you jealous. To punish you for messing with the Irish girl. You remember you said you liked her? I remember your exact words: 'She is my kind of girl.' Hah, Jackie?"

He smiled, shaking his head, "Ester, Ester. You always let your temper rule. Never did you take the time to think things over."

She started to stop him, "Jackie, don't give me—" but he cut her off, putting his index finger to his lip while making the sound, "Shh." Then, speaking softly he said, "Let me finish. You—the most beautiful girl I've ever known, and that still holds true today—how could I have loved anyone but you? I didn't love that girl. I liked her because she was from Ireland. And to be honest, I thought I could get from her what I couldn't get from you."

"Did you?" she snapped.

"Of course not," he said, smiling and shaking his head. Then he continued, "I wanted to make you jealous."

Luke and Juan stood in front of the stoop, blocking Jose's way, brandishing their weaponry; neither showing their fear nor knowing what to expect. At the same time, they were ready to pounce on him if he tried to get by, which they hoped he would do.

"I want a piece of this guy," said Luke.

"Amen. I wouldn't hesitate to do some serious damage to the sonofabitch," agreed Juan. "If he makes me."

Jose was becoming more agitated by the moment. He stomped about shouting in Spanish, feigning blows at them with the pipe, grinning with contempt as he did. When he charged at Juan the second time, Juan countered by utilizing bayonet fighting tactics he had learned in the army. Pretending the baseball bat was a rifle with bayonet affixed, he thrust forward the narrow end of the bat, intentionally stopping just short of Jose's open mouth—Jose was moving in—then delivered a vertical butt stroke that again purposely stopped just inches from the same target, sending Jose stumbling backwards, looking like a fool, almost falling to the ground.

Although he was mad to get at Mulligan, he was wise enough to know he would be in over his head to take these guys on. *There will be another day*, he thought as he retreated back across the street, but not without making a threat:

"I'll get you Irishers." Then, he pointed at Juan and shouted, "And you too, *maricon*."

Juan and Luke said nothing, just stood their ground, all the time grinning. Carmen was watching, relieved that Jose had withdrawn. Mulligan and Ester had no idea of what was going down outside.

"I got to ask you, Jackie. Were you ever going to ask me ..." She hesitated. "Were you—" She went silent.

"Was I going to ask you to marry me?" he asked, surprising her.

"Yes," she said.

He answered, "Yes. The day you dumped me ... Oh, how I was crushed."

Ester just looked at him for a moment, her eyes welling up with tears. Mulligan moved closer, gently taking her hands in his. She didn't resist him as he kissed her tears.

"Can you ... ever forgive this jerk?"

He smiled, nodding, at the same time muttering, "Yes," then again kissed her on the cheek.

"Would you see me again?" she asked him.

"Yes! Yes, I'd love to. Just say when."

"Tonight! About eight. In front of Santana's."

"I'll be there."

She put her glasses back on, only to have them removed by Mulligan. "Ester! You're more beautiful than ever. When I saw your ponytail and you walking that walk ... I just knew something good was going to happen."

"You better go. Tell my friend Carmen to come up, please."

"Sure ... see you tonight," he said.

Outside Luke and Juan sat in the car, waiting.

"I wish he'd shake his ass," said Juan.

"Yeah, that Jose scares me," said Luke.

"I don't know what this crazy dude is up to. Maybe he's going to fill us with little holes," continued Juan. "Where the hell is lover boy?"

At that moment a happy-looking Mulligan—a cool dude once again—came strutting through the entranceway and down the stoop. Once again as happy as a pig in shit, his face aglow, he burst into song. "The sun is shining, O happy day; no more troubles, no skies are gray ..."

"Hurry, Jackie. We got problems," he heard Juan shouting from the driver's seat. "Let's go, let's go!"

Seeing Juan's worried look and his fast-waving arm beckoning to him said it all. "What's the problem?" he asked.

"Just get in the car. We'll tell you when we get moving," said Juan.

"One sec." Stepping into the car, Mulligan turned to Carmen. "Ester needs you upstairs." Before he closed the door the car was moving.

"Juan and I had to hold that crazy Jose at bay while you were with your sweetheart. He came after us with a piece of pipe. He was pissed. Luckily, you had some equalizers in the car."

"What the fug! One of these days I'll get that bastard. I'll get him good," said Mulligan.

From Charlotte they headed to Miniford Place.

"Lukie baby, what do you think? He looks like a new man," declared Juan.

Mulligan smiled but kept looking straight ahead. "Why not? She invited me out tonight."

"Good man, Jackie. I'm happy for you," said Luke. "And by the way, she thinks the guy that accosted her, Jose, is the guy who torched Coburn's daughter's house."

"My man Coburn also thinks it was him," Juan added. "But he's not sure. He thinks he was wearing disguises."

"If he ever touches her again, I'll have to do something … I'll break his ugly face."

"What! You're going to wait till he does something first! That's crazy. Get him first!" Juan insisted.

"You're probably right, but I just can't work that way, man. I've always been a counter-puncher. And besides, I don't wanna lose this job … my man."

"Coburn also backed out on us. He's afraid for his family. Guess I can't blame him. Especially when the fire marshals let him down," said Luke.

"Man, that's terrible," said Mulligan. "Now, what do we do … I was depending on him to get this nut off the streets. I'm afraid for Ester. That he'll go after her. I just know it, man."

"Like I said, man. Get him first … there's no other way to stop him. The marshals, the police, they don't do shit. Wouldn't it be nice if we caught him in the act, in a gasoline-filled apartment? And we threw a match in. Puff the Magic Dragon!"

"You're crazy, man, to even think like that," said Luke reprovingly.

Chapter 18

Memorial Day, 1972

"Today we become fire marshals," joked Mulligan, as he stepped out of the firehouse with Luke and Juan at his side. They were on their way to Dorney's to meet up with Molletti.

Juan was wearing a new tee-shirt with an American flag on the front and *Support the Troops* on the back. "Everybody should wear these," he said. He often wore similar shirts, as did many of the firefighters, to show their support for the troops fighting in Vietnam.

The firehouse door flung open with a bang and out jumped Jimbo. "Wait for me! Wait for me!" he shouted.

"Sure. Jump in! But understand we're going to do a little arson investigating. Get a rough count of how many buildings have been burned out in our district."

"What for?" asked Jimbo. "That's not our job."

"No, not us. We're going to Dorney's to get a fire marshal friend of Juan's. Said he'd help us. But he thinks we're exaggerating about the number of fires. After the investigation we're going back to Dorney's for a little Memorial Day party. Can you handle that?"

"I think so." Jimbo climbed into the car. "Mama's down the shore with the kids." He rubbed his hands together with a little devilment in his eyes. "I got time to play with the boys."

"This should be interesting," said Luke. "I never really looked closely at the destruction around here. Juan, you think Molletti will get involved? He's our only hope, now that Coburn's gone."

"He's cool, man. He'll come across for me. Probably waiting for us," said Juan.

Mulligan double-parked in front of Dorney's. Juan ran inside. The door to the bar had hardly closed when it swung open again. Juan, then Molletti, who had a glass of beer in his hand, hustled out and got into the car.

"Hi, fellas. I'm—"

"Cool it, my man. That's my job," said Juan. "I'll do the intros. Gentlemen! This is my main man, Ritchie Molletti."

They greeted Molletti, a man in his mid-forties.

"I'm Jimbo."

"I'm Luke White." Luke shook his hand.

"Your name," he paused, stroking his chin with three fingers, "begins with an M, right?" Molletti said as he spied Mulligan.

"Hi, Ritchie. It's Mulligan." They shook hands. "I guess you know what we want. You're going to help us, I hope?"

"Let me see the situation first. I find it hard to believe it's as bad as Juan says."

"We'll make you a believer," said Mulligan.

Driving along Jerome Avenue, they passed an old hangout of Mulligan's. "See that place there? Used to be the Red Mill. I spent a lot of time there doing some smooth footwork. A lot of good-looking Irish broads hung there. But I had to stop going there."

"Why?" asked Luke.

"Isn't it obvious? The broads wouldn't give me a break. 'Dance with me. Dance with me,' they pleaded. They wouldn't let up."

Luke laughed. "You got me, you bum you."

Mulligan started singing along with "Guantanamera" that was playing on the car radio. They all joined in, and in unison rocked in their seats to the beat, except for Molletti, who simply smiled. They were in good form, ready to have a wee bit of a party.

Luke was a little uneasy, concerned that a few drinks might turn into an all-day session. "Hey, guys?" He lit up a cigarette. "I don't wanna hang around too long. The old lady will kill me."

"I thought you called her and told her. What kind of lame-ass are you, man?" asked Juan.

"Yeah! But you know how they are. They don't like to see us have a little fun … You know, sometimes I wonder why it is that after a tour at work, I feel I got to have a drink. That didn't happen when I worked downtown."

"Me too! A couple of beers seems to make it okay. You know, all the bad shit we see," agreed Mulligan. He continued, "I'm getting too insensitive to people's suffering. Like a dead body means nothing anymore. And that's not good! If I ever transfer out of this crazy place, that'll be why. I'd rather be where people still get upset at the sight of a DOA."

Still heading east on Tremont Avenue, they crossed Webster Avenue, then drove under the Third Avenue elevated train, where they were cut off by a gypsy taxi. Mulligan cursed the driver to himself, but Jimbo yelled out the window, "Get a license, you imbecile."

They passed the once thriving Third Avenue shopping district with all its storefronts, a small few of which were still open for business. And as expected, many were burned-out shells.

"You know what that used to be?" Juan asked, pointing to a lone-standing, burned building on the southeast corner of Tremont and Third Avenues. It looked like a miniature of the nation's Capitol, only it was brownish in color. "Jackie, you should know."

"Yeah! Bronx Borough Hall."

"Right! That's where people went to get their marriage licenses," said Juan.

Next they entered Crotona Park, which was once well-maintained, but was now totally neglected, perhaps because it was such a dangerous place, especially after dark.

"Man, when I was a kid I used to swim here. There's a great pool up the other side," said Mulligan.

"Been there many a time, my man," said Juan.

Once through the park, they came to the intersection of Boston Road and Wilkins Avenue. Proceeding slowly along Wilkins, they observed the devastation. Molletti stared in silence.

They passed 170th Street on the way to the next corner, Jennings Street, on one side of which stood a row of burned-out storefronts. The sidewalk was buried beneath tons of bricks from the building's frontage that had collapsed during a fire.

Continuing slowly, they drove two more blocks, then turned into the other end of Miniford Place. This was the worst part of Miniford. Here most of the buildings were empty of tenants and ravaged by fire. The street was like one big pothole that seemingly served as a graveyard for the charred remains of cars, most of which were stripped.

"Man, they really strip these cars clean," said Molletti. A look of disbelief covered his face. Never before had he seen anything like the destruction.

From the rooftop of one of the tenements, five-and-a-half floors above, a twenty-foot-wide section of the roof cornice hung precariously down the face of the building. The next windstorm would bring it down, unless the firefighters were called to remove it first.

A rusted-out skeleton of an auto lay on its roof, extending diagonally out into the street. There was hardly enough room for traffic to get by; not that there would be any traffic. For the most part, only fire trucks traveled these streets. And when there were such blockages, the firefighters would physically move the offending car. If the car was on its roof, all they had to do was spin it.

Many pairs of sneakers hung from the utility wires that crisscrossed the streets.

The firefighters continued through Miniford to the next block, 170th Street, then onto Seabury Place, a short block strewn with debris and garbage, looking like a garbage dump. On the right side of the street stood a vacant public school with black burn marks on many of its glass-less, frame-less windows. Across the street in the middle of the block stood the fire-blackened shell of a synagogue.

Overriding the smell of the garbage was the sickening stench of the remains of a large, fly-covered, decomposing dog, lying in the middle of the street. A rat that was chewing on its anus ran for shelter as the car approached.

Almost in unison they gagged, distorting their faces.

"Close the fucking windows," shouted Juan.

Mulligan puffed out, shouting, "Oh God, Luke! Did you shit in your pants?"

"Jackie, please! Close your mouth," retorted Luke.

They laughed and gagged, trying not to breathe. But not Molletti. Holding his nose, he kept his head out the window, taking in everything there was to see.

Of the seven apartment buildings still standing on the nearly deserted block, only one was occupied. There were also three vacant lots where buildings once stood. Piles of bricks covered the lots. No people were in sight.

"Man, it pisses me off! What the slumlords have done to these neighborhoods. My neighborhood," Mulligan bitched. "Let's go back to Jennings by Charlotte." He wanted to see the house where Ester's aunt used to live.

Upon entering Jennings, the car hardly moving, they passed the ruins of a three-story private dwelling.

"That place there," said Mulligan, "I hung out there a lot." Pointing to a spacious lot overgrown with wild vegetation, he said, "There used to be a convent in there."

"Was this an immigrant neighborhood?" asked Luke.

"Sure was. But I never thought of it that way," answered Mulligan. "There were all kinds of accents, man: Micks, PRs, Greaseballs, even Polocks. At the time I didn't know the difference. Where I lived there were mucho Irish. After dinner during the nice weather, they'd sit on the stoop; the men bullshitting, and the woman gossiping. There was plenty of community spirit. When I think of it, it was great."

Mulligan's cheerful look was replaced by one of anger. "This is a bitch," he continued. "All the people's tangible memories, their roots, all gone! Nobody has the right to do this. To destroy everything that means so much to so many people."

Charlotte Street between Jennings and 170th was deserted, no evidence of normal life. It was also littered with ADVs and rubbish, and was home to many more potholes.

There was a group of derelicts hanging out, who were stoned or near stoned. Two people lay on the sidewalk, passed out. One was a young, stunning-faced Hispanic girl no more than sixteen or seventeen.

"Look at that beautiful face," said Luke. "God help her parents."

Another young girl, this one white with blond hair, with her clothes disheveled and dirty, stumbled aimlessly across the street, struggling to stay on her feet.

"What's she doing here?" asked Jimbo.

"My man doesn't dig that shit, hah, Jimbo? A nice little *chicata blanca* down here with the skells," Juan needled him.

"You got that right. What's she doing down here?" asked Jimbo, shaking his head in sorrow.

"How you think I feel when I see beautiful young Rican girls all messed up on this shit? Like that broad there?" Juan pointed to the Puerto Rican girl.

Two men in the group were watching Mulligan's car. They called the others' attention to it. One of the group stepped into the street. Staggering slightly, he walked toward the slow-moving car and yelled, "What you muddafucking pigs doing around here?"

Luke smiled. "They think we're cops."

"You hear me, man?" the man again shouted.

"Four whiteys and one Hispanic, all men, in a car in the ghetto. What else would they think?" said Jimbo.

"I think it's time we make it. Before the shit hits the fan," said Mulligan.

"Yeah," said Molletti. "You don't have to show me any more. I'm a believer. I've never seen anything like this."

"Good man, Ritchie. Then it's back to Dorney's we go," said Juan.

"I was wondering when you'd say that." Jimbo beamed.

As they neared 4401 Charlotte, Jose appeared at the entrance to his hangout across the street.

"Sonofabitch! There's the guy," said Mulligan, turning to Molletti. "He's the torch."

"First lesson: with arson you have to catch the person in the act. Or have a reliable witness that saw him in action," said Molletti. "We'll talk in Dorney's."

✳   ✳   ✳   ✳

It was noon when they walked through the door into the bar, where it was already jumping.

"It's party time," said Mulligan, as he and the others joined his neighborhood friends.

"Jerry D, give these tigers whatever they want. They surely deserve it," said Molletti.

"And what's the occasion?" asked Jerry D. He wiped the bar counter where the men made themselves at home.

"I just witnessed for the first time what's happening in the South Bronx, and it's unbelievable. Arson out of control is the best way to describe it. This pro has never seen anything like it. Looks like it's been bombed out."

"Not to change the subject, but before I forget," said Jerry D, "here's a message from Charlie Boland. He'll meet you all here at 7:00 PM on the nineteenth to discuss the arson problem."

"That's encouraging. But we can't wait for the union and the City," said Mulligan.

"That's right," said Luke. "The Mayor will decide what happens, if anything. And you know what he's going to do … zippo!"

"Ritchie, my man! Now that you've seen the shit, will you help us catch the bastard, or bastards?" asked Juan.

"Yes! Definitely. I got a vendetta for his ilk," said Molletti.

"What do you mean?" asked Mulligan.

"Remember the brother that was killed last year when that vacant collapsed in Brownsville?"

"Yeah, sure. I remember it," replied Mulligan.

"Jessie Johnson. He was my car pool partner … I owe it to him, to his family. His parents still live in that ghetto."

They all thanked him for his commitment to help.

Mulligan welcomed Papi and Maria, who followed them in. "What's happening, my friends?" he said while putting his arm around Lucita's shoulder. "I got news for you."

"What's that?" she asked, her smiling eyes opening wide.

"I found that girl."

"Ester," she said.

"Yeah. And I'll be seeing her tonight."

"You kidding?" she asked.

"No. I saw her at a fire in her building, mind you," said Mulligan.

"You going to bring her up here to meet your friends?" Lucita asked.

"If things work out, sure."

"Ah, man. Now I'm jealous," she said with a wink.

"Hey, Jackie! Come here," shouted Luke. "Molletti's devised an initial strategy."

"What you got, Ritchie?" asked Mulligan.

"Juan told me that guy was spotted several times at the vacant where we saw him just before. He also said the people in the neighborhood had pointed him out as a suspect concerning a couple of recent fires. I'm inclined to believe he's working for one of those arson-for-profit gangs I told you about. You know, the bums that do the landlord's dirty work. There's just too many buildings involved for one person."

"Yes. Yes, of course," agreed Mulligan.

"First thing I want to do is get a good, clear, close-up picture of his face. I have a Fire Department camera in the car that's perfect for the job. And the car I got is the one I was talking about. Now can you guys go back there today? The sooner the better."

Mulligan said, "I guess that means we're going today. How's about we go in about an hour's time?"

"That's fine with me," agreed Molletti.

"And me too," said Luke.

Then the beautiful voice of the gifted Irene Hogan filled the bar, bringing with it complete silence from the customers. Blending in, just like a pro, she sang along with an instrumental version of "Patriot Game" that played on the jukebox. When singing, this woman displayed total confidence: she stared people in the eye almost as if she were challenging them to tell her she wasn't good. People got goose pimples listening to her.

"My favorite song," Luke whispered to Mulligan.

"That's beautiful, Irene. Beautiful," Mulligan urged her on.

Then Lucita, Papi, and the others provided harmony. And they too were good, as good as any professional concert. It was apparent they had practiced many a time.

Mulligan got great pleasure out of two Puerto Ricans and two Irishers singing Irish songs. When they finished they received a well-deserved ovation.

"Jackie, aren't you going to sing with us?" Irene called out.

Just then a mambo started playing.

"Listen, my friends. Let's get going. Let's do what we have to do. Something tells me if we don't go now, we won't be going," said Molletti. "We'll take my car."

Before Molletti finished, Lucita was tugging on Mulligan. "Time to mambo, Jackie."

"Ritchie, after this dance we go, okay?" said Mulligan.

✳   ✳   ✳   ✳

Jose was again in the clubhouse where he was preparing for yet another torch job. He had his containers of petrol at the ready in their green shopping bag. And, as always, he took a quick look at the street below, checking for possible problems before he took off on his cowardly mission that could prove deadly for some of his neighbors. He did not like what he saw: a strange car parked on the opposite side of the street near 4401. In it he saw what looked like four white men. *Who are they?* he wondered. *Prob'ly fucking pigs.* He hurried from the apartment down to the first floor. He rushed into an apartment with a street view from where, unnoticed, he could watch them. The car pulled away.

Rushing out to the stoop, he hid himself behind one of the entranceway columns, giving himself a good vantage point to check out the block.

Molletti again drove into Charlotte, this time from the opposite end, and parked about thirty feet short of Ester's building, which provided him a clear view of the stoop.

"How'll you get a close shot of his face?" asked Mulligan.

"No problem," answered Molletti. "This camera has a zoom lens for that purpose."

When Jose saw the car returning, he returned to the first floor apartment to continue monitoring their movements. This time he saw Mulligan and Juan. *Maricons! They're looking over here. They're looking for me, man*, he thought. *I teach them a lesson.*

With that he took off to the roof, scampering recklessly hand over hand, pulling himself along what remained of the stairway railings; foot over foot, stepping on the one-inch-wide riser braces that once held the missing steps and half-landing slabs.

Never once did he hesitate or stumble as he made his way onto the roof, where he went right to the bulkhead of the adjoining building. There he picked up a metal garbage can that he placed on top of the roof cornice. He then gathered up loose pieces of parapet coping and bricks, and put them in the can to give it weight.

Standing near the edge of the cornice, six floors above, with one hand gripping each end of the garbage can and his eyes glued to the car, he raised it over his head and heaved it straight out at Molletti's car. With a loud thud, it crashed off the side of the car.

"Holy shit!" bellowed Molletti, jumping in his seat.

"What the hell was that?" Luke shouted. He saw the garbage can hit the street.

Then there was a loud thump on the car's roof accompanied by the sound of a breaking bottle. "Whoa! Let's get the hell out of here," Molletti shouted. The car burned rubber as it sped from the block.

Look at them run, the maricons. Jose laughed.

"That *cabrone*. If that was Jose, he is crazy," said Juan.

Molletti parked the car on Wilkins Avenue, where people still moved about and where there was still some traffic, then got out. "You have to forgive me, guys. That scared me shitless."

"And me too. Imagine if he hit one of us?" said Luke.

Mulligan and Juan were reluctant to admit that they too were shaken by the incident.

Molletti rubbed his fingers over the sizable dents. "Luckily this is not a new car. Look at that. Enough of this," he continued. "Can we work our way back there through the yards without being noticed?"

"Why? What for?" asked Mulligan.

"We can plant ourselves in a vacant and wait for him. Now it's doubly personal … now he's damaged my car."

"You're the boss. Juan and I'll take you through the yards. Luke and Jimbo will watch the car. Okay, guys?"

They weren't ten feet into the alleyway of a vacant building when Juan began dancing what looked like an Irish Jig. But his fear-filled eyes gave him away. He wasn't dancing; he was scrambling to avoid the startled, monster rat he had stepped on. "Get him away from me," he screamed.

They picked their steps, working their way through the rain-soaked, months-old decaying garbage that was dotted with disposable diapers, to the vacant building next to Ester's that they wanted to enter. Finding that the stairway from the alleyway to the main-floor hallway was lacking steps, they went to the rear yard and climbed the fire escape. There they got inside and walked straight through to a front apartment with a street view, where they watched for Jose.

Jose returned to the clubhouse to pick up the shopping bag. When he left the building he stopped momentarily on the stoop for a scan of the block.

"Shit! There he is," said Molletti, snapping a picture. "I can't believe my luck. In less than a half hour."

"You get the green bag?" asked Mulligan.

"Of course! I'm a pro," joked Molletti.

"What do you think is in it?" asked Mulligan.

"It's heavy. I'd bet gasoline," said Molletti. He kept watching Jose.

"So we got the picture, man. Now what do we do with it?" asked Juan. He cleared the windowsill with his hand.

"Now we follow him," said Molletti. "Maybe get picture of him torching a building."

Jose walked south on Charlotte. The three of them worked their way along the street after him. They ducked in and out of doorways and alleyways and behind cars, like an infantry squad moving in on the enemy.

Just below 170th, Jose stopped opposite the only occupied tenement left on the block. Again he checked the sidewalks for possible witnesses. Then he crossed the street and entered the building, with the green shopping bag in hand.

They monitored Jose's movements from inside a doorway on the other side of 170th. Several minutes passed before Jose came back out of the dwelling.

"Where's the bag?" asked Mulligan.

"He left it inside," said Molletti, snapping off several quick shots of Jose. "Make sure you let me know if this place gets torched anytime soon."

"Yeah. Sure. Why?" asked Mulligan.

"I got a hunch that he planted gasoline in there," said Molletti.

"Why would you think that?" Juan joked.

"That bag didn't contain food. What was in it was in one piece. It was heavyish, just like a gallon of milk." Molletti grinned. "With the telephoto lens I could see the outline of the container through the bag."

"I told you my main man would help us," Juan exclaimed. He offered his comrades cigarettes, which Mulligan accepted.

"Let's get back to Dorney's," said Mulligan. He lit the cigarettes.

"I've never been so fortunate tracking a perp," said Molletti. He closed the cover of the camera case.

"It's progress, but I'm still nervous about him," said Mulligan. "It's my girl's safety I'm concerned with."

*   *   *   *

After finding a parking space near the front of Dorney's, the four of them bolted from the car to the bar. Molletti just shook his head and smiled. "Can't you wait for me, for God's sake?" he shouted.

Voices singing in harmony greeted them as they entered Dorney's.

"Sounds like there's a good time to be had," shouted Mulligan.

"And why not?" said Jimbo. "We Tigers deserve a good time. A couple of drinks, you know."

Mulligan laughed. "When was the last time we had a couple of drinks?"

"I can't remember." Jimbo observed the crowd with beaming eyes.

"Hey, don't get any silly ideas," said Luke. "We're only having a couple." But his warning didn't carry much weight. Right then Jerry D backed them up with a beer and a ball.

Irene, Lucita, and Papi sang "Black Velvet Band."

Luke raised his glass and made a toast. "Here's to New York's best damn fire-fighters."

The men raised their glasses and cheered him on.

"Come on, Jackie," called Lucita. "Sing with us."

Mulligan eagerly joined in. Papi sang lead to "My Girl." They were now nearly encircled by the patrons. They sang with feeling. They swayed with the beat, as if performing on a stage.

"Damn! You guys are good," said Luke.

Mulligan was on a high: singing four-part rhythm and blues harmony with a beer in his hand. What more could he ask for, other than a good, tough fire?

When they finished, Lucita insisted that Mulligan sing something Irish. She suggested the "Wild Rover."

"No! You sing it, Lucita. You do it better," encouraged Mulligan. "And besides, everybody wants to hear you sing an Irish song."

At that moment Bull, Packy, and Copper entered the bar, grinning from ear to ear. They headed right into the commotion. "It's party time. I love it, I love it," shouted Bull.

Some patrons joined in the singing. Others danced and swayed to the beat, as did Bull and Copper, who clowned around, dancing cheek to cheek. "This is absolutely fantastic," roared Bull.

At the sight of Bull, Luke near panicked. "Let's go, Jackie. Finish your beer," he insisted. "We're out of here. It's after two. If Bull gets a hold of us, we'll never get out."

"What?" shouted Lucita. "You going to be a party pooper again, Lukie baby? And drag everybody away just when the party's getting good?"

"Yeah! As much as I want to stay, I got commitments. And besides, I got to keep him straight. He's got a heavy date tonight."

"Jimbo! Juan! Let's go," shouted Luke.

"You guys go. We're staying," said Juan, speaking also for Jimbo. "The party's just too good to cop out on."

When the group started singing "Wild Rover" Jackie turned to join in. But Luke grabbed his arm and pulled him toward the door. "That's it! We're leaving!"

"Hey, Jackie! Luke! You'll miss the party!" they heard Bull shouting after them. "Where the hell you guys going?" he wanted to know.

"I got to go," said Mulligan. "I don't want to be responsible for Luke getting his ass kicked by his darling wife."

Once outside the bar, Luke apologized. "Sorry for taking you away. But I must get home. The old lady's waiting on me." Luke knew how Mulligan loved harmonizing.

"No problem. I had to leave. I got to be straight when I meet my date. You know, first impressions."

Chapter 19

"There's me darling Mama," Luke said, on approaching his house. Dorothy stood in their small front lawn that was bordered with all kinds of colorful flowers, including tulips, violets, and rose bushes that had not yet blossomed. It was enclosed by a freshly painted three-foot-high white picket fence.

"She must be happy about your promotion, hah? More money for Mama," said Mulligan.

"I'm sure she'll think of ways to spend it … but she won't like it when she hears I'm staying in the Tin House. How am I going to tell her? Yi, yi, yi," said Luke, who then groaned, "Oh God."

Luke had lived in the Bronx since right after he got assigned to Engine 85. It was a short fifteen-minute trip to the firehouse when traffic was moving, and about five minutes from Dorney's.

They were greeted by Dorothy, standing there smiling, holding their two-year-old daughter Fiona in her arms. A warm, happy person, she was very much in love with her Luke. When he came home from work she would be all over him, just like a newlywed.

They had been in love since she arrived from Ireland as a young teenager and had married right after Luke got out of the Navy. Both had lived in Middle Village, a working-class section of Queens, where they attended high school and courted. But they'd bought their first house in the Bronx because that's where he worked.

"How's me darling? And me beautiful little Fiona?" he asked while getting out of the car, carrying his soiled work clothes. Mulligan also got out.

Dorothy embraced Luke, kissing him on the lips. "How's me hubby?" Her Irish accent was pronounced.

Luke blushed slightly. "Just fine, Mama … and how are you, me love?"

"As happy as ever! Especially when you're home on time." She smiled wryly.

"Hi, Jackie! How are you?" she asked. She gave him a hug and a peck.

"Just fine. And hows about herself?"

"Can't complain. Luke's on his good behavior … home early, as promised." She gave him a stern look, then smiled, "And that's what counts. How about a tea or coffee? Maybe something for the holiday."

"Nah! No, thanks," said Mulligan.

Luke's sons—Shane, five, and Sean, four—came running from the house.

"Pick me up, Daddy!" shouted Shane.

Sean jealously mimicked Shane, "Me too, Daddy! Me too!"

While Dorothy and Jackie exchanged small talk, Luke dropped his work clothes on the lawn and scooped up his sons, kissing them. "Did you guys miss Daddy?"

"Yes, Daddy. Will you play with me?" asked Shane.

"Me too, Daddy, me too," said Sean.

"All right! But first I got to eat."

With his boys in his arms, Luke again kissed his wife and daughter, then put the boys down and took Fiona from Dorothy. "How's my Fiona? Daddy loves his little girl." Luke put his free arm around his thirty-two-year-old, Irish-born wife, and whispered in her ear, "Time for a matinee, darling?"

Dorothy kissed him, then whispered, "What'll we do with the kids?"

With a smile she quickly changed the conversation. "Lukie baby!" she said. "You've been promoted for two weeks now. When are you getting transferred to the slow firehouse?"

"I'm not going anywhere. I'm staying where I am."

"What?" she snapped, almost screaming. "You told me you'd be leaving that goddamned place when you got promoted! Now you're staying there? That's bull! Bullshit!"

Jackie threw his hands up over his head as if surrendering and hustled over to his car. "Uh-oh, it's time to go. Take care, Dorothy. Bye-bye kids. Luke, I'll see you on the day tour."

"If I'm still in one piece," Luke joked, forcing a smile.

Just like the wives of most firefighters who worked in busy firehouses, Dorothy had been after him to transfer. There was just too much danger there, too many opportunities for him to get hurt. Worrying herself sick about him when he was at work was a normal part of her life. The majority of firefighters kept their wives in the dark about their work experiences. But still the wives had a good idea of what went on. It couldn't be avoided.

On one occasion when Luke was working, while watching the nightly news, Dorothy saw several firemen from Ladder 59 rushing off the roof of a burning building just before it collapsed.

On another occasion, television network news aired footage of firefighters being pulled from a collapsed six-story tenement, in which both their companies were involved. Miraculously, nobody was killed. Several of the wives saw it, and immediately spread the word by telephone.

In the kitchen as they bickered back and forth, Dorothy prepared him a cup of coffee. Their children watched with fear-filled eyes.

"Mama, please don't worry. How many times must I tell you, there's nothing to worry about! I don't take chances."

Shane shifted in his seat, scratching the back of his head with his fingernails. "You going to get hurt, Daddy?"

"Now look what you've done. You got him upset … Ahh no, Shane. Don't be worrying about Daddy."

"Why don't you get out of there? With all your time on the job, certainly you can transfer to a slow firehouse. You know how I worry about you … What would we do without you? Did you ever think about that?" Tears welled up in her eyes.

"Honey, I've made many close friends there. It took a lot of fires to build that bond. They're my safety net. We protect each other. That's what keeps me safe. I wouldn't have that protection in a slow firehouse. So please, don't ask me to give it up."

They stared at each other without further comment, the children still looking on.

*   *   *   *

Mulligan drove to the car wash. He wanted everything in the best of shape, including himself. Then he went to his barber to get his hair trimmed by Fred. He was full of anticipation, couldn't wait to see Ester; kept wondering how she would act toward him. *Does she dig me, or was she just being nice to an old boy-friend?*

He tried taking a snooze, but with Ester on his mind that was impossible. Later he showered and shaved, applying an overdose of aftershave, then headed to Mugavin's Diner for a quick bite.

Man, I feel like a million bucks. Mustn't forget to be the cool stud. He wanted it to be just like the old days.

In the diner he sat at the counter and was immediately greeted by Gina. She asked right away, "Any luck yet? Did you find her?"

"Yeah, yes, I did! I found her. She appeared out of nowhere."

"Oh, your Irish admirer will be heartbroken."

"Oh, don't say that. I never led her on."

"Just kidding," said Gina.

"How do I look?" he asked. "Tell me the truth. I'm seeing her tonight."

"Don't worry. You'll do just fine. Now what'll you have?"

"A hamburger." He emphasized, "No onion. Just in case I get real close to that lucky young lady."

*   *   *   *

It was eight on the dot when Mulligan pulled up across the street from Santana's. Right in front of the store stood Ester, talking to Carmen. She wore a tight, short skirt and a form-fitting sleeveless top over her body that drove him crazy. Her dark brown hair was in a tight ponytail.

"See you later," said Carmen.

"Mmmmm," he groaned softly, gawking at her. Thoughts of the two of them in bed naked ran through his mind. At the same time he tried to park his car. The front tire mounted the sidewalk before he pulled himself together.

Watching him made her smile, knowing exactly what was on his mind. That's why she dressed as she did, wanting very much to turn him on. She laughed aloud when the car jumped on the sidewalk.

Jackie was still gawking when she reached the car.

"What! What's wrong?" she asked.

"God, you're beautiful. More so than ever." He jumped out and opened her door.

Ester smiled, "Haven't you ever seen a beautiful girl before?"

"Not like you. How you arouse me."

"Control yourself, Jackie."

"Where do you wanna go?" he asked.

"How about the Dugout? It's a mixed crowd there," she said.

"That's just fine," he said. He just kept looking at her.

After sitting her in the car, he got in. He treated her just like he did when they dated. Once in the car, he again stared at her. Starting the car, he proceeded slowly down the block.

"You're stunning," he said. But she cut him off.

"Listen to me," she said, with pain in her eyes. "Over and over I thought about what you said. About me dumping you for Ricardo. I feel so bad that I hurt you so much. For so long … and all the time I was angry with you. Thinking you dumped me. You, the nicest guy I ever knew. And you were going to ask me to marry you." She choked up. "And when your parents died, I wasn't even there for you. When you needed me most." She turned away.

"Stop this, Ester." He hit the brakes, then pulled her to him. "I don't care about the past. Just about today … About you."

"For six years we would've been married," she said.

*   *   *   *

"Jake, sometimes I think you're a real schmuck," said Izzy Katzshoe. He dropped a Styrofoam cup with an inch of coffee still in it into the wire wastebasket. Most of it spilled out on the carpet.

"What do you mean?" asked Jake Lipper. He looked down at Katzshoe's mess.

"You never ask questions. Don't you want to know what we're doing?"

"I know enough," said Jake. "But what I don't understand is how you get away with it?" Jake Lipper scratched his head.

"Jake, it's all about friends in the right places."

Jake Lipper, an obese, rather jovial man in his late thirties, was the go-between for Izzy Katzshoe and his associates, and the arson-for-profit gangs they used, from different South Bronx neighborhoods. He handled the dirty work; selecting the buildings for burning and making sure the appropriate gangs took care of them. This way Katzshoe and the others were protected from knowing the cruel results of their crimes.

Katzshoe had the list of all relevant properties and Lipper knew which ones were located in the targeted areas. Katzshoe's associates had faith in him to protect their interests and Katzshoe had full confidence in Lipper to take care of the unwanted buildings.

Katzshoe's associates were not aware that people were being hurt, even killed, at these fires. Even Katzshoe and Lipper tried to stay aloof of such information whenever possible, by not asking questions. They didn't want to know. And when they did hear about a tragedy at one of their fires, they would yell and scream at Miguel and his cohorts, and that helped ease their guilt.

Katzshoe had his Arcows Realty office on the second floor of the Platz Building, which he owned, on the east side of the Grand Concourse near 188th Street. His office was sloppy, just like the clothes he wore that were often food-stained.

Newspapers were strewn around the carpeted floor, as were empty Styrofoam and paper coffee cups. Inside one of the cups was a fuzzy layer of mold.

"Did you find out if your friends will take care of our business over here too? Or do we have to get somebody else?"

"I'll find out today," said Lipper.

Lipper bid farewell and headed to the door.

"One more thing," Izzy called after him. "We don't want people getting hurt. That makes people ask questions. Tell them we are very angry. Give them a good scare. Make the schmucks think you'll get somebody else."

∗   ∗   ∗   ∗

A just-off-the-assembly-line, two-door Chevy sedan pulled up in front of the El Tico. Its fire-engine-red color and chrome spoke wheels got the immediate attention of a couple of bad boys standing out front. They started toward the car. Jake Lipper quickly closed his electrically operated window, the only window to have been open, and locked the doors, confining himself inside a very hot space. He heard one of them shout, "Hey, mister! Why you closing the window?"

Lipper's eyes darted nervously in all directions except at the bad boys. Beads of sweat quickly formed on his forehead.

The man pounded on the window, shouting, "Hey, mister! Open that window! I wanna talk to you!"

To Lipper's instant relief, the El Tico door opened and out stepped Miguel, meticulously dressed, wearing a bright yellow flowered shirt with black pants and black French-toe shoes, going right to the Chevy, waving off the bad boys. Lipper stepped out; pretending to be unfazed, but his pale coloring gave him away.

"You're all sweat," said Miguel, a cynical smile on his face. "Why you driving around in this heat, man, with the windows all closed up?" He knew exactly why Lipper had closed the windows. He was afraid of the guys who approached him.

"Oh, I was locking up the car to join you and the boys," Lipper lied.

"Come on, my friend," said Miguel, placing his arm around Lipper's shoulder. "Let's go." Miguel said not a word about the new car.

They passed through the bar, empty except for the bartender and a drunk who had a hard time keeping his head from slamming the counter top, and went into the back room.

The neatly dressed torch men, Jose and Tito, greeted Lipper. The only thing they liked about him was that he paid them.

"How you doing, my amigos?" Lipper asked, lighting a cigar. He too was well dressed, wearing a khaki-colored suit over his large, bulging frame, three rings flashing on each hand.

"Muy bien," answered Miguel. "You got an envelope for me, my friend?"

Lipper nodded yes while retrieving the envelope from inside his jacket. Miguel opened it and started counting.

"Don't you trust me yet, Miguel?" asked Lipper. He was offended.

Miguel smiled. "Of course I do. But isn't it wise to count the money in front of the deliverer, Mr. Jake?"

"If you say so. Now down to business. I want three more buildings torched ASAP—2431 Charlotte, 313 Miniford and 4044 Seabury. Do 2431 first. The others you can do at your convenience, but don't take too long. And remember, top floor and heavy damage. Is that clear, my friends?"

"No problem, man. We can torch every place you want," said Miguel, while writing down the addresses. He continued, "You said on the phone that the people you work for have buildings all over the west Bronx that they're going to want torched. Tell them we'd gladly take care of all the places. They don't gotta give them to anybody else. You dig what I'm saying, Mr. Jake, my friend?"

"Yes. I'll tell them exactly what you said. But I must advise you we got a serious problem. They are pissed at you guys," warned Lipper. He looked nervous; his eyes darted all over the room.

Why?" asked Miguel, his neck stiffening.

"A man was killed. People are getting hurt. That's not part of the deal. They're afraid City Hall might do something. If it continues, we can't do business anymore."

Miguel glared at Jose. He could not conceal his fury, which Lipper detected.

"Don't worry. I take care of that," said Miguel.

"My friends, this is a very serious matter that must be dealt with right away," Lipper continued.

"I take care of it. Tell your boss not to worry, okay, Mr. Lipper?" Miguel reassured him.

"Whatever you say, Miguel … and congratulations to you all." Lipper smiled, happy to change the subject.

"For what?" Miguel asked. He was caught off guard by Lipper's complimentary tone.

"I understand you people bought some properties where—"

"No. Not us. Just me." Quickly Miguel cut him off and glared at him, sending a chill through Lipper. "I bought them, man." He did not want Jose to know about the corporation he formed with Tito and George.

"That's what I meant. You, you bought them. You did a smart thing," Lipper continued. "And you got them at bargain prices. You won't regret that. That property will be worth a lot of money when they start rebuilding. You'll be rich."

"It's great." Miguel tapped his chest. "We get paid to burn them and you guys collect the insurance."

"Yeah," said Lipper. "And the people who burned them buy them el cheapo. It's a great country." He smiled. "Just don't forget—2431 Charlotte. Do it right away. With that I'll say good day, my amigos."

As soon as Lipper left the room, the cocky Jose insisted, "I'll take care of 2431."

"Don't you screw up again," warned Miguel, glaring at Jose.

"Who you talking to, muddafucker?" Jose was pissed. "Why you no tell me you bought some of these places?"

"Why the fuck should I tell you what I do, *maricon?*" Miguel returned Jose's glare.

"Look at all the addresses, man," said Miguel, the glare leaving his face. "Look where they are. All over! Simpson, Fox. They got Vyse Avenue, Freeman Street too. Even down on Aldus. And look, all the way down on Caldwell Avenue."

"Let George do Caldwell and Aldus. Okay, Miguel? Once we get 2431 out of the way," said Tito.

✳   ✳   ✳   ✳

The Dugout Bar was a friendly enough place to go for a couple of drinks, without the fear of trouble of any kind. It was one of the few joints in the area where blacks, whites, and Puerto Ricans still mingled. There was a decent crowd of men and women this night, mostly Puerto Ricans. A merengue played on the jukebox and a few people danced in the dark. The Dugout was always dark, having a black ceiling and black walls. Even the front windows were mostly blacked out.

Mulligan and Ester sat at the bar facing each other, she sipping a Seven & Seven and he a bottle of Schaeffer. He was surprisingly well relaxed, considering the situation.

"That guy Jose gave you a hard time," said Mulligan. He held the bottle of Schaeffer so that he could see the label, then raised it to his mouth and took a long swig, like he had a mean thirst.

"That's not the first time. He wants me to be his girl. I hate him. Did you know he came to get you the other day, when we were talking in my building?"

"I know. My friends told me … I got to get him off the streets. Before he kills somebody else … before he hurts you."

Gently she took hold of his wrist. "Oh, how nice of you. But stay away from him. He's crazy. He'll kill you."

"There's a safer way. We got a fire marshal helping us. Earlier today we got pictures of him. We think he was setting up a building to be torched. But the marshal told us that we have to have people willing to point him out in a courtroom."

"The people won't do that. They're afraid of him," she said. "And you know the people just won't tell you guys anything. So that idea is no good."

"He gets away with murder," said Mulligan. "And that little girl, Lucita. I just know he set that one."

The bar was alive, the music played and the people danced. The clock showed nine-thirty.

"Let's dance," she said. She got to her feet.

Mulligan smiled. "Love to. We're here to enjoy ourselves."

Taking her by the hand, he ushered her to the dance area, where they danced a slow dance. "You smell so good," he said while closing his eyes and inhaling.

She laughed.

"Why you laughing?" He chuckled.

"It's cheap crap I got at work."

"You haven't changed. There's no pretense. No bullshit with Ester. There never was, was there? Unless it was to make me jealous." He shook his head. "Where's work?" he continued.

"S&S, on 174th."

"A decent job, I hope?" he asked.

"It pays the bills," she said.

When the music stopped, they returned to the bar. For a moment they stood there smiling at each other. Then Mulligan grasped her hands, gently placing her arms behind her back, and pulled her to him, their bodies touching. Her face was but a few inches from his. "Ester. I … I still dig you, you know."

She pulled back from him and turned away. A look of dejection shadowed her face. "Jackie! Too fast. I don't know if we're right for each other anymore."

"Why? What's the matter?" He turned her around, facing him; his heart sinking. "What's the problem?"

"We ain't got any future together," she said.

"Why do you say that, 'no future together'?"

"You know … I mean—you forget? I'm a spic, you're a mick, you know. Our people don't want us together."

"Screw the bastards!" Mulligan said.

"Stop cursing!" she said.

"Sorry about that," he replied sheepishly.

"Listen to me. We could never get married because of that." Then she looked him hard in the eyes. "And your job! Ever since I met you I've been worrying about you. When I see you at these fires, it scares me terrible."

"Why? I told you not to be afraid. All we do is put the fires out," he said.

"Don't give me that baloney! What you think, I'm stupid? I see your friends getting hurt. Heck, I worried about you even when I was angry with you."

"Let's not ruin a good thing. What's the expression? What will be, will be," he said.

Still standing, he again put her arms behind her back and pulled her close to him. They gazed at each other.

"I must love you too. All I think about is you." She looked at the clock over the bar. "You better take me home. Work comes early."

Chapter   20

Tuesday, June 1, 1972

Fire Commissioner James Steele sat at a long, glossy mahogany table in one of City Hall's conference rooms. He appeared uptight, puffing fast and hard on a cigarette, creating a lot of smoke.

Directly across from the commissioner, next to Terrence Rubin, sat the upbeat Martha Johnson. A petite twenty-eight-year-old with short jet-black hair, Martha was wearing her usual smile. No wonder the Mayor told Rubin to make sure this whiz kid was the representative from Planning. She had the kind of face and charm that would light up a room, put a little cheer into one's day.

Mayor Nicholas Dunlap stood by the window, and as usual was observing the view out front on Broadway outside the security fence, where there were people, people, and more people. He enjoyed the hustle and bustle of the area at 7:30 AM, even when there were demonstrations or protest marches, as there was this day. Gathered in front of the gated main entrance, hardly noticed by the passersby hurrying to work, and being held at bay by a large contingent of police, was a small but vocal group of protesters.

"Look at that. Today it's the blacks demanding we bus Brownsville kids to Canarsie schools. Yesterday it was the whites insisting there be no bussing. Last week we had the hippies and the anti-war crowd. Since I've been Mayor, there's been nothing but marches, rioting, demonstrations—protest after protest. It never seems to end." He turned to Steele. "And of course fires, fires, and more fires." Shaking his head, he continued, "The City's ungovernable. Crime and disorder. It's out of control. How would the public react if they knew just how bad things are? Thank God the media cooperates with us. God, if the people knew the extent of the destruction." He shook his head.

"Sir!" Rubin interjected. "It's not as bad as in many other cities. And that's because of your popularity with the minorities. In other cities they fight the minorities. But not you, sir. You go to them. You walk, you talk and you listen.

Then you do something. They trust you, Mr. Mayor. That's what helps keep the lid on our long, hot summers."

It had been a tough six years for Dunlap since he took over as Mayor. Crisis after crisis, and no money.

He started off as an inspiration to the nation. But that image was long gone. He emerged as pro-minority and anti-cop, which didn't sit well with most Americans. The strain of the years showed on his face. He was tired, distraught.

Without looking at Commissioner Steele and Ms. Johnson, he thanked them for coming. "I know you both have busy schedules, so I'll be brief. I've just a couple of questions for you."

Looking directly at Steele he continued, "Jim, I know you're most concerned about the arson problems. And don't think I've been ignoring you. Or that I'm not concerned. But I need more info on that situation. How many arson-related deaths have there been this year in the South Bronx? Between January first and April thirtieth, I mean."

The commissioner glanced at his stats. "Thirty-nine, sir. Another five persons succumbed subsequently from their injuries, but statistically they don't count as fire deaths."

"Then I'm not interested in them."

The Mayor's response startled Martha Johnson, which was detected by Rubin.

"Martha." Rubin leaned close to her and whispered, "The City doesn't consider the cause of death to be fire-related if death occurs more than twenty-four hours after the fire."

The young woman still looked puzzled.

"How about injuries, Jim? And what kind?" continued the Mayor.

"Two hundred and one reported injuries. Mostly smoke inhalation, burns, broken bones, and lacerations. But I must make the point, sir, that many people *don't report* their injuries, especially minor ones. Either they're afraid they will have to pay for it or they are illegally in the country."

"I'm only interested in what is on the record," said the Mayor.

"Of course, Mr. Mayor. Also, these reports don't include the injuries to firefighters, which are numerous."

"Not now, Jim! How about vacant buildings? How many?"

The commissioner continued, "Some fire companies report as many as a hundred in their district, sir. Vacant or partially vacant that is. Some of them have entire blocks that are burned out and vacant. In certain areas the buildings in question are sound structures, not more than thirty years old."

"Uh ... how many families were relocated?" asked the Mayor.

"Mr. Mayor, if you don't mind, I'll defer that one to Martha." Commissioner Steele was annoyed at the Mayor's lack of concern regarding injuries to his men. He never yet addressed that issue with him.

Martha Johnson, a recent member of Planning's Neighborhood Development Team, was delighted to be asked to attend the meeting. She was grateful to be called upon by the Mayor. This was her opportunity to shine for "His Honor." A chance to get appointed to his staff, a highly esteemed position.

"Thanks, Commissioner," she said. She knew exactly where to look on her fact sheet for the answer to the Mayor's question.

"Mayor Dunlap, sir. It's impossible to come up with an exact number. But going by the pace of the destruction and the ever-expanding size of the South Bronx, we estimate that thousands of families have been permanently relocated. Since January that is. On Charlotte Street alone, which is just three blocks long, there have been over one hundred and sixty families displaced during that four-month period."

"My God! I find this hard to believe," said the Mayor.

"And please bear in mind, these figures are on the low side because there are many cases where several families shared an apartment."

Again the Mayor looked out the window, tapping the windowpane with his fingers. "How—how many people displaced throughout the City since the troubles started? Any idea of that figure?" he asked.

"I only have the figure for the South Bronx. That's heading for three hundred thousand, from when the problems started in '66 to now, mid 1972. And that number is rising all the time and will get much worse before it gets better," she replied.

"Why's that?" he asked.

"Because the same thing is now beginning in the west Bronx," she answered.

"Oh my Lord! Is there anything to compare it with historically? Anywhere?" Dunlap asked.

"Not that I'm aware of. Not in peace time," she said. She looked at the other faces to see if anyone else had an opinion on that question.

"It's like a war zone. Terry, you better schedule more 'walks with the people.'"

"Excellent idea, Mr. Mayor."

"Martha, if I'm not mistaken, this is within the area earmarked for redevelopment?" asked the Mayor.

"That is correct, sir. That's the heart of our Hunts Point project," she said.

"*Our* Hunts Point project? You mean Mayor Dunlap's South Bronx Revitalization Master Plan, don't you, Miss Johnson?" snapped Dunlap.

"Y-y-yes, sir, Mr. Mayor! All part of your ingenious South Bronx Revitalization Master Plan," she said.

Waving his hand, he silenced her. "I'll tell you, Miss Johnson. This is my pride and joy. If I ever get the promised money from the feds, it'll be my legacy. I'll create many thousands of new jobs. Many local workers will be needed to construct the Hunts Point Industrial Park. Once completed, the industrial park will generate many more permanent jobs. At the same time we'll be building new housing and renovating some existing housing throughout the area. This too will bring about employment. And fine housing will have been built for the people. Construction of several schools is already underway. My plan will serve as a model for the rest of the nation."

The faces around the conference table looked as though they were impressed.

"Jim, Martha! That'll be all for now. I'm sure I'll have more questions for you in the near future."

"But Mr. Mayor," said Commissioner Steele. "About the injuries to the firefighters and the arson for profit …"

"Jim, that doesn't concern me right now … and besides, most of our firefighters don't even live in the city. They don't vote here. What the hell good are they to me?"

"Yes, sir. But what does that have to do with it? They're our firefighters." The Commissioner was angry with the Mayor's contempt for the firemen and responded accordingly. But he was cut off with a firm wave of the Mayor's hand. Dunlap snapped, "That'll be all, Jim. The discussion is over."

Commissioner Steele managed to keep his demeanor as impassive as possible. He said no more, not wanting to put his highly regarded position on the line. He also understood the Mayor was doing what was expedient, for the good of the masses; so they said.

With Steele and Johnson gone, Dunlap roared, venting his anger. "I'm sick and tired of hearing about this 'arson for profit' bullshit! It's been going on far too long. What, four, five years?"

"In the Bronx, at least six years, sir," said Rubin.

Mayor Dunlap knew well how fragile the situation was for him. If the public ever became aware of his hands-off policy concerning the arson, it would be his political demise. And his slumlord friends wouldn't even be affected. And he also had to worry that the arson for profit would spread outside of the ghettos.

"How long can I look the other way?" muttered Dunlap.

Again Dunlap looked out the window at the demonstrators. "I wonder when they'll be out there protesting against the fires. Carrying 'Stop the Burning' placards." Turning to Rubin he said, "We must do something. Jim was upset. He's under a lot of pressure from his men and their unions; to expand the Department of Fire Investigation … I've got two years to go. I'll stall it for the duration. Besides, we don't have the money for that. What we have goes to the Urban Coalition and similar projects. Whatever it takes to keep the cool. No disorders, disturbances. You understand that, Terry?"

"Yes, Your Honor."

Dunlap never referred to the large-scale disturbances as the riots they were, many of which included burning and looting. He played them down, and the news media went along with him. The riots were often called *minor disturbances*.

"That's right, sir. Let the next Mayor take care of the arson. And if I may say, sir, don't concern yourself with the firemen. They're not your friends. Your friends in real estate are much more important."

"Yes! My friends … they're a band of bastards. The backbone of the arson-for-profit headache." He thought for a moment, then continued, "Yes, Terry, I think you're right. Stalling has another significant advantage. It will enable us to clear the areas of people, make it totally vacant, that is, so we can get on with rebuilding. My South Bronx Revitalization Program will make all concerned happy. And that should get me elected governor. That's why the deaths and injuries will be tolerated. Because of the end result."

"Yes, sir, Mr. Mayor. I am sure that by taking 'no action,' you'll be helping your political career," said Rubin.

"But I'm bothered by the deaths," said Dunlap.

"Yes, Mr. Mayor. But not all fire-related deaths and injuries are due to the arson for profit. Many, yes, but not all. Most are the result of accidents."

But there were many incidents of homicide by arson and arson used to cover up homicides. The two most common examples were jealous lovers and drug deals gone bad.

There was an irony to it all. There could have been a lot more casualties in the ghettos, but the affected people had so many unscheduled fire drills with all the fires they had experienced that they were up and out of the building before the fire and smoke became too much for them. They anticipated the next fire.

"And there's something else Jim told me," said the Mayor, "about the brazen bastards in those gangs. That his men detected a new tactic they're using: telling the people when to vacate the premises. Recently his men found that when arriving at a fire in a tenement, the tenants were already out in the street with their belongings. The people had been forewarned to be out by a certain date, the date when the building would be set afire."

The Mayor continued, "Yes, it is time to arrange a couple of those 'walks with the people.' That usually makes them feel good; most of them anyway."

At the same time, large commercial interests in the area were also being threatened. Most of them went out of business, wiping out badly needed jobs and sources of tax revenue. Those that resisted were burned out.

"One more thing, Your Honor. Senator Blackburn called to inform you that that piece of legislation you want has been introduced in the Senate and Assembly. He wants to assure you that he is confident it will become law."

Dunlap smiled broadly.

✳   ✳   ✳   ✳

Just off duty from a day tour, Mulligan and the brothers stood outside the firehouse, waiting for Luke. They were heading to Dorney's for a scheduled, but unofficial, union meeting between South Bronx firefighters and Charles "Chucky" Boland from the City Uniformed Firefighters Association.

"Where's Luke? Why can't that man ever be on time?" teased Mulligan. That's when Luke came through the door. Mulligan good-naturedly pointed to his watch and then to Luke, shaking his finger in a scolding manner. "You're late again. You are not setting a good example for us, Lieu."

The guys laughed.

"What do you got in the bag, Copper?" asked Mulligan.

"Six cold ones," he answered.

The men piled into Luke's car. Mulligan rode shotgun, smoking a cigarette, as was Luke. Copper passed out the beers, which they popped open as fast as they got them.

"Hey, Jackie! Anyone ever tell you, you gots a rather large head?" asked Copper.

Big laugh.

"The shit's on, baby. Lookout!" said Juan.

They pulled onto the Cross Bronx Expressway, which was a sea of slow-moving traffic.

"Yeah, Copper! The other night there, some broad I was banging commented on the size of my head."

"And who was that? Do I know her?" asked Copper.

"Yeah! Sure you do. It was your old lady," said Mulligan.

"You got him gooood, my man," said Juan while cheering.

The men's laughter irritated Copper. Staring narrow-eyed at the back of Mulligan's head, he drew on his cigarette, then snapped, "'It was your old lady.' Oh, he's so fucking funny."

"You're so easy, Copper," said Mulligan. "Who's coming from the union tonight?"

"Chucky Boland," answered Luke.

"WHOA! Look at the face on that broad. That's the ugliest face I've ever seen. Uglier than Jackie!" said Copper. "Catch up with her. I wanna get a closer look."

Luke accelerated the car.

Luke, the gentleman of the crowd, shook his head, disapproving of Copper's sense of humor. "Copper! You're ruthless. You ever look in a mirror?"

Luke pulled the car alongside the woman's vehicle. Copper leaned out the window, resting his chin on his arm. "Look at that face. What an ugly face … I mean ugly," he said, loud enough for the guys to hear him, laughing as he did.

"She knows what you're saying. She's giving you some dirty looks," warned Luke.

The woman opened her window.

Copper shouted, "That's a face only a mother could love."

Luke was startled. It was hard for him to keep his eyes on the road. "What's wrong with you?" he snapped. "Leave her alone!"

She shouted back, "Hey, you! Shit for brains."

Big laugh from the men.

"Shit! She's talking to me?" Copper's face flushed.

Luke laughed. "Well, she's not talking to me."

Copper regained his composure, looked hard at her, then shouted, "You talking to me, lady?"

"That's right, you little shit. What are you laughing at, you fat-assed faggot!"

For a moment Copper just stared at her, openmouthed, not knowing what to say. That's when she hit him hard, right in the mouth with an orange, then sped off, giving him the finger.

Dumbfounded, he grabbed his open mouth, as his lip immediately started swelling. He yelled after her, "Fa-fa-funny face."

"Fa-fa-funny face!" Mulligan mimicked, and then roared with laughter. "You got to be shitting. Is that all you got to say? Funny face!"

"Copper, you're ghost white. She scared you," laughed Packy.

Copper did not appreciate being ridiculed. He opened another beer.

"You got what you deserved," said Luke, who was genuinely annoyed with Copper.

"The last time I saw such a look of fear, it was on Jackie's face. But he had reason to be scared. Almost fell off a roof," said Juan.

"Jackie, tell us what happened," said Luke. "I never heard that story. But please! Don't turn it into a dramatic bull-crap story."

Mulligan sipped his beer. "I'd love to. As soon as I get everybody's attention, thank you." He looked around to make sure everyone was focused on him.

"It was 3:00 AM Christmas morning, 1970," he began. "A bitter cold night. We had a third alarm in a row of wood-frame houses. Sixty souls were left homeless. Fire was consuming several of the buildings, working its way from house to house through the cocklofts. My job was to get to the roof of the corner building. The safest, fastest way for me to get there was by the tower-ladder bucket. Thick smoke pushed out of the front windows on the top two floors. Heavy fire and smoke shot upwards into the sky from the rear of the building."

"Already you're starting to drift into the bull, Jackie," warned Luke.

"How dare you!" Mulligan feigned reprimanding Luke. "As I was saying, I got the Haze from Thirty-One to take me to the roof via the bucket, right up through the choking smoke to a location about fifteen feet from the scuttle. I had to open it to begin venting. Meanwhile, we were being sprayed with water that froze on contact."

Mulligan turned around in his seat, a big smile on his face. "You had to see the Haze. The white crystals formed on his eyebrows and mustache against his black skin. It looked rather weird. Of course he told me I looked weird too."

"You do look weird, Jackie," mumbled Copper.

"But what I didn't notice in the smoke and darkness was that the water was turning the roof into an ice skating rink. And that the roof pitched down toward the rear of the building, where fire was everywhere. I opened the bucket gate and stepped onto the icy surface, using my halligan and six-foot hook to help keep my balance. Haze maneuvered the bucket back down to the street. He didn't see me as I struggled to keep my footing."

"The bull is getting real heavy," said Luke.

"I bullshit you not. Wait till you hear this. I slipped on the ice, slammed face down and busted my nose. And my helmet slid right off the roof. Worst of all, I started sliding on the ice toward the back of the building, heading right for that fiery hell."

"Such courage. He's my hero," laughed Juan.

Mulligan laughed too, but continued: "Fortunately enough, I had the presence of mind to use my halligan tool to stop my slide. With all the force I could muster, I drove its point into the roofing. It all happened so fast, I didn't really have the time to think of what was transpiring. But when I stopped sliding, that's when I got scared shitless. That's when I realized what almost happened. That's when I decided to get the hell off the roof. But not before I got over to the scuttle and popped it open. Then I called the Haze, who returned to get my trembling ass. Since then, I have had the utmost respect for ice."

A big smile broke across Luke's face when he commented in jest, "Jackie, truly you're a man among men. A hero among heroes."

"Superman," said Packy.

Mulligan turned to Luke, and in a pleasant tone said, "Thank you."

Everybody got a chuckle, except Copper, who was into himself, still stinging from his experience with the young lady.

Packy shouted, "We're here, brothers! Kindly place your empties into the bag provided us by Smiley. Oh, excuse me, I mean Copper." By then, Copper was sporting a swollen upper lip.

"Copper, that's a big lip you got there. She really got you good," said Mulligan.

"Up yours, you hump."

Chapter 21

Like follow the leader, Mulligan, Luke, Juan, and Packy marched military-style into Dorney's, stomping their feet, with Mulligan counting cadence. Sour-faced Copper followed, keeping a distance, looking at the floor.

The noisy, smoke-filled joint was overflowing with people, mostly off-duty firefighters who had turned out for the meeting, some unfamiliar faces among them. Bull and Jimbo were already there with several other men from the Tin House.

"Look at the turnout, man. Must be a hundred guys," observed Mulligan. The large crowd was uplifting to him, as was the tune "Crystal Chandelier" that played on the jukebox.

"I just hope it helps our situation," said Luke.

Chucky Boland, decked out smartly in a beige-colored suit, entered the bar and joined them.

"What's with the suit, big guy?" joked Mulligan as they shook hands. Boland was a big man, standing at six-three, weighing in at 220.

"What do you expect me to wear? Dungarees? Have respect for your union, will you," barked Chucky. As usual he took a joke seriously even though everybody in their group was laughing, but he quickly recovered his good-natured way.

There were some verbal greetings and handshakes, mixed with a little more banter and a couple of digs. Mulligan yelled, "Jerry D, give this important union representative a drink."

"Make it a soda," said Chucky. He looked around the room, checking out the crowd.

"And make sure he pays for all the drinks," continued Mulligan.

Chucky Boland was well liked by the firefighters.

"How you doing, Chucky?" Mulligan asked. "Guess you wanna get right down to business, hah?"

"Absolutely. As soon as I get my costly soda … I see you did your homework. Got a good turnout."

"Yep! The bigger the turnout, the more the union listens. Isn't that right, Chucky?"

Boland nodded. "That's how it works."

"Why don't we head into the back room?" suggested Juan.

Jerry D, the usually mild-mannered owner, placed the drinks in front of the men, then scooped up Boland's ten-dollar bill, which prompted some "gotcha" smiles from the men. With a biting grin that eventually turned to a smile, the big man scanned the smiling faces.

Mulligan toasted Boland. "Here's to a good man. Thanks for the drink, Chucky."

Boland grinned while saying, "It's my pleasure—brothers." Then he leaned close to Mulligan and whispered, "You won't do that again."

"Everybody," barked Bull, "move your fat asses into the back room. Pronto!" From somewhere up front a high-pitched voice shouted, "Anything you say, lard-ass." Laughter filled the room.

A lectern was in place, as were chairs set up in rows across the floor, but not enough. It was a standing-room-only situation. Boland stepped up to the lectern, where he laid out some papers, killing time as the troops piled into the room. Pounding the sides of the hollow lectern with his hands like it was a drum to get the men's attention, he shouted, "Let's get started. Let's go, brothers." He then fidgeted with his tie.

At the same time Juan began shouting with his hand up, waving, "I got a question. I got a question."

Boland responded with a chuckle. "Whoa! Whoa, brother! One minute, please. Before I take questions," he gripped the sides of the lectern top, "I want to say hello, you know. And give you guys some new info I have relating to the arson. It's quite informative."

"Let him speak," somebody shouted.

"Brothers, I want to thank you for turning out tonight," he said, his eyes checking the crowd. "For those of you who might not know me, my name is Charles Boland. I am your Bronx Trustee. I too work in the South Bronx. I started in Engine 46 and crossed the floor to Ladder 27, to which I am still assigned. And we're also confronted with a lot of arson." Then he began to read a prepared statement.

"Over the past seven years, the increase in structural fires throughout the ghettos has been staggering. The arson," he looked out at the men, "torch jobs as we call it, has impacted dramatically on Fire Department related statistics." With a believe-it-or-not look on his face he continued, "Listen to this. In 1961 there were less than 62,000 fires. About 10,000 were structural, and they were spread throughout the city. In 1968, there were 128,929 fires, in '69 there was 126,204 and in '70, 127,249 fires. In each of these years there was well over 40,000 structural fires, more than four times the number in '61."

Again he looked out at the brothers. "And the vast majority of the fires have been in the ghettos, like here in the South Bronx. The ghettos represent only a small portion of the City's land mass. Yet, a couple of million people, out of New York's more than eight million, reside in them."

Somebody shouted, "Not no more. Now it's like seven million and change, according to the news."

"My God. It's worse than we thought," said Boland.

"Yeah, man. The donkeys and guineas are fleeing the City en masse," shouted Juan to a roar of laughter.

"All right. Let me continue," said Boland, who was still laughing. "Most of the fires were torch jobs. And many of them were major fires. And the arson is spreading rapidly to the surrounding areas, which were not ghettos. Like right here in the west Bronx."

Boland paused to check the reactions of the men, then continued, "There was never a publicized, accurate accounting by the City of the number of arson-related fires. Many of the obvious arson fires in occupied buildings in the Bronx, Brooklyn, Harlem and the Lower East Side, were marked suspicious (pending investigation), but were never investigated. And in vacant buildings, hell, every fire is a torch job. Some vacants had thirty, forty or more fires in them. And there have been thousands of vacants over the years. They too were not recorded."

Changing the charged tone of his voice to a soft and deliberate tone, he continued, "And you know why there have been no investigations?" Raising his voice to a shout, "Because there's not enough goddamned marshals to do the job. Why? Because the City refuses to deal with this crisis. That's the Mayor I'm talking about."

He resumed speaking in his normal tone. "A problem that has been extremely detrimental to us. And the City hasn't even carried out, for the public's consumption, an accurate accounting of how many civilians and firefighters were injured or killed due to the arson. Your union has now initiated such a study. We've also been looking into what's behind the arson with the help of good friends in important places. This arson-for-profit scheme is much bigger than we thought. Very politicized, involving politicians at every level of government. They are intertwined with our real estate and insurance industries. Some of the pols are heavily invested in ghetto real estate. Many have just bought in, mind you. It's scandalous. Especially when so many people have been screwed … This crap pisses me off."

Boland had their full attention.

"How does it work?" somebody shouted.

"From what we got so far, it's very simple. The slumlords set up phony companies just to sell their buildings back and forth to themselves. This way they raise the value of the properties." Boland looked around the room. "Shall I continue?" he asked, enjoying their enthusiasm.

"Yes!" was the overwhelming response.

"Then, through friends in the insurance business, they get the buildings insured for much higher prices. And many of them take out multiple policies on the same building, collecting in full from each insurer."

"That's legal?" a brother shouted.

"That's right, brother. Imagine recovering more on a building than it would be worth, even in the best of times. For a building they can't give away."

"No wonder they won't hire more fire marshals. Everybody's in on the bonanza, raking in all the money," shouted Mulligan.

"Yeah," continued Boland. "And as I said before, as the people who are burned out move to the west Bronx, the arson-for-profit gangs follow them. This plague is going to go on for years if left unchecked."

After a brief pause to let what he said register with the men, he said, "I will keep you updated." He nodded and waved in appreciation as the men applauded him.

Boland felt good about himself, being able to provide the men with important information they hadn't already known. It showed on his face.

"Now it's time for questions." Pointing to Juan, he asked, "How about you, brother?"

"Yesterday we had another bad job. A torch job. A few of the brothers got hurt, as did three civilians." He held up three fingers. "Including an infant."

A firefighter in the back shouted, "And one of the adults died since."

"I didn't know that," said Juan. "It's obvious the union agrees with us that too many of our people are getting injured at these fires. But do you guys care about it?"

"Absolutely!" insisted Boland. The contented look on his face disappeared.

"Let me finish, man," said Juan while holding up his hand. "I mean like your research will take God knows how long. But we need action now! You dig what I'm saying?"

"Yeah, I *dig* what you're saying. As far as the union's concerned, we're constantly pushing the City. But to no avail. We get the same old story: they're going to hire more marshals. But, as you know, that never happens. And our commissioner simply echoes the Mayor's message, even though he's sympathetic to us."

"He's nothing but a yes man," shouted Bull.

"Absolutely!" agreed Boland.

"Is that all you got to say: 'absolutely'?" asked Luke. "I mean, you don't even know what the City plans to do about it. Don't you guys talk to them?"

"Sorry, guys! But there is nothing new to tell you on that issue. It's that simple," he replied nonchalantly, with a smirk on his face that the men did not like.

With that he was bombarded with boos. Over the boos Bull roared: "This is bullshit, Brother Boland. You guys don't give a shit. What the hell we paying yuz for?"

Boland's face soured; his neck reddened. Gripping tightly the lectern top, he moved his lips, wanting to shout back, to tell them all to go to hell, but he thought better of it. He let them finish venting, then continued.

"Guys, please! Hear me out. It's not that we haven't tried to get the City off their butts. God knows we're constantly calling them on it. What do you want us to do?"

"Whatever it takes, Chuck," shouted Mulligan.

Several voices called for a strike.

Bull shouted, "That's right! If the bastards don't give a damn about us, screw them. Maybe we should call a strike. That'll get their attention. And the public's too. After all, they don't give a damn either. Then maybe we'll get some results."

"Brothers," Boland paused, looking around the room, waiting until he got their full attention. "Rumor has it that nothing significant will be done to combat the arson until the properties of the shyster landlords—some of whom are political heavyweights—have been burned out and the insurance collected. We've also heard the City wants the areas in question cleared for redevelopment and that the arson is doing the job for them."

Mulligan nudged Luke and Juan. "Exactly what Molletti said."

Again Luke raised his hand.

"Go ahead, brother," said Boland.

"But up here this arson crap has been going on for years. And many brothers have been hurt since it started," said Luke.

Jimbo raised his hand, but before being recognized, yelled out, "Is this an exercise in futility? Or is it an exercise in futility? Get my drift, brother?"

"Hold on there, brother. Wait till I've acknowledged you." Boland paused. "Okay. What's your question?"

"I've been my company delegate for the past three years. And I've been proud to represent my union. But now I'm pissed with it. You guys," he shook his head. "You aren't looking out for our interests."

Boland pounded his ham-hocks-like fists on the top of the lectern. "Easy there, brother!" With a glare in his eyes, he pointed his finger at Jimbo, then roared, "I'm with you. Damn it! I know your concerns. I know there have been many injuries, serious injuries … My company was caught in that vacant that collapsed the other day. Every one of the injured is a personal friend. How the hell you think I feel?"

Jimbo stood up and pointed back at Boland, shouting, "Yeah! Well, let me tell you." But before the shouting match between Jimbo and Boland could get started, a commotion erupted in the back of the room that got everybody's attention. A man with *half-a-jag-on,* his neck wrapped in gauze and an arm in a cast, entered the room and started shouting at Boland. Although slurring a little, he made his point loud and clear. "You guys aren't worth a shit, Chucky. What has the union done for us?"

There was total silence as Boland calmly spoke to the man. "Easy now, Lombardi. Take a seat."

"I'll sit when I'm ready to sit. You union guys haven't done diddly-squat about it," the man continued, still shouting. "That collapse should never have happened."

The silence was deafening. All eyes were on Lombardi. Boland decided it would be prudent to let the man have his say, whatever it was.

Lombardi continued, his voice lowered, no longer shouting. "You know I was in that collapse on Jennings. Trapped in smoldering rubble, choking. Thinking for sure I would die before the brothers got to me. I'm the only one that wasn't hurt seriously. We were almost all killed." He then shouted, "At a fucking torch job! In a fucking vacant that should have been demolished a long time ago."

Boland was caught between a rock and a hard place. He wanted to cut this guy off. But how could he? They worked in the same firehouse. And he was talking about something most important to ghetto firefighters. "Is that all, Lombardi?"

"I'm not finished."

One man shouted, "Let him talk!"

"You got the floor, brother," said Boland.

"Do you know what it's like to be trapped? Upside-down, pinned under tons of debris, hardly able to breathe or move any part of your body … with smoke choking you, with water constantly running over your face, sometimes almost smothering you? Always on the verge of panic. And hearing fire crackling below you, wondering if it will get you. All the while listening to your brothers moaning or crying out for help. It's a horrible experience I wish on no one."

The men were riveted to their seats, hearing every word he had to say.

His eyes moistened as he continued. "You know what saved me from going crazy?" His body trembled for a moment. "Prayer. I turned to my Maker and prayed like hell. I turned my life over to him and asked only that he take care of my family. Then, like that," he snapped his fingers, "I was able to accept my fate … which gave me peace of mind. I was no longer afraid. But we were lucky. They pulled all of us out. But I'm so pissed off that I had to go through this hell. For almost six hours. In a vacant!" Then, his voice filled with emotion, he shouted, "A vacant torch job!"

Having spoken his piece, Lombardi left the room. There was momentary silence, then a gradual applause that became a thunderous one.

Boland spoke in a conciliatory tone. "But what can we do? They have the power, and they do as they please. And there's nobody checking them. Not the press. Not even the public, who doesn't even know what's going on."

Bull asked, "How about if we ourselves go after these people?"

"I'd advise against that. You'd get yourselves into a major civil rights jam. And the City won't back you."

Bull continued, "If I was so fortunate as to catch one of these scumbags, the City would never know. There'd be a terrible accident."

Luke stood up to speak. "I want to make a point."

"Absolutely, brother! You got the floor," said Boland.

As Luke started talking, Juan smiled and poked Packy in the ribs, then whispered, "Man, like what's all this 'absolutely' bullshit?"

"Chucky, you know what's going to happen," said Luke.

"Absolutely!"

Juan and Packy laughed.

Luke continued. "One day one of our guys will get seriously hurt, maybe even killed. And then what? I'll tell you what! The union will be just as responsible as the City. Unless you guys start pressuring them to take real action against these bums."

"You tell them, Luke," shouted Mulligan. "That's what it's all about!"

Luke continued, "So, I ask you to make a commitment here, right now, that you'll do all you can, as our rep up here, to get the union and the City to move on this. What do you say, Chucky?"

Luke's words brought loud cheers and applause from the men.

"I got the message, brothers … and for your info, the union has made its mind up to take strong action against the City. Of course, we don't yet know what that will be. So please give us a little more slack."

Juan shouted, "Absolutely!"

There was an outburst of laughter, with one exception: Boland, who mumbled something under his breath while gazing coldly at Juan.

"Any further questions?" shouted Boland. There were none. "I guess there's nothing else then, except to remind you to turn out for the next citywide meeting and put your position before the general membership. I'll do the same."

Boland didn't look too happy when he stepped from behind the lectern, but then a shout came from Bull, "But we still love you, Chucky baby," to which the men applauded.

A big smile broke across Boland's face. "Thanks, I needed that."

With the meeting over, the men went to the bar. Now the fun would start. This would be a night out for the boys. Or as Luke's wife would call it: "Children's night out."

The men were back at the bar with their drinks. Mulligan had changed to club soda, about which he had one word to say: "Boring."

"The Mayor and his cronies don't give a damn about us," said Bull.

"Yeah, all they give a damn about is the dudes with the money. We're their servants. Cannon fodder," added Juan.

"Why do we risk our lives? You know what I mean? Why?" asked Bull.

"Ah! For the good people, Bull," said Mulligan.

"Where *we* work? What good people?" Bull asked.

"They're just like us, Bull," Mulligan continued. "All they want is a little dignity. A decent job, a place to live, and an education for their kids. Just like us."

Juan frowned, but didn't get excited. "That's right, Bull," he said. "Most of my people are just like you, and want the same things for their families as you want for yours. Just like Jackie said."

"I know that now, Juan. You educated me on that shit. But you have to be honest. I mean the shit that happens down here's just too much. And it happens much too often. You don't see that happening where I come from, where whitey lives. But you're right. And I mean that."

They slapped five. Then Bull turned to Mulligan and said, "Sometimes I think you're becoming a lib. You know that?"

"The City should demolish the damned vacants. That would prevent many of our injuries," said Juan.

"I'm out of here. Got to pick up Ester," said Mulligan.

"Yeah. I better go get Mama," said Luke. He finished his beer. "Did you notice the size of Copper's lip?"

"No!" said Mulligan, turning to Copper. "Wow! Your lip got bigger—"

"One of these fucking days," said Copper, rubbing a tissue on his lip.

"Damn! Can't you take a joke?" With that, Mulligan turned and headed out the door. He heard Copper shouting after him, "Sure. But you don't know when to stop."

✶   ✶   ✶   ✶

When Mulligan pulled into Charlotte Street heading toward Ester's, he heard what sounded like an argument between a woman and man. *That's Ester's voice.* Then he saw her and Jose. Stopping abruptly, he hopped out of the car and rushed to her side.

Jose threw up his fists. "Come on, muddafucker. I kick you ass." He started dancing with his guard up. Mulligan was quick to oblige, putting up his fists, but Ester stepped in front of him. In a flash, he side-stepped her, shouting, "Come on! Hit me with your best, you puta."

Ester put her arms around Mulligan and pushed him back. "Stop it! Stop it," she shouted. She would not let him go.

The two raging bulls exchanged angry looks and taunts.

"Are you all right? Did he touch you?" Mulligan stood poised to brawl, but no longer pushed for a fight. Jose had also backed off, but continued to threaten. "You fucking *maricons,*" he pointed to Mulligan, "better stop following me. I'm warning you, mister."

Mulligan was taken aback, but his response was sudden. "We know you're the torch. And we're gonna get your ass. One way or the other."

"Fuck you!" He gave Mulligan the birdie. "I get you first, mister. All you guys. You put my father in jail. You took him from me. I don't forget that."

Storming off, Jose turned and shouted, "What kind of a Puerto Rican woman are you? Going out with an Irisher!"

Ester was shaking. "I wasn't afraid for myself. It was for you. If you guys had a fight he'd pull his knife. And he'd use it," she emphasized.

Mulligan pretended the knife bit didn't faze him. "What's he talking about we took his father away?"

"He blames all firemen for his father going to jail. His old man started a big fire on Southern Boulevard. It was a fireman who identified him. So he blames all you guys."

"Did he touch you?" asked Mulligan.

"No! He just yelled at me, wanting to know why you guys are following him." Then she gave a puzzled look and asked, "*Are* you following him?"

"Yes. We want to catch him. To stop him. But let's not talk about that. I'm here to enjoy you. To look at your pretty face."

"You know, he's crazy," she said, getting into the car. "Most people around here are scared of him. And I mean it, he will cut you."

"No big deal. I'll take care of him," he said, getting into the car. His hands trembling, he struggled to get the key into the ignition. "So let me see that face," he continued, smiling, trying to appear calm. "That beautiful face that you denied me all these years."

"Don't say that. Please," she insisted. She slapped the back of his hand.

"Just kidding," he replied.

"And pay attention. He'll hurt you. And your friends."

"Yeah, yeah. I hope you don't mind meeting my friends," said Mulligan.

"Listen to me," she insisted, cutting him off. "Be afraid of him. He'll kill you, Jackie."

"All right, all right! I'll be careful. Do you mind meeting my friends?"

"No, I don't mind. I want to meet them. I like your friends," she said. "The guy, Luke, and the tall, red-headed guy. What's his name?"

"Packy! A good man. They're all good men," he said.

"I don't know what Jose would have done to me if they didn't come over," she said.

"One of these days, we're going to go at it. Me and him," said Mulligan.

"No, no! Don't do that. Not over me, please," she insisted.

"Do you know people who'd point him out in court?" He changed the subject.

"No, I told you before. They're scared. But I'll go to court."

"No! No! Not you," he said.

"Why not me?" she asked.

"I don't want anything happening to you."

"He's already threatened me. Before you came tonight, he told me he'd get me if he couldn't get you and your friends."

"What! I'll get that sonofa … You know, if you don't feel safe here, you can stay in my place."

"No, no. I got to stay with Carmen." She kissed his face. "You're so kind."

$$* \qquad * \qquad * \qquad *$$

There was a full house in Dorney's when Mulligan returned with Ester. A real party atmosphere with a lot of laughter and people talking. Even a couple of people were singing along with the jukebox.

"Gads. Look at that smoke. Looks like we got a working fire here," said Mulligan. Most patrons hardly noticed the thick cigarette smoke that had banked down from the lightless ceiling to a point just above their heads.

They joined Luke and Dorothy, who were with Mulligan's neighborhood friends. Shortly, they were surrounded by Juan, Packy, Bull, Copper and Jimmy Bannon.

Jerry D put up a couple of drinks for them compliments of Luke, and Mulligan introduced Ester to the group. "Hey, everybody," he said, "This is my old friend, Ester Gonzalez. The most beautiful—"

"None of that shit here," she protested in whisper, while driving her elbow into his ribs. "Don't embarrass me."

"Hi," she said with a smile, shaking hands with Luke and Packy. "Thanks for helping me the other day."

Then Lucita stepped close to Jackie. "I see you have good taste. She's a good-looking Puerto Rican girl. Just like Lucita Morales."

"Good gal, Lucita," shouted Dorothy.

Mulligan smiled, and Ester blushed—a little.

"And I'm Irene Hogan. A beautiful Irish girl," said Irene upon returning from the bathroom.

"Yeah, and if I was a single guy," said Bull, to Irene's pleasure, "I'd be chasing you."

"The Black Velvet Band" started playing on the jukebox. Immediately Papi started singing. He was joined by Lucita and Irene. Ester was fascinated with their talent and the sound.

"What kind of music is that?" she asked Mulligan.

"Ah, poor Ester. You've been in the ghetto too long. You forgot what good music is. That's Irish music! Don't you remember? From the old neighborhood."

"Oh yes, of course. But it's been so long. And besides, not everybody listens to Irish music, you know."

"I didn't know that. I thought everybody did," said Mulligan.

As soon as the song finished, a mambo started playing. In this bar it seemed that every time an Irish tune played, it was followed by Latino music.

Lucita grabbed Mulligan by the hand. "Ester, we always do the mambo. Do you mind?"

"Please join me." Dorothy welcomed Ester in her Irish accent.

"Oh, you're Irish. What a nice accent you have."

"Why, thank you. Jackie talks a lot about you. And if I may say so, you're every bit as pretty as he said you were."

"Thank you. And your husband's a nice man. He, and that big man over there," she pointed to Packy, "helped me the other day."

"Yes. Luke told me. Some crazy guy went after you, or something like that," said Dorothy.

"Yes."

"How long have you known Jackie?" asked Dorothy.

"Since we were kids. We went steady for almost two years," she said.

Dorothy's tone changed. "I wanna give you a word of advice. If you have any long-term plans for him and wanna sleep at night, make sure he transfers from that crazy firehouse."

"What do you mean?" asked Ester.

"Make him move to a slow firehouse. It's too dangerous where they work. They're always getting hurt."

"Okay. I know what you mean … I'm already worrying about him. I saw him almost get killed."

"What! Luke never told me. That devil. Did Jackie tell you one of their good friends was killed in '69?"

Ester shook her head. "Uh, uh."

"Mike McGarry was his name. A young guy with a wife and two small kids. Very sad."

"That's terrible. Why don't they work where it's safer? Or just get another job?"

Dorothy smiled. "Because they're a bunch of assholes. That's why. And my husband Luke is the biggest asshole of them all. But I love him dearly."

Ester returned the smile. "I see them all the time doing crazy things. I hope they get paid well."

"Not at all. They have to work side jobs to pay the bills. Sometimes Luke's like a walking zombie when he goes to work at the firehouse, when he goes in from his other job. It's just not right."

The music stopped. Lucita brought Jackie back. "Here, Ester. He's all yours."

"You're not mad, Ester, are you?" asked Mulligan.

"Why should I be mad?"

"Remember, Ester? It was you who taught me to mambo," he said.

Juan cut in on their conversation. "The union's not too cool, man," he said. "Boland didn't do shit for me. Like nothing changed. They're still talking about how to bring pressure on the Mayor, and the Mayor's still studying the arson situation. The place will be gone before anything is done."

"Well, Chucky pretty much leveled with us when he said the Mayor has the power, not the union," said Mulligan.

*   *   *   *

Mulligan and Ester sat in the car facing each other, with their backs against the door, parked around the corner from her place. They didn't want to be seen by Jose should he be hanging out at the vacant.

"Man, you turn me on. Just like you always did. You look so good." He reached for her, only to be pushed back.

"Hold on there," she said. "So I turn you on, hah? Well, how do you feel about me?"

"Now what's wrong?" he asked, not knowing whether or not to smile.

"You heard me. How do you feel about me?" she repeated. Stone-faced, she stared him in the eye and waited for his reply.

"Just like I felt about you when you dumped me."

She stared in silence, making it obvious she wasn't satisfied with his answer.

He laughed a nervous laugh. "I love you."

"You love me enough to go to a slow firehouse?"

"Go to a what?" Mulligan paused, looking her in the eye. "Who were you talking to?"

"Never mind! And don't feed me no more of that bull that it's safe there. We've been through this before … and you never told me about your friend Mister McGarry."

"I don't want you worrying about me."

"Well, I do worry about you."

Chapter 22

August 12, 1972 was a hot, sticky day that required maximum air conditioning. At 1:00 PM sharp, a battered older car parked at the corner of Boston Road and Charlotte Street. A derelict stumbled from the car. Scary to think that this person was driving.

Upon closer inspection, the derelict turned out to be Ritchie Molletti, and he was stone sober. The fire marshal was driving a friend's car that he often used for surveillance. With a several-day growth on his face; unkempt clothes; dirty, worn sneakers; and his hair a mess, he looked like, and smelled like, a real live skell. Molletti was still tracking Jose, hoping to finally get a picture of him in the act of starting a fire.

Several passersby paid him little notice. Acting the drunk, he staggered sideways from the car to a corner utility pole, all the time glancing at Jose's hangout. Then, as though losing his balance, he hooked one of his arms around the pole and proceeded to stumble around it.

Since he first started trailing Jose, Molletti twice saw him enter a building with a green shopping bag. And shortly thereafter, when he exited the building, the bag was empty. On both occasions, early the next morning a fire occurred in the buildings. The blazes began in vacant, top-floor apartments.

Keeping up with Jose was tough for Molletti, being twelve years older and thirty pounds heavier. Especially when maneuvering through vacant buildings with stairwells that had steps missing and when cutting through garbage-filled backyards and climbing fire escapes.

Just what to do with the picture once he got it was Molletti's dilemma. Trailing Jose was unauthorized.

"There'll be no investigation in the South Bronx until the Mayor calls for one. And that's final," was the order he received from his superior when he sought permission to track him. The only way to nail Jose was for someone to catch him red-handed starting a fire.

Molletti had been trailing Jose for three days, posing as a drunk and wearing the same clothes. Most of the time he spent watching the entrance to Jose's hangout.

Three men with an air of cockiness about them ambled along Charlotte, then stopped in front of Jose's hangout and conversed briefly. Molletti used a small telephoto lens camera to get close-ups of each of them. The small camera, taped to a bottle of wine, was concealed in a paper bag.

He then staggered into Charlotte for a better view of things. And he did it well; slamming sideways into a six-foot-high wrought-iron fence in front of Ester's building, almost falling to the ground. He could see the cool dudes across the street chuckling at him.

Upstairs in their so-called headquarters, Jose was picking up another container of gasoline, when there were three soft knocks on the door. After checking the peephole, he let them in: Miguel, Tito, and George, the men Molletti had observed on the street.

When Miguel saw the gasoline, he right away asked, "What's that for?"

"For the one on 170th," snapped Jose. "Why you ask me that?"

"Because I don't trust you. You're nothing but trouble, man. I'm afraid you're going to bring us down."

"You bet you ass, man. If I go, you go too." Jose turned and walked out of the apartment, bringing the Red Devil's drink with him in the shopping bag.

"That fucking guy. He's crazy," warned Miguel. "He's gonna get us in big trouble, man. If we let him." He pounded the table.

Lying prone on the stoop of the charred remains of Coburn's daughter's home, Molletti saw Jose exit the building, then stop momentarily. Getting to his feet, he staggered across the street, keeping his eye on Jose, who was too occupied with his own anger to notice him.

Molletti sprawled on another stoop, hitting it hard enough to cause him some pain, this time faking a swig from the wine bottle. His eyes followed Jose to the corner, where he turned into 170th and entered an Acrows-owned corner building, the last building on that block with a full complement of tenants. Molletti snapped a picture of him going inside. A few minutes later Jose exited the building minus the gasoline, the green bag under his arm.

Beautiful! He planted the gasoline, thought Molletti. He snapped another picture.

Jose headed across 170th on his way to Wilkins.

Molletti ducked into the alleyway to continue his tail of Jose. Perspiring and breathing heavily, he worked his way through the alleyways and backyards to Wilkins. When he emerged on the street, Jose, who was almost right in front of him crossing the street, spotted him. He stopped and faced Molletti. *Is this guy following me?* he wondered. But his suspicion vanished when he saw Molletti start picking through a garbage can. Jose continued across the street to the El Tico.

*   *   *   *

It was almost two-fifteen in the afternoon when the two fire companies returned to quarters from a nasty automobile wreck. An auto had crashed through the six-foot-high steel safety fencing of the Penn Central railway tracks on Park Avenue, plummeting thirty feet to the track bed below, sending three people to a fiery death, one of them a child. The men went right to the kitchen.

"Man, you took that real bad, Lieu," said Juan.

"I always do, when it's a kid. Having kids of my own, it hurts to see an innocent one killed," replied Luke.

"You are a good man," Juan continued. "I'm proud to work with you."

Luke didn't know what to say. "I ... you ... I'm—"

"Spit it out, man," said Juan.

"I'm proud of you guys too," said Luke. "To work with you, all you guys. You're the best. We're the best. We got a great thing here. So many smiling faces. When we're not fighting fires, we're enjoying each other's company. One big happy family."

"We might as well enjoy ourselves while we're here," said Juan. "Once we go out that door we don't know what's going to happen, man. Pull out a roast ... maybe a broken body from a wreck! Or maybe one of us getting fucked up."

"I love me, who do you love?" said Copper. "What do we got here? A couple of faggots getting sentimental on us. Give me a break!" Copper laughed.

"You know, Copper!" said Luke. "That tiny young lady that hit you in the mouth with the orange was right."

Copper did not know where Luke was going with this. "Yeah ... About what?" he asked.

"You do have a fat butt."

*   *   *   *

In the El Tico, Jose and Tito stood towards the front of the bar while Miguel and George stood at the far end.

Tito warned Jose, "We won't take any more of your shit, man. You've made a fool of me and I don't like it, *maricon.*"

"Fuck you muddafuckers! I don't need you guys," Jose challenged, staring defiantly into Tito's eyes.

"That you're my cousin doesn't mean shit anymore. You screw us again …" Tito formed a gun with his hand and mimicked shooting it. That was the end of their conversation. Tito joined Miguel and George.

Sitting on the stoop of a vacant on the other side of Wilkins Avenue, an unusually wide street, directly opposite the El Tico, Molletti's patience was fast dissipating. *When's this guy coming out?* he wondered. It was 4:00 PM, a long day for him tracking Jose, sweating almost continuously in his funky derelict attire, stinking of body odor, which lent credibility to his disguise. It was when he got to his feet to leave that the door to the El Tico opened and out stepped Jose, his eyes immediately zeroing in on Molletti.

Holy shit! Molletti thought fast. *Now what do I do?* Molletti did not look back at him. He staggered a few feet, then fell back down on the stoop, again hitting hard; again hurting himself. Next thing he saw was Jose's red shoes on the street right in front of him.

"Mister," he slurred, "you got a quarter?" while extending his hand, making it tremble like the hand of an alcoholic desperate for a drink. He gave Jose a hopeless look.

Jose replied in a tough, growling voice, scaring Molletti. "Hey, mister. I don't like you dirty face. If it wasn't for the way you stink, man, I'd think you were a cop. If I thought you was a fucking cop," Jose handed him a dollar with one hand, and with his other hand, flashed and flipped open his switchblade knife, "I would cut you deep and continuously." With that he continued on his way.

Walking toward 170th, Jose kept looking back at Molletti, who was again searching through garbage cans.

Where's the crazy bastard going now? thought Molletti. *It's got to be to 170th.* Once Jose turned into that street, Molletti took off down the cellar steps, working his way back through the rubbish-filled alleys and backyards to the yard behind the tenement where Jose dropped off the gasoline. When about to slip through a hole in the wooden fence leading to its rear yard, Jose appeared in front of him on the other side of the fence.

Freezing in place, his heart pounding, he listened to the metallic rattling of the fire escape drop ladder Jose was climbing. Excited, he asked himself: *Is this it? Am I going to catch the sonofabitch?* On impulse he felt for the camera … and his gun.

*   *   *   *

Luke was one of Mulligan's staunchest fans when he sang and played his guitar. "Jackie, me boy! Give us a couple of rebel songs, will you?"

"Yeah, that's exactly what we need," shouted Bull, "to liven up this dull, uneventful firehouse … It is show time!"

"Thank you, gentlemen, thank you," replied Mulligan, reaching into the kitchen food closet for his guitar. "But I must demand," he pointed at Frank and Copper, who stood at the kitchen counter with Packy and Jimbo, "total silence from all, including the two jealous miscreants over there."

Frank Healy grinned, then shouted in his high-pitched voice, "Oh, I'm so excited. Mulligan's again going to bore us to death with some of his horrific noises. Already I feel nauseous. Ha, ha, ha." He crossed his arms and legs and leaned against the kitchen counter.

"Let the music begin," commanded Bull. He looked around the room to make sure everybody was paying attention.

Mulligan did some finger picking then went right into singing the Patriot Game.

"I love it! I love it!" Luke complimented Mulligan.

Then came a shout from Bull, "This place sucks," followed by laughter.

Mulligan continued.

Mulligan had their complete attention, even that of Copper and Frank. When he finished they applauded him, then requested another tune.

"Thank you, gentlemen." He spoke with confidence. "If you don't mind, I will now sing the song that catapulted me right to the top. That kicked off my career. As," he waved his finger in the air, "you probably realize, if it wasn't for the Fire Department, I'd be another John McCormack."

Frank Healy couldn't resist. Again his high-pitched voice called out, "Catapulted you right to the top of what? A pile of shit. Ha, ha, ha."

Mulligan started his next selection, "The Wild Colonial Boy."

Also enjoying the entertainment were Packy and Jimbo. They stood by the kitchen counter, whispering at a mile-a-minute pace. They were hatching a scheme.

"We got to devise a special treat for Peanut Head," said Jimbo. "Imagine that hump not in on the meals so he doesn't have to pay. Yet, when nobody's watching, he's in the refrigerator devouring the leftovers." Jimbo wrung his fingers and cracked a devious smile. "Yep—yep," he said. "Let's teach him a lesson."

They liked Peanut Head, but couldn't stand his miserliness, which he called being 'economically clever.'

"When's he working?" Packy asked in a whisper.

"Tomorrow morning," said Jimbo.

"Good," said Packy. "Let's make up some kind of a dish, something real shitty, but tasty-looking, and leave it in the refrigerator. Sound good?"

"Keep it down over there," shouted Bull. "You're upsetting the concert."

"I still have a can of dog food in my locker." Packy took off for the locker room.

Jimbo perused the refrigerator. *Let's see what we got. Hmm! Look at that crusty, white creamy shit.* He removed the "crusty, white creamy shit" along with a green-molded glob and a bottle of Worcestershire sauce. *We'll mix these together and sprinkle it with sauce.*

Meanwhile, Mulligan continued singing, with Luke and Bull cheering him on.

Packy returned, waving the can of dog food in the air

Bull and Luke joined in the singing. The kitchen was alive.

Man, these are good times, thought Luke. He took great pleasure in seeing his men enjoying themselves. *And why the heck not? We might as well enjoy ourselves while we're here.* He recalled what Juan had said about what could be awaiting them once they go out that door. Mulligan started marching around the room.

"Follow me, Irish Tigers," Luke shouted, stepping in behind Mulligan. Bull, Frank, Juan, and Copper joined in. Mulligan sang:

Jimbo was pleased. Raising the neatly wrapped plate in the air, he shouted a toast: "Here's to you, Peanut Head. May you shit your brains out." Then he placed the dish into the refrigerator, making sure it was clearly visible, almost ready to jump out at Peanut Head.

*   *   *   *

From his vantage point behind the fence, Molletti watched Jose enter a vacant apartment on the third floor, from the fire escape. There he waited, hoping for the worst: that Jose would set a fire. Moments later Jose reappeared.

Molletti waited as Jose leaned over the side railing of the fire escape. He began snapping off photos when Jose set a pack of matches afire and threw them into the nearby window. Another picture got the flames exploding from several windows, presenting a clear shot of his face. Molletti was ecstatic.

*   *   *   *

The kitchen was energized. Mulligan and the others marched around the room to the beat of the lively tune, while Jimbo and Packy boasted about the dish 'not fit for a king' they had prepared for Peanut Head.

Spoiling their fun, the telegraph alarm banged in fire alarm box 2–7–4–3, followed by the dispatcher's voice snapping out that familiar message: "In the Bronx, stand by the following units …" Once again they were on their way to "Charlotte and 1–7–0."

"Get out! Everybody goes," shouted the Housewatch.

The dispatcher called back: "Ladder 59, be advised we have reports of people trapped above the fire."

"Sounds like we got a worker," shouted Luke. "Let's go."

They bolted from the kitchen to the apparatus floor.

Bull shouted, "This place sucks. Can't even have a singsong in peace."

It was adrenaline-pumping time; the men had begun psyching themselves up for a good job. They charged out to the apparatus floor—suiting up as they did. They continued right out to the street to control traffic. Most times they would be in the fire trucks responding to the fire in a matter of seconds after receipt of the alarm.

With Ladder 59 leading the way, the rigs moved onto the sidewalk, flashing their emergency lights. A speeding car passed them, almost hitting two of the men, narrowly missing the rig. The men hardly reacted.

With everybody on board they shouted to the chauffeurs, "Go, go, go." And the big red fire trucks took off, making maximum noise with their sirens and air horns, bullying the heavy traffic just ahead of them to get it out of the way. If they hadn't maximized the noise, they would have been ignored. And with a possible "people trapped" situation awaiting them, the two companies were in a hurry.

In the cab, the Bronx dispatcher was heard communicating with Luke, "Ladder 59! Battalion wants you to go to the floor above, where several children are reported to be trapped. Be aware the fire has extended to that apartment."

"Just as I expected—kids," shouted Luke.

"Just be careful, Lieu," warned Packy. "Don't forget, you got kids of your own."

Luke opened the sliding Plexiglas window between the cab and the firefighters' compartment. "Listen up," he shouted. "We're taking the floor above. The dispatcher says there might be kids up there. And there is fire up there. So we got to get in and get out, real quick like."

"We're ready, Lukie baby," Mulligan shouted back.

"Jackie! Try to get inside from the fire escape. But don't get yourself in trouble."

"Sure thing, Lieu," said Mulligan.

Mulligan felt the jitters coming on. In a couple of minutes he would be in a deadly atmosphere, a burning apartment above the main fire, filled with scorching heat and killer smoke. The sounds of the air horn and siren helped condition him for what lay ahead.

Mulligan continued, "Sounds like we're going to have our hands full."

Through the cab windshield the men saw up ahead a large column of smoke rising high above the roofs on Charlotte Street.

"Check it out, guys. Looks like a biggy," said Luke, while working the air horn and siren.

This was the kind of action that made the job worthwhile for these men, even with all the abuse from the neighborhood punks. They would be getting a chance to save lives. This is what firefighting was all about. And the bigger the risk they were taking when saving a life, the better they felt about themselves.

Last year on Medal Day, Luke had received one of the medals for bravery awarded that year, the James Gordon Bennett Medal, for rescuing a young girl. It was a big deal and his brothers were proud of him.

Packy floored the accelerator, swerving in and out of traffic along Boston Road, forcing his way into a busy intersection against a red light. Tires squealed as cars skidded to a halt.

Packy parked the truck directly across from the burning tenement.

"Let's go, Irish Tigers," yelled Luke, bolting from the cab. "Let's show them what we're made of."

As a group they exited the rig in quick fashion, hurrying toward the fire.

Mulligan broke from them, heading for the fire escape. With a firm push of his six-foot hook, he dropped the ladder and started climbing.

Luke, Juan, and Copper rushed through the courtyard, where they were joined by Chief Powers. "Luke, you aware there's children trapped on the floor above?"

"Yes, Chief."

Several tenants rushing from the building ran past them. They were calm, as though they had been through this exercise before.

"It's bad up there, so be careful," advised the chief. "I'm sending Eighty-Five up with another line to cover you guys."

Shards of glass rained down on the courtyard as they ran through it. Wisely, the firefighters stayed close to the wall, avoiding most of the falling glass. The lightly dressed tenants weren't so lucky. They were cut by the glass.

Another man wearing slippers received a bad gash on his foot. He hobbled his way out to the safety of the street, leaving a trail of blood.

Mulligan started up the fire escape, his eye on the worsening situation above. *This is going to be a bitch.*

Weighted down with equipment, Luke and the others were already huffing and puffing, as they worked their way up the interior stairs.

"Copper, if we have to pass the fire to get to the kids, it'll be up to you to hold it back with the can until Engine 85 arrives with the line," directed Luke. He paused to catch his breath. "And remember, Jackie'll be in there!"

Several people hurried past them on their way down the stairs.

Luke quipped, "This doesn't seem right. They're running away from the inferno; we're running towards it."

Chapter 23

Lt. Bilcot and his men hurried through the courtyard, pulling their lengths of hose. Their mission was to protect Ladder 59 on the floor above the main fire, where fire was also raging. Engine 82 was already operating a hose line on the main fire below.

"Hustle up, guys," Lt. Bilcot barked at his men. "They're depending on us up there for water."

Mulligan was on his way up the fire escape. To get where he was going, he had to bury himself in some nasty smoke. On reaching his objective, he was blinded by the smoke, but that didn't prevent him from getting into the apartment. In one swift motion, he pried the window open.

This is crazy, he told himself. He thought of Ester, when she asked him to transfer to a slow firehouse where it would be safer. And how he lied to her when he told her that firefighting wasn't half as bad as it looks.

The hot smoke that rushed from the open window was a signal to him that there was a good fire raging inside. He heard voices from the street shouting: "Don't go in there, fireman." "You crazy, mister!"

On reaching the fourth floor, Luke, Copper, and Juan ran smack into a wall of dense, acrid smoke.

Luke ordered, "Check your masks," to which they complied, checking to make sure each other's mask air bottle was turned on.

"Okay, let's go find that apartment," he directed, sounding like a boss who knew his job well.

They advanced up the smoky stairway to the fifth floor. And when they could no longer see where they were going, they felt their way. Luke felt along the wall with his bare hand until he felt a door that was hot to the touch. "Here it is. Get it open," he barked. He held the doorknob to prevent it from swinging open, which would allow any fire that might be right at the door to jump out at them. Juan and Copper used their tools to pry open the locked door.

"Come on! Let's go find those kids," shouted Luke, urging them on.

One after the other they crawled into the apartment on their hands and knees, surrounded by the bloodcurdling sounds of a fire they knew was closing in on them. Besides his regular tools, Copper dragged a twenty-four-pound, water-filled fire extinguisher.

The smoke was so dark and thick that their vision was zippo. To improve his vision, Luke tried removing his mask, but that caused him to gag violently on the smoke. And their flashlights were just about useless.

"It's getting hot in here," warned Copper.

At the other end of that apartment, Mulligan crawled around conducting his search, keeping his nose close to the floor. He cursed himself for not bringing his mask, but then assured himself that he did the right thing, knowing that the time it took to put on a mask could be the difference between life and death for a trapped victim.

"Anybody here?" he shouted. "Anybody here?" *If only I could find the kids and get out.*

It's a scary situation for a firefighter to be in Mulligan's predicament. Operating alone, in a burning apartment, unable to see or breathe properly, he has to search for a victim (or victims) he doesn't even know exists.

Luke and Copper crawled along the hallway floor toward the kitchen. Juan felt his way into the bathroom, probing with his hands. He reached into the tub: nothing, then behind the toilet: again nothing. There were no bodies.

"We got fire up ahead," shouted Luke. Right in front of him he saw the glow of the fire through the smoke. Moving closer, he saw flames lapping out of the kitchen into the hallway.

Then the flames started rolling along the ceiling and dropping. Momentarily the hallway would be impassable, unless Copper could protect them with the spray from the water can.

"Let's go, Juan," said Luke, deciding to pass under the fire.

"Cover our asses, Copper," shouted Juan.

"You're covered! And you're crazy!" Copper shouted. "Just move fast. This thing doesn't hold much water."

Copper managed to half close the kitchen door, which, combined with the spray of the water can, held back the fire just enough to enable Luke and Juan to pass under the fire. They decided to put on their masks, but quickly found themselves having difficulty communicating with each other.

Heck with this! This thing is more of a hindrance than anything else. Luke again removed his mask, opting instead to use it when he needed a quick breath of air.

*   *   *   *

Mulligan slithered through the blackness all around him. He was looking for a window or two in which he could break the glass and vent the smoke. He kept jabbing at the wall with the point of his six-foot hook. It wasn't long before he found the glass. He sprung to his knees, thrust the point of his hook through the glass and cleared the window of the remaining shards. In an instant he was back of his belly, crawling another few feet, where he banged into a bed on which he did a proper bed search. Still he found nothing.

Continuing along the wall—the sounds of fire now more prominent—he found a passageway to another room where the smoke level had not yet reached the floor, making visible the fire on the other side of the room. The closer he got, the larger were the flames that rolled up the wall and across the ceiling and the louder was the crackling and popping of the fire. That room was hot and getting hotter. He feared if it got much hotter, the room would burst into flame.

Where the hell are they? His nerves were rattled; his stomach a ball of knots. *I got to get out of here.* Then right there in front of him were several prone bodies, silhouetted against the glow of the fire. "Luke! If you hear me," he shouted, "I found them! In here!"

"Keep talking, Jackie! We're coming," he heard Luke shouting.

Mulligan quickly crawled to the three child-like forms. Grabbing two of the unconscious bodies, one under each arm, he rolled over on his back. Digging his heels into the carpeted floor and tugging with his elbows, he started sliding his body away from the fire, toward what he hoped was the hallway. But he was in for a terrible surprise.

At that very moment Copper ran out of water and the fire shot right back into the hallway, engulfing their escape route. Copper was scared. The situation was getting out of hand and Engine 85 was not yet in position with the hose line. He ran to the apartment door and was screaming to Engine 85, "Get that fucking line up here right now! We're in big fucking trouble!"

Jimbo was on the landing below when he heard Copper's frantic call. He shouted back that they were on the way up. Jimbo still had his arm through the folds of hose, pulling it along when the line was charged. He got knocked around by the hose—thrown against the wall, his helmet knocked off—as it jumped and kicked, but it didn't stop him. "Let's go! Let's go! Five-Nine's in trouble!"

"There's another kid," shouted Mulligan as the three found each other. "Just straight ahead."

"I see it," said Luke, doing a fast crawl towards the remaining child. "It's bad in here. Real bad."

"How are we going to get out of here?" asked Mulligan. He could not hide his fear.

"Have no fear, Engine 85 is here. They'll put it out and we'll get out," said Juan. But his voice lacked its usual cockiness.

Chapter 24

It didn't take Luke but a few seconds to find the third child. In one quick motion he was on his knees holding the child in his arms, his mask over its face, rushing life-saving air into the little one's lungs. But all that joy and excitement vanished the moment he felt himself being smothered in scorching heat. "Oh my God," he shouted, plopping down on his side, his arms still wrapped protectively around the child.

This time he found no relief at the floor level. Instead, the heat intensified; its severity was like nothing he'd ever experienced before. Quickly his face and ears began to burn; the heat penetrating his firefighting gear was unbearable. He was overwhelmed with fear. He screamed a horrible squeal. Then visions of his wife and children filled his mind. He pictured Dorothy yelling, *What would we do without you?*

Abruptly, the room burst into flame lasting a matter of seconds.

"Oh Jesus," he screamed. "I'm fucking burning!" Again his wife's face appeared: "Mama! Mama! Oh my God," he prayed, "I'm heartily sorry for having offended thee—"

The scorching heat from the flashover reached into the adjoining room, scaring the wits out of Mulligan and Juan. Dropping flat on the floor, they covered the kids.

"Whoa, it is hot! Real bad," said Mulligan.

"Where the hell is Engine 85?" yelled Juan. "We're not getting out of here without them."

They heard Copper assuring them that 85 was on the way.

They were caught between two bodies of fire.

Copper rocked in place, anxious to get past the fire. "Get water on that fucking fire," he screamed. "They're roasting in there." He moved toward the fire as if to go through it, but backed off, his arms protecting his face. Again he roared, "Start that fucking water."

"Here she comes," shouted Jimbo, throwing himself on the floor almost directly in front of the fire. He opened the nozzle, releasing a powerful stream of water that drove the fire back into the kitchen, making the hall once again passable, but that made it hotter for Ladder 59.

"Cover my ass," shouted Copper.

"Go, go, go," shouted Jimbo.

With the water now attacking the fire, Copper was finally able to go to the aid of the others. As scared as he was, he would not let them down. And he knew Jimbo would protect their escape route at all costs. With fear churning in his gut, he crawled forward into the hell-like atmosphere, feeling his ears and cheeks burning. *Get out, get out*, he told himself, but he kept advancing. *Got to get the brothers … got to get the brothers.*

His arms reaching out ahead of him feeling for bodies, he felt a large, pliable bulk over which he ran his gloved hand. "Who's this?" he shouted.

"It's me, Jackie," the groggy Mulligan responded.

Juan mumbled from right nearby, "Get us out. Get us out."

"Get up! Get up!" Copper screamed, slapping Mulligan's helmet, then Juan's, shocking them into reality, out of their smoke-induced stupor.

The whooshing, crackling sounds of fire were everywhere, as was the smoke.

"We're over here, Luke. Just follow us out," shouted Copper. He continued shouting, "Let's go! Let's go! Just follow me."

On their feet, on their knees, they followed Copper. Stumbling, they dragged and pulled each other and the kids, scrambling past Engine 85 out onto the landing, where they collapsed in the midst of a group of surprised firefighters.

"Luke! Where's Luke?" shouted Mulligan, realizing he was not with them.

There was a brief silence.

"Let's go," snapped Mulligan.

Exhausted but determined, they hurried back inside. Once again on their stomachs, they snaked across the floor, grabbing at anything and everything, searching for Luke; ignoring the flames that rolled along the ceiling in front of them.

Copper sighed, "I just assumed he was with us." He was already blaming himself for whatever happened.

"Hssst! Hssst!" muttered Mulligan. "Oh God," he moaned, reacting to what were gurgling sounds. All he could think of was that Luke's lungs had been seared.

His hand came down on a body. It had to be Luke; he felt the metal clasps of a turnout coat. Moving closer to the body, he came face to face with Luke, his facial flesh blackened and peeling. Mulligan gagged at the sight of him.

Juan and Copper joined them.

"Lukie baby! We got you. We'll have you out of here right away," whispered Mulligan.

Luke was helmet-less, lying on his side. When they rolled him over, they found the body of a small girl with Luke's mask covering her face.

"Jesus, he looks awful, man," said Mulligan. "Luke! Luke! Come on. Say something, will ya?"

"C'mon, let's get him out of here," Juan demanded.

The three of them, exhausted, on all fours, struggled with Luke's body, dragging him along the floor until out of danger. They then scooped him up and carried his sagging body out of the apartment, where they laid him out.

"Look at his face. God!" Mulligan's voice broke. "It's all burned. Where's his hair?"

The smell of his burnt flesh and hair was very upsetting for them.

Mulligan got no pulse from his aorta. He began mouth-to-mouth resuscitation. Copper started heart compressions.

"This kid is breathing. Would you take her to the street?" Juan asked a member of Engine 50. He sounded like he was talking about a rag doll. He had no interest whatsoever in the child. All he could think about was keeping his buddy alive. "I gotta be with Lukie baby."

They could hear Lt. Bilcot calling over the Handie-Talkies: "Urgent! Urgent! Engine 85 to Battalion. We got to get Luke to the hospital right away. He's not breathing."

"Come on, Luke!" Mulligan cried out, then began bawling uncontrollably. He pounded on Luke's chest.

Copper grabbed Mulligan's hand. "Easy, Jackie. Easy."

"Damn it to hell! Why isn't he responding? Say something, Lukie baby," Mulligan continued.

Reality was setting in for them. They were accepting that Luke was gone.

"Like this is all wrong, man," said Juan. "This shouldn't happen."

"Why Luke?" shouted Mulligan. "He's the best of us all … and this is what he gets for being a good guy. How about his family?"

Two firefighters arrived with a Stokes basket stretcher. While reaching to pick up Luke, they were intercepted by Mulligan's arm. "We'll take him down," he said with a firm voice.

Juan cut in with an explanation: "Brothers. If you don't mind. He's our boss."

After securing Luke to the stretcher, Mulligan and Juan lifted it and started down the stairs with Copper on their tail.

Jose stood watching on the other side of the street, as defiant-looking as ever. The damage caused by this fire gave him great satisfaction. He would get paid handsomely for this job. The destruction was total, guaranteeing a maximum payout from the insurance company.

Bull and Packy met them in the courtyard. Packy rubbed tears from his eyes.

"Is he dead?" asked Bull.

They simply shook their heads, yes.

"What happened to our Luke? He's all burned," sobbed Packy.

Water and debris rained down on them. Tiny charred splinters and dirty water settled on Luke's face. Bull leaned forward over Luke to shelter him.

"I don't know," said Mulligan. "We found him on top of the kid. He sheltered it with his body. Gave the kid his mask."

"Our Irish Tiger was a hero right to the end," said Bull. Then looking to the sky—his clenched fists trembling—he shouted, "Let me find the bastard," he choked up, "that did this."

They rushed Luke to the waiting chief's car. Jimbo, Lt. Bilcot, and the rest of Engine 85 hurried from the building to be with Luke one last time. The crowd followed them. An elderly black woman approached Packy. "Is he going to be o—" she stopped, then continued, "Oh Lord. Look at that poor man. He's all burned."

"He gave his life for one of those kids." Packy sobbed as he spoke.

"I'm so sorry, fireman. He mustta been [sob] a good man," said the woman.

Packy nodded, and spoke softly. "That he was. That he was."

Upon reaching the chief's car, they lowered the Stokes basket to the pavement. Bull jumped in the back seat. Mulligan and Copper lifted Luke out of the stretcher.

They placed Luke inside, resting his head on Bull's lap. Bull would go with Luke to the hospital.

"What will Dorothy do?" Mulligan asked no one in particular.

The grief-stricken men of the Tin House stood in the street, their eyes following the chief's car as it sped from the block. Their looks reflected their anguish over the quickness of Luke's demise. They were overcome with that terrible pain of knowing they would never again see him alive.

This was the end of a wonderful era for these men. Their close-knit team, like a family, was shattered. But as past experience had taught them, they would heal and get on with what they did best: fight fires.

"Men, I want you all to return to quarters," ordered the grief-stricken Chief Powers. "You're relieved of duty. Go back and plan for Luke's funeral."

That's when the men saw Jose, who had watched the procession of injured—three children and several firemen—being helped from the building, and Luke's lifeless body being placed in the chief's car. He returned their hard looks.

"Juan! You see what I see?" said Mulligan.

Juan simply nodded with narrowing eyes. His fists clenched. In fact, every muscle in his upper torso tightened, to a point his arms started shaking.

Chief Powers sensed their fury. "If you know he did it, get him for the police. If not, don't you dare touch him," he warned.

"Shit. If I only knew for sure," said Mulligan, gnashing his teeth while raising his halligan tool over his head and slamming its pointed tip into the street's asphalt surface.

"Oh yeah? Well, there's no fucking doubt in my mind!" Juan bolted for him.

Jose saw him coming and was unable to sidestep him. Juan was on him like a bolt of lighting: punching, kicking, slamming him to the street, driving the wind from his lungs. "You killed my buddy, you sonofabitch," he screamed. His screams quickly turned to sobs. Tears welling in his eyes.

Juan's mates ran to the action. Several of them looked back to see if the chief was watching; he was. Exactly what they were going to do wasn't clear, but the chief was taking no chances. "Don't you dare touch that man! Don't you dare!" he repeated his orders.

Mulligan and Packy struggled to pull Juan off of him, as they wrestled around on the ground pounding each other. But not before Juan got one more kick in on Jose, a solid blow to the ribs that again knocked the wind out of him. "You disgrace us, *maricon*," Juan yelled.

Mulligan felt like a wimp. *I should have been the one to get him. But I wasn't sure he did it. I'm never sure. What am I supposed to do?* While Mulligan debated with himself, Jose was shouting to the crowd, "Look, everybody! These *bomberos* are messing with me because I'm Puerto Rican. These people don't like us Puerto Ricans or our black friends. You know what I'm saying, my friends?"

Mulligan faced the crowd, making eye contact with them. He shouted for all to hear: "We believe he set this fire, and many more around here." The people locked eyes with Mulligan, giving him their full attention.

Jose shouted, "Don't listen to him! He's a liar! Lying to you, that's what he doing, my friends."

Mulligan again faced Jose, and said in a high-pitched voice, "You got to be kidding," then looked back at the crowd. "People," he shouted. "We believe this man has set fires to many buildings and people have been killed. Your neighbors!"

As Mulligan spoke, Jose shouted to the people, defying them: "Don't listen to him, amigos. You listen to Jose!" He tapped his chest. "And you won't get in trouble."

Mulligan continued, "One of our men was just killed here." A muted sigh came from the onlookers. "And we just know he did it."

Murmurs came from the crowd. Some people were genuinely sympathetic; a few didn't give a damn. After all, the firefighters represented the establishment.

An eerie, crying-scream of a child grabbed everybody's attention, firefighters and civilians alike. All heads turned to see young Chico running after the chief's car that was already gone. Wonderment, even heartache showed on some of the people's faces. Except Jose, who squirmed, trying to hide himself.

"Mr. Luke," Chico wailed. "My friend, Mr. Luke."

Mulligan and Juan rushed forward to intercept the kid. The crowd watched in silence.

"Chico. Chico, my friend. What are you doing here?" Mulligan spoke softly.

In a fit of hysterics, Chico wrapped his arms around Mulligan, crying aloud. "Why? Mr. Luke? I want to see my friend!"

"Easy, Chico," Mulligan said softly. "We'll all get through this. Together."

Juan spoke comforting words to him. "You're his best friend, Chico. He loved you like a son."

"Mr. Luke's with God now. In heaven. With your dad," said Mulligan. "Where we'll all be one day." Then holding up three fingers, Mulligan again shouted to the people. "And he almost killed three kids today."

Then Juan joined in. "Yeah! Three little Puerto Rican kids. Just like me," he tapped his chest, "and just like many of you."

Jose's cousin, Tito, stepped forward from the crowd, faced them and shouted to get their attention, allowing Jose to slip away. "Hey, fireman, how you know who started the fire? You see somebody starting it? Hah, mister?"

Tito wasn't interested in protecting Jose by letting him get away; he was protecting his own interests and those of his partners. He did not want the police to get their hands on him, afraid he would tell everything, which would implicate them.

"No! But he's been seen at the other fires," answered Juan.

"Big deal, man," said Tito. "That means nothing."

"Yeah, but we also know," continued Juan, "he hung around with the guy who got burned at the fire on Miniford. And the guy who sets the fires has been seen carrying a green shopping bag, just like the one he's carrying now."

Heads turned, looking for Jose, but he was gone.

"Hell, he probably just left gasoline at another place he's going to torch," shouted Juan.

Chico's teary eyes bulged with disbelief. "I saw him with those green bags all the time," he shouted between sobs.

"Hey, people," said Mulligan. "Remember! We're your friends. We put the fires out. We risk our lives to save your family when they are in danger."

An older woman agreed. "Yes, Mr. Fireman. We know you're our friends. I hope you catch that bad man who did this terrible thing. I'm so sorry. I will pray for him and his family."

Several people openly agreed with her.

Jose stood just inside the entrance of the hangout, watching Juan, who was looking for him. He heard Juan shouting, "Wherever you are, you coward, if you did this, we'll get you."

Chief Powers stepped in and addressed the firefighters. "That's enough! I'm ordering you all right now to get your equipment and return to quarters. You're good men. I don't want anything to happen that could jeopardize your jobs."

Tito kept the focus of the crowd on him and away from Jose by repeatedly taunting the firefighters, who more or less ignored him. The tactic was effective.

Jose was undaunted. For him it was just another well-done torch job. That is, until he was approached by Chico, who came out of nowhere. Jose would have hidden if he saw him coming.

Sobbing, Chico asked, "Jose. Did you kill my friend, Mr. Luke?"

"No, Chico, my friend. Don't say that. Please." Jose was deeply upset by Chico's accusation. "Please. Don't listen to those firemen. You know they don't like us Puerto Ricans." It was difficult for him to look Chico in the eye.

"No. They are my friends. Mr. Luke takes me to his house. He said he wished I was his son."

"No, no, Chico. I didn't set the fire."

"But I saw you with the bag. The green bag."

∗   ∗   ∗   ∗

6:00 PM THAT EVENING—"Jake, you sonofabitch you! You schmuck! You putz," roared old-man Izzy Katzshoe. "Look at the mess you got us in." Suddenly he gasped, grasping his chest with both hands as he stomped around his private, backroom office. He kicked at an ancient wire wastepaper basket that he missed, causing him to lose his balance. He reached for the edge of his desk, but it was out of his reach. With a thud he crashed down on the floor in a sitting position, a hard fall in spite of the cushioned carpet. With his two arms raised, he continued shouting, "Look what you're doing to me! You schmuck, you!"

"But, Uncle Izzy—" a meek Jake Lipper tried to cut in.

"'But,' my ass! Shut up," continued seventy-two-year-old Katzshoe, his flushed face a scary sight. "Now you really got us up shit's creek. You killed a fireman. It's all over the news."

"But Izzy, they did it, not me," said Jake.

"You did it! What do you think? It was you and your Puerto Rican friends!"

"*My* friends?" Jake gasped. "You mean *our* friends, Uncle Izzy."

"No," he snapped. "Your friends. You understand that? My partners and I, we got nothing to do with them."

Lipper did not give a verbal response, but his nearly deranged face said it all. He was outraged and terrified.

"I just got a call from Rubin. He's crazy mad, I tell you," shouted Katzshoe. "He's shitting in his pants. What am I going to do, spend the rest of my life in jail? Oh my God!"

By now Katzshoe was standing immediately in front of the office's large window that faced the Grand Concourse. He appeared to be shouting at the window with his arms flailing about.

"What did Jerry Rubin say?" asked Lipper.

"He said somebody in the council is calling for an investigation. This is crazy!"

Herb Kaufman didn't even knock on the office door. He slammed it open, causing several cracks to track through the door's large glass pane. "What the hell is going on? No one's supposed to get hurt, let alone killed. A fireman! What kind of a jackass are you, Izzy?"

"Wait a minute. Let me get him out of here," said Izzy, nodding at Lipper. "You go to those friends of yours and tell them to stop everything. To make sure something like this can never happen again."

"How can they make sure?" asked Lipper, still meek in tone, but still angry-looking.

"Whatever it takes. That's how to make sure. Now go," shouted Katzshoe.

Carefully Lipper opened the shattered glass door and disappeared, without looking back.

"Schmuck! You schmuck," Izzy yelled after him.

"That fireman that was just killed over on Charlotte Street. That was one of our buildings, right?" asked Kaufman.

"Yes. And Rubin from the Mayor's office told me that Malloy in the Council is calling for an investigation. The unions are pushing him. I'm so afraid," said Katzshoe, his hands trembling.

"Calm down, Izzy—before you get a heart attack! Are you forgetting who you are? Don't worry about an investigation. At the end of the day it won't happen. We got too many friends there. I've already made some calls. And if they really push it, your friend in Albany will take care of it."

"Who, in Albany?" shouted Katzshoe.

"What! Has your brain gone dead?" asked Kaufman as he started dialing the phone. "Your good friend and partner, one of the most powerful men up there."

"Herb, my friend, you make me feel so good." Katzshoe smiled, relief beginning to replace fear on his face.

"Hello, Terry. It's good to hear your voice." Kaufman spoke into the phone, then listened for a moment. "And how's my good friend, Nicholas?" Again he paused. "You heard about that poor fireman that was killed in the South Bronx?" After listening to Rubin's response, Kaufman continued, "We understand that Mr. Malloy is already calling for an investigation into his death. He's concerned that the fire was arson."

Kaufman sat down, a smile breaking on his face. "Thank you, Terry. Tell the Mayor we fully support him and will once again support his campaign with a very generous donation." He paused, then said, "Goodbye."

"Well, what's going on?" asked Katzshoe, his eyes bulging.

"Calm down, Izzy. He said the Mayor is confident that his good friend Malloy will not push the investigation if the Mayor asks him not to. And they will be meeting shortly on it. But, please, no more problems! There will be a thorough investigation the next time, and the council will insist that the Mayor hire more fire marshals."

Herb Kaufman was a partner in the Bronx-based Webster Building Supplies, a major supplier of building materials for New York City and elsewhere, including the recently completed Coop City and many of the City's housing projects. Their real estate interests alone owned many hundreds of tenements and commercial properties.

"I do feel bad about the fireman," said Katzshoe.

"So do I, but these things happen in business. We didn't want this to happen, but we have to protect our interests. Don't we, Izzy?"

"Of course, Herb," said Katzshoe.

"If they have a collection for the fireman's family, we'll give a nice donation. That'll make things right," said Kaufman. "And remember. It was an accident."

✳   ✳   ✳   ✳

Miguel sat at a table in the back room of the El Tico, glaring at its Formica surface. He then stood up and threw the heavy glass ashtray he was using at the wall.

"Hey! What you guys doing back there, man?" a Hispanic voice shouted from the bar.

Ignoring the voice from outside, Miguel glared at Tito. Springing to his feet, he shouted, "Mr. Lipper, that Jew muddafucker. He screamed at me. Like I was a piece of shit, man. He called me a dumb spic. All because of that sonofabitch," he pointed at Tito, "your cousin. He should be dead … not the fireman."

Tito couldn't look Miguel in the eye. Instead he focused on a pack of Lucky Strikes he was inadvertently crushing with his hands. He jumped when Miguel pounded the table. "We in big trouble, man! Your cousin! Why didn't he start the fire on the top floor? Then there would have been no kids. And the fireman wouldn't have been killed."

"But they don't know he did it," said Tito, now looking Miguel in the eye.

"Bullshit! They got a picture of the muddafucker," said Miguel.

"What?" shouted Tito. He jumped to his feet.

"Yes! A picture of him starting the fire." Miguel pulled from his back pocket a handmade wanted poster and threw it on the table. "Look at that! Somebody left it here."

The poster showed a clear picture of Jose, and read: "WANTED FOR KILLING A FIREMAN." It gave several phone numbers that people could call.

Miguel continued shouting, "Lipper said his people are going crazy. Thinking they're all going to prison for your cousin, who wouldn't listen."

Again Miguel pounded the table. "Our empire, man. The three of us, you know. Finally making big money. And that muddafucker is going to take it all away from us. Remember what he said he would do if he went down."

Tito and George nodded their heads.

Miguel continued, "He said he would 'take us all down' … You know what that means for us? Big jail time, man!" Miguel paused, looking coldly into Tito's eyes, then calmly said, "But not if we take him down first." Miguel took his seat at the table, and placed his hands to his chest like he was praying. He said to Tito, in a near-whisper, "He must go, man. And you must take care of it."

Nodding his head, Tito said, "Yes, boss."

Tito left the backroom as Lipper stormed in. He laughed to himself on hearing Lipper shouting, "What are you guys trying to do to me? Give me a heart attack? They blame me—"

But before he could continue, Miguel, maintaining a cool, calm, but deliberate disposition, warned, "Jake, my friend. Don't you ever yell at me again. And don't ever call me a spic. It is not nice to treat your friends with such disrespect."

"They blame me for what you did, killing that fireman," Lipper continued shouting.

The sight of Miguel getting to his feet with a mad glare in his eyes made Lipper uneasy. Raising both hands defensively, he said, "Wait! Wait a minute. What are you doing? Don't get excited."

"I won't tell you again. Don't ever yell at me," Miguel threatened, standing almost face to face with him.

Lipper became very civil. "My boss is scared shitless. He blames me for what happened."

"Did you kill the fireman?" asked Miguel.

"No! Of course not."

"Then what are you worrying about?" Miguel portrayed himself to be very calm, when in fact he too was worried about going to jail. "We know who killed him, and we'll take care of it," said Miguel.

"My boss wants you to stop the fires," said Lipper, going right over what Miguel said. Lipper continued, "To lay low until we see what happens. He's terribly afraid this could happen again."

Miguel grasped Lipper's hand and shook it. "My friend, Mr. Jake," he said, "you tell him not to worry." Wrapping his free arm around Lipper's shoulders, he continued: "Tell him we are making sure this cannot happen again. And that everything will be okay. Okay, Mr. Jake? You tell him that."

Chapter 25

7:30 PM THE NEXT EVENING—Mulligan and Juan wore their FDNY dress uniforms, as did most of the firefighters present at McGlogan Brothers Funeral Parlor paying their respects to Dorothy White and her family. Numerous floral wreaths lined the walls, some of them bearing the green, white, and orange colors of the Irish tri-color flag. Two were green and shaped like a shamrock. Other wreaths came from neighboring fire companies, the unions, and fire companies where he once worked. The Tin House wreath read: *Always in our hearts.*

When Mulligan and Juan presented themselves to Dorothy, she began weeping uncontrollably. Mulligan embraced her. "I'm—I'm so sorry," he said, finding it very hard to refrain from shedding a tear himself. "So sorry for your pain … Luke was a good man … the best." He raised his voice slightly. "He didn't deserve this … You didn't deserve this. I'll miss him." Mulligan began to sob.

"Thank you, Jackie," she said. "Thank you for your kindness. He loved you guys. All he ever talked about was you. His 'Irish Tigers.'" She looked at Juan, "And his Puerto Rican Tiger."

Then Juan embraced her. "So sorry. I'll keep you, all of you, in my prayers." He managed to hold back the tears.

"Thank you, Juan. Please do pray for us." She dropped her face in her hands. "Why did this have to happen? God, I'm going to miss him. Terribly."

The viewing room was filled. The waiting line extended out onto the street.

Luke was well liked, having many friends both on and off the job. Hence the large crowd and the many floral wreaths.

While Mulligan and Juan comforted Dorothy, Packy and Bull talked with her sons, Sean and Shane. Just beyond them stood a two-man Fire Department honor guard, standing at attention, one on each side of the coffin.

Luke White was laid out wearing his FDNY dress uniform. Affixed to the left breast of his coat were three citations for bravery. Lying centered on his chest, with the ribbon around his neck, was the medal he had won.

Mulligan and Juan knelt in front of the coffin. Mulligan grasped Luke's wrist. *Sorry I never got to tell you what you meant to me. How working with you made my day … Of course, maybe you knew that all along.* He whispered to Juan: "I thought they'd keep the coffin closed."

"Yeah, man. They did do a pretty good job on him. But you'd still know he was burned."

Mulligan stood up, took several steps back from the coffin, where he stood staring at Luke. His memory flashed back to the death in 1969 of another close buddy, Mike McGarry.

At the time of his death, Mulligan had just gone off duty. He was hanging around the firehouse when word came back that Mike McGarry had just fallen from the fire truck, that he was being transported to the hospital.

Mulligan jumped in his car and sped to the hospital, a short distance away. He wanted to see Mike before he went off on his three-day swing, to make sure he was okay. When he arrived at the hospital he hurried through the waiting room to where emergency cases were treated. Looking through the door that he cracked open, he saw two fire officers and no less than eight doctors and nurses working frantically around a table. He wondered why there were so many people working on him and began to feel queasy.

Through the door he went, almost in a trance, walking toward Mike, slowly at first, then faster. Just before he was noticed, he got a quick look at Mike's swollen, blood-covered face; there was blood everywhere.

"Mike, Mike!" he yelled. Then he cried, like a baby, struggling to ask, "Is he all right? Please, say he's okay." *I feel dizzy. I don't feel good at all.*

The next thing he knew he was being escorted out of the emergency room by Chief Rafferty and the other fire officer. "Sorry, Fireman Mulligan, but you can't be in here."

"How's Mike? How's Mike, I got to know!" demanded Mulligan.

In a soft, solemn voice, Chief Rafferty responded. "Jackie … Mike McGarry is dead."

At the time, twenty-six years of age, Mulligan had never lost a close friend under such violent, bloody circumstances. That night he drowned his sorrows in booze, getting drunk and sleeping it off in his car.

Mulligan's thinking returned to the moment; he was still staring at Luke's remains in the coffin. *I promise you I'll never forget you. We'll never forget you.*

*   *   *   *

9:05 PM THAT NIGHT—Mulligan, Juan, Packy, Bull, and Jimbo entered the Parkside Saloon directly across the street from the funeral parlor.

"I need a stiff drink," said Mulligan. Juan agreed. "And we won't have Luke to rush us out of here," said Mulligan.

On walking into the bar, they were greeted by the song, "Patriot Game." Mulligan stopped in front of the jukebox. There he stood and listened to the music. A minute later he was at the bar, where he and the others joined a larger group from the Tin House.

"It's ironic, isn't it?" said Mulligan.

"What's that?" asked Juan.

"That Luke's favorite Irish rebel song should be playing," said Mulligan.

"Yeah, right. And I didn't even hear it." Packy continued, "It broke my heart to see his boys. Those innocent little faces that only a child could have. What are they going to do without their daddy?"

"Yeah, man. What's Dorothy going to do?" said Juan.

Too bad you didn't listen to your wife, Luke. She was right to get pissed at you for staying with us. She was right, Luke, to want you to go to a slow house. A tear rolled down Mulligan's cheek. *You'd be alive today, Luke, wouldn't you? If you'd just listened to her.*

"What a way to go, at an arson job. Where's justice?" asked Jimbo.

"How about a toast." Mulligan raised his glass. The rest of the guys followed suit. Packy and Bull removed their hats, placing them over their hearts.

"Here's to you, Lukie baby! You'll always be with us," Mulligan toasted.

Juan made his own toast, holding his empty glass high over his head: "To my Irish Tiger."

Bull finished the toast with an "Amen, brothers!"

"Am I glad to see you guys," shouted Ritchie Molletti, dressed in civvies, pushing his way through the crowd, which got him some dirty looks and a "Who's this jerk doing all the pushing?"

"Sorry I didn't get to you sooner," Molletti continued. "Sorry for your loss, brothers. I didn't know Luke but for a few days. But it was obvious he was good people."

"What's up?" asked Juan. "Why you all excited?"

"I got the bastard red-handed, setting that fire," said Molletti.

"You mean where Luke bought it?" asked Mulligan.

"Exactly," said Molletti.

A rush of questions interrupted him.

"Let me talk. I'd been working the neighborhood undercover, tailing that guy Jose for days. Then, yesterday, I followed him from his hangout to a joint on 170th by Charlotte Street, where he planted the gasoline. And he carried it in the green bag. From there he went to a joint called the El Tico."

"Yeah, we know the place," said Juan.

Molletti continued, "He met three of his amigos at that bar." He showed Mulligan a picture of them.

"I saw this one a couple of times," said Mulligan, fingering Tito's face. "Always near Jose. When I had words with Jose after the fire, this guy took his side."

Molletti sipped his beer, then continued, "About an hour later he left them. Then he doubled back to the rear yard of that building. That's where I got the pictures."

He showed them the picture of Jose lighting the fire and the one with the fire shooting out the window over his head. They all picked up on the critical evidence; the fire escape stairway handrail was painted red with the top of it bent outward, which was unique.

"Great, now we can get him," said Mulligan. Then turning to Juan, Mulligan said, "Now I would feel justified in doing the bastard."

"Yeah, right, Jackie. But that's not the problem. What are you going to do with these pictures?" Juan asked Molletti. "You can't use them. Like you're not authorized to do what you did."

"Just listen to me … I got two plans of action. One is already underway. First I want to try and let nature," he chuckled, "I mean *human* nature take its course. And if it doesn't work, I'll make sure the pictures get into the right hands in the PD." Molletti tapped his empty glass on the bar.

"Hold your horses there, will you," the bartender snapped.

Mulligan asked, "What's the other one?"

From a manila folder Molletti withdrew a crude "wanted" poster. "I've left a few of these in the area, including one at that El Tico joint."

"What good is that? Those people probably patted him on the back," said Bull.

"Oh, stop that shit! I'm sick and tired of you attacking my people," asserted Juan.

"So you don't like the truth, hah?" countered Bull. "Well, that's too bad."

"Too bad. Well, fuck—"

"Will you guys let me finish," Molletti interjected. "You're directing your anger in the wrong direction.

"Not that it's my intention," Molletti continued, "but my preference is that Jose's gang—that is, the people he was with in the El Tico—that they will see him as too much of a threat to their survival. This, hopefully, will provoke them to take tough action against him." With a wild look in his eyes, Molletti paused and looked them in the eye. "Remove him from the face of the earth, that is."

He continued, "I don't think anybody would give a shit if this scum got done by his associates. Right, fellas?"

"Right," said Juan. "Now I see what you mean by letting *human* nature take its course. You're to be lauded for a job well done. Like you're cool. Like you're my man. Slap me five."

"I'm not finished. I got some good info from Boland."

"Yeah, Chucky. What did he have to say?" asked Mulligan.

"The union got a promise from Councilman Malloy. He said he'd ask for a full investigation into your buddy's death. Such an investigation can blow this whole conspiracy apart."

"This sounds like great news. He's a good friend of the union's," said Mulligan. "Am I right?"

"Don't put all your eggs in one basket. I hear he's also a good friend of the Mayor's," said Molletti.

"Hey. There's Boland now. Let's ask him," said Juan.

"Yo! Chucky! Over here," shouted Mulligan, waving his hand.

Boland acknowledged Mulligan with a nod of the head, then made a beeline to them, greeting a few firefighters on the way.

"Glad I caught up with you guys," he said. "I'm really sorry about Lt. White. All the board members are across the street right now."

The guys nodded, listening to what he had to say.

"Please tell his wife that after things settle down, I'll be in touch to advise her on his benefits. And tell her not to worry about a thing. The union will be there for her."

"That'll be of great consolation to her," said Mulligan.

"Shit. What can we do for her?" asked Bull.

"He told me he was going to paint the outside of the house. Why don't we do that?" suggested Packy.

"Done!" said Bull. "Right, fellas?" He got a "count me in" from them all.

"It would be an honor for us," said Mulligan. "Mr. Bartender," he shouted. "When you have a moment to spare, give us a round of drinks over here."

"You're paying for mine this time. Is that right, brother?" Boland insisted, getting in Mulligan's face.

"Chucky. We got a question. Councilman Malloy promised the union he'd call for an investigation into Luke's death. The arson for profit, that is."

"Yes, that's right," said Boland.

"But I'm not finished. I understand he's a good friend of the union. But according to Ritchie Molletti here, who's with the marshals, Malloy's also a good friend of the Mayor's," continued Mulligan. "Where does that leave us regarding the investigation?"

"Well, we helped get Malloy elected," said Boland, his voice rising. "Our men worked the streets for him. We manned the phones for him. He won't betray us." Nobody said anything, waiting for Boland to continue. He paused, looking them in the eye. "I guess we got to wait and see."

"Yeah, I guess that's all we can do," said Mulligan. Then he asked, "What time we leaving for the church tomorrow?"

"Listen up, everybody," shouted Bull. "We're leaving from the Tin House at eight-thirty sharp."

"I better go," said Mulligan, who then gulped down the beer and ball sitting in front of him.

"What's the rush?" Bull shouted after him.

"Got to see somebody," answered Mulligan.

✶   ✶   ✶   ✶

9:55 PM THAT NIGHT—Ester and Carmen sat on the front stoop exchanging small talk while sipping sodas. The street smelled of burned debris and was quiet, all but deserted of people, except for the superintendent next door who was trying to tidy up the trash cans that were overflowing. His was the only building where trash cans were still put out on the street. But he never had enough cans to handle all the garbage, so it piled up, just sitting there, often being knocked over by cats and dogs. The problem was that the Sanitation Department rarely came into the street to pick up the trash, treating the area as if it was completely vacated.

And for the most part anymore, the block was empty of people. Only nine of the twenty apartments in Ester's building were occupied.

Carmen offered Ester a cigarette.

"What are you doing? You know I don't smoke anymore. You trying to make me smoke again?" said Ester.

"No. I just forgot," said Carmen. "How is your friend Jackie?"

"Very upset. They were good friends. And he's worried about the man's wife and kids," said Ester.

Across the street, hiding just inside the darkened entranceway to the alley of his former hangout, stood Jose, downing a can of beer while watching Ester. He had been keeping out of sight ever since Luke's death, knowing he was a wanted man. His desire for Ester consumed him, sometimes to a point of madness.

Mulligan drove into Charlotte Street with extreme caution, closely scrutinizing the street ahead. He did not want to draw people's attention. A lone white person would be an easy target for local bad boys, especially at night, when few people were on the streets. He had no problem finding a parking space. Hell, hardly anybody lived there anymore, and most of those who did, didn't own a car. Carmen stood, yawned while rubbing her eyes, then took a last draw on her cigarette and ditched it on the sidewalk. "I'm going up. I have to get some sleep. You coming up soon?" She walked into the building.

"Shortly." Ester watched Carmen disappear in the hallway. When Carmen was out of sight, she reached into her pocket, pulled out a single cigarette, putting it to her lips. A flame from her lighter lit it. It would be her first cigarette today and her last cigarette forever.

Once Jose saw Carmen leave, he crossed the street, never taking his eyes off Ester.

"Oh shit. That sonofabitch is back," Ester muttered, regretting she hadn't gone with Carmen. She was nervous, but that was muted by her surging anger. *I wish a cop car would come now and catch him.*

"Beautiful Ester, how are you?" he said.

She gave him a hard look.

"Why don't you let me take you out, hah?"

"Why would I go out with you, you bastard you?" she snapped. "You are a killer. You're wanted by the police."

Jose's eyes filled with rage. Grabbing her ponytail, he twisted tightly, making her scream, then yanked her head so that her face was right in front of his. "You fucking *puta,*" he shouted, spraying her with his spittle. "What you waiting for? That *donkey* muddafucker?"

"Stop! Let me go, you're hurting me," she screamed.

Ester! That's Ester! Mulligan stopped the car so abruptly that he hit his forehead against the steering wheel.

"Bitch, I let you go when I ready. And when I finish with you I'll get your fireman," Jose roared.

"Leave him out of this," she shouted. Again she screamed from the pain.

Mulligan was out of his car and running before he knew it. Ester's sounds of distress put him into a terror blackout. He didn't bother to close the door, nor turn off the ignition. *I'll kill him.* Somehow he knew her attacker was Jose.

By the time he reached them, he was set on doing some serious harm to Jose, after which he would tie him up and turn him over to the police. As Jose started backing down the stoop, pulling Ester along by the hair—her screams adding to Mulligan's rage—Mulligan charged up behind him, stopping just in time to slam several hard punches into Jose's kidneys.

Jose squealed like a pig, the pain was so intense. While letting go of Ester and clutching his kidneys, he stumbled sideways, hitting against a car. "You sonofa-bitch," he roared. "I going to kill you."

Mulligan's first impulse was to attack wildly; kicking and swinging, but his instincts told him that it would be a big mistake. Jose was too smart a fighter. Keeping his composure, Mulligan took a boxer's stance, and with his hands motioned Jose to him. "Come on, girl beater. I should have done this before."

"What are you doing?" Ester shouted. "He will kill you."

"He'll be chopped liver when I'm finished with him, the murdering bastard," Mulligan shouted.

Jose squared off, also maneuvering like a pug. "Let's go, *maricon*."

"You're mine, you lowlife," said Mulligan.

"Screw you, *donkey*," laughed Jose.

"Screw me, hah ..., I'm going to waste your ass. You *maricon, pato*," said Mulligan. Jackie continued to verbally assault Jose, hoping he would lose his cool and drop his guard. But he didn't. "And I'm going to drag your ass to the police station."

Jose jabbed with his left, which Mulligan sidestepped. And he deflected his next jab with a flip of his right hand, then countered effectively with his own left that made a slapping, thud-like sound, snapping Jose's head back, momentarily replacing his look of defiance with a dopey grin.

Jose lunged for Mulligan, only to be caught with a quick left jab, then a straight right-left hook combination to the face. He staggered back, blood dripping from his nose and mouth, feeling his back pocket.

Jose did not know he was being watched from a second-story window by Harry Coburn, who called out, "Hey, boy! You better fight clean, or you'll be fighting two of us."

Without looking up, Jose shouted: "Fuck you, mister."

Jose threw his own combination of punches, which Mulligan easily evaded. Jose then landed a shot flush on Mulligan's face just as Mulligan was lunging at him. But his momentum knocked Jose on his back, with Mulligan landing on top of him. They wrestled around on the sidewalk, at the same time punching at each other.

"You pull a knife," groaned Mulligan while gripping Jose's arm, preventing him from removing the knife, "I'll—I'll cut your fucking balls off," Mulligan was screaming, "and shove them down your throat." Jose kept reaching for the knife.

"Stop! Stop fighting," Ester shouted. "Somebody, please! Call the police!"

Up in his apartment, Mr. Coburn pulled in from his window. "That's the fireman who saved our baby. He's fighting that bastard that started the fire. And he has a knife."

"Don't you get involved! He'll kill you," Coburn's wife implored.

"I've got to help that man. I betrayed him once. Not again."

"You didn't betray him, baby. You was protecting your family. Just like he'd a done."

Mr. Coburn hurried to the street, taking with him a baseball bat. "And call the police," he shouted on the way down the stairs.

"Be careful, baby," shouted Mrs. Coburn.

The two combatants were back on their feet, punching it out toe to toe. No one at this point was winning; both were taking a beating. Both were bleeding from wounds to the face.

Suddenly Mulligan's left hook got through to Jose's chin, flattening him; his chance to revenge Luke's death. He would beat him to death. He dropped knees-first on Jose's shoulders, then proceeded to pound on his face. Jose's face kept snapping from left to right, blood splashing everywhere. "You killed my buddy. Now I'll kill you." He didn't hear Ester screaming for him to stop; screaming for him to wait for the cops.

Not satisfied, the crazed Mulligan jumped to his feet, grabbed one of the trash cans, dumped its contents, then raised it over his head, directly over Jose's face, then shouted, "Die, you bastard!"

But before he could pound Jose's face with the edge of the trash can, Ester stood over Jose, blocking Mulligan. "Stop it! Stop it! What are you doing? If you kill him, you'll be no different than him."

Mulligan tried to get around her, but she wouldn't let him.

"Stop!" again she screamed. "He's not worth it."

Coburn stepped onto the stoop, holding the baseball bat. "She's right, fireman. That rat's not worth it."

Their coaxing calmed Mulligan, but presented an opening for Jose. When Mulligan dropped the can clanging to the street, Jose quickly got to his feet with an open knife and lunged at him.

"Not so fast, rat bastard," roared Coburn, crashing the baseball bat down on his arm.

Jose screamed in agony, dropping the knife. Mulligan and Ester turned in time to see the knife fall to the sidewalk.

"Oh that sonofa—! He was going to cut you," cried Ester. They watched Jose run away holding his arm. But he wasn't finished. "I'll get you," he threatened.

Mulligan was all wound up. He trembled. He voice cracked. "Thank you, Mr. Coburn."

"I owed you that, sir." Coburn turned and started back up the stoop, then turned again to Mulligan. "You know, fireman. I felt like hitting him again and again."

"I wish you did, Mr. Coburn," said Mulligan. "Then he wouldn't have got away."

"What do you mean?" asked Coburn.

"He's the one that started the fire where the fireman was killed."

"That bastard. May he burn in hell … We are terribly sorry about what happened to your friend." Grim-faced, he walked back into the building, the bat at his side.

Chapter 26

"You are crazy. That's what you are," Ester scolded him.

It bothered him to see her so distraught, but what was he to do? He had to protect her. "Are you okay?" he asked.

"Oh yeah. I'm fine." She shook her hands in front of her. "You almost got stabbed and you're asking me if I'm okay. I'm shaking. Just look at me. You're driving me crazy."

She sat on the stoop and wiped her tears. Pointing to the step right in front of her, she said, "Sit here. Let me look at your face and your head." He sat between her legs, leaning his head against her bosom. Blood oozed from a gash on his right eyebrow and a busted lip. She worked her fingers through his hair. "You got a couple of lumps." She kissed them.

"Ouch! That's sore."

With her handkerchief she cleaned the blood from his right eyebrow that was starting to swell. "Ever since you come back in my life, all I've done is worry about you. First the fires, then him wanting to kill you … It's like we'll never have peace. We're not meant for each other. You're Irish and me a Puerto Rican. It's always been a problem for me."

"How about me? How many fights did I have because of that shit?" he snapped at her.

Mulligan was often challenged because he was going out with a Puerto Rican, not just by white kids who called him a "spic lover," but by some Puerto Rican kids who resented him going out with one of theirs.

"I'm willing to accept it, why can't you?" he asked, while kissing her arm that was now wrapped around his shoulders. "And as far as his threat to get me, well, I don't see that happening. The man is on the run. And they will catch him shortly and put his ass away for a long time."

"I just don't want to go through this worrying. It's not for me." She sobbed quietly, dabbing her bloodied hankie to her eyes. "Dorothy told me about how she and the other wives worry all the time about their men. And then to see Luke in his coffin. My God, that made it all so real." Her sobbing got heavier. "Poor Mrs. White. Now what does she have?" She shook her head, pulled her arms from around him, placing her face in her hands. "No! No! It's not for me."

"What're you talking about?" he asked.

"Jackie, please don't give me any more of your bull. You know exactly what I'm talking about. I can't stand you working in this crazy place. It scares me all the time. Why do you think I don't watch the fires anymore?"

She got to her feet and shook her head. "I have to go. I'm tired. Tired of worrying about you. I want you to get the hell out of this place!" she demanded.

He, too, got to his feet, upset with her sudden outburst. He did not know what to do.

With that she bid him farewell and walked into the building. Mulligan started after her, but stopped. *Screw it!* He threw his hands in the air. He controlled his anger; wanting first to think about what happened. *I'm not in the mood to listen to this bullshit.*

Mulligan was in a bad way; overwhelmed with the emotional pain of Luke's death and now thinking he was about to lose Ester. What he needed was another drink to keep his mind numb, not a good night's sleep. He was heading to Dorney's, where he would find someone to talk to for another opinion on how to handle her.

Dorney's was quiet when he got there. Only a few people were about, no one from his gang. Jerry D was standing idle behind the bar. He appeared as though he was waiting for Mulligan.

"Give me a whiskey and a beer."

"Coming up," said the bartender, all the while looking at Mulligan's face.

Mulligan lit a cigarette, then offered one to the bartender that was declined.

"What happened to you, me boy?" asked Jerry D. "Looks like you been through a meat grinder."

As soon as the bartender gave him the whiskey, Mulligan downed it, ignoring Jerry D's question. Then he downed the beer and ordered another one.

On the jukebox "Patriot Game" played. Again thoughts of Luke surfaced in Mulligan's mind.

"Jackie, me boy. When you going to answer me question? What happened?" pushed Jerry D.

"I got that bastard who," he took a deep breath, "who killed our Luke." His voice quivered.

"Sure, I'll miss that lad. He often brought a smile to me face," said Jerry D. "I hope you got your receipts in?"

"Oh, I did."

"You don't look too happy, me boy. What's the problem?" Jerry D asked.

"Two days ago I lost one of my best friends. Tonight I had a fight with my girl," said Mulligan. "Like nothing is going right."

"Now what happened?" He handed Mulligan the beer.

"She doesn't want me working in a busy firehouse."

"Why?"

"Said she worries about me. That's her neighborhood. Sees too much … said she saw me being carried from a building."

Raising his hands, Jerry D cut him off. "Hold it right there, me boy. You ever think, maybe she's right? 'Tis Luke not the second close friend you've lost down there?"

Mulligan listened attentively.

"So you lost two good friends," Jerry D continued. "And now you're going to lose, or should I say give up, the love of your life. For what? Do you think anybody gives a shit about you boys down there? Not at all."

Mulligan responded, "I know you're right. But what am I to do?"

"Here's me advice, boyo," said Jerry D. "Go to that gal. Tell her—I don't want to get too mushy here—tell her how you feel about her. That she's more important than working down there in that hellhole. And one more thing … they don't pay you guys enough for what you do."

Mulligan finished his beer, hopped off his stool, stumbled slightly, but not bad. *That's what I'll do. She's worth more than all that gung-ho bullshit.*

"Thanks. That's just what I needed to hear." In a matter of seconds he was out the door and in his car on the way back to Ester's place.

It was 11:45 PM when Mulligan returned to Charlotte Street. Not a soul stirred anywhere; ideal for a mugging. Making hardly a sound, he entered the dark, dingy hall of Ester's building and climbed the stairs to the second floor. Once again the stench of urine attacked his nostrils. He tapped softly on her door, then waited. Hearing the peephole open, he whispered: "It's me, Jackie."

The door opened just enough for her hand to reach out and grab his shirt and pull him inside. A tempting sight she was, dressed only in a man's red flannel shirt over her panties. Her eyes were red as though she'd been crying. She walked to the couch, where she sat with her legs folded at her side.

"I'm glad you came back," she said, bursting into tears. "I was wrong what I did. Walking away from you when you needed me most."

Kneeling before her and staring her in the eye, he held her hands to his face and kissed them. He began to sob. "No, no, Ester!"

"Let me finish, Jackie. When you were grieving for Luke, I should have been there for you. Please forgive me."

"But it was my fault," he said. "I shouldn't have walked away from you. I love you too much. I don't want to lose you again … All I ask is that you wait till I get promoted. Then I'll go to a slow firehouse. And that may be in a couple of weeks."

"Yes. That'll make me very happy," she said.

"Hold me, Ester … Tell me you love me."

She wrapped her arms around him, pulling him closer. She kissed the top of his head. "I love you dearly, Jackie. I never did stop loving you."

"Would you consider marrying me?" he asked.

Not one bit startled, a slight smile crossed her lips. "Would it be right for us?" she asked.

An ear-to-ear grin covered his face. He laughed. "Look! You're not a bit excited. I feel stupid."

"I am. But is it right for us?"

"Ester! You got to get over this Irish/Spanish shit."

"I don't know. But I do love you … enough to marry you," she finished with a grin.

With her hands placed on the back of his head she pulled him to her and kissed him, which he returned, passionately. She straightened out on the couch, not worrying about what was showing. As he kissed her all about the head, he started unbuttoning the red flannel shirt.

"Where's Carmen?"

"Sleeping. And she's a very heavy sleeper."

Chapter 27

Rays of sunlight penetrated Mulligan's kitchen, revealing just how many crumbs he had missed on the table. The glare caused him to change seats while he worked on a cup of decaf coffee. The table was cluttered with cereal boxes, newspapers, cups, and silverware. Surprisingly, the limited counter space in the kitchen was almost spotless.

On the radio a newscaster spoke about Luke White: "A hero fireman, who gave his life saving a child in the South Bronx, will be buried today. Thousands of firefighters are expected to attend the funeral Mass that will be held at Saint Brendan's Roman Catholic Church in Middle Village."

From one of the kitchen cabinets he pulled a bottle of Jamieson's Irish whiskey and poured a shot into his coffee. He then capped the bottle and put it back in the cabinet.

"Here's to you, Lukie baby." Raising the cup to his head, he finished the contents. Images of some friendly faces appeared to him: Lucita, Juan, and Jimbo. At the same time he thought about life without Luke. It was a sad time. He looked over at the crucifix that hung on the wall. *Thank you for bringing her back.*

Ring! Ring! Ring! His apartment buzzer rang. The brothers had arrived and were waiting for him.

Mulligan donned his uniform jacket, took a quick look in the mirror: he didn't look bad considering he'd been out late, had a few drinks, and been in a fight. Ester did a good job cleaning his lacerations and bruises. Still, he had some swelling on his face and a black eye that he covered well with the makeup Ester gave him.

He took his uniform hat from the counter, left the table as it was and started out the door. In less than a minute he was down the stairs and out on the sidewalk, where the brothers waited for him. There he got into Jimbo's car, joining

Juan and Packy. They too wore their freshly cleaned and pressed dress uniforms, with their citations affixed, looking real smart. And why not?

These guys were proud of that uniform; a uniform that represented the ultimate brotherhood with a tradition of great courage.

"Did you hear?" Jimbo asked. "Another brother was badly burned last night."

"No. No, I didn't," said Mulligan. "Who? What company?"

"John Liso. Squad 4."

"How bad?"

"The news said he's critical," said Jimbo. "And he's a father of four."

From then on they remained mostly silent. This carpool had none of the usual banter. No chop-breaking. It was a real downer for them. All they thought about was Luke and his family.

Once again the boys were carpooling through the Bronx, as they did many times before, but this time they weren't taking Luke home. They were going to bid him a final farewell. They sped along the Cross Bronx Expressway heading to Luke and Dorothy's old neighborhood, Middle Village.

Middle Village was a far cry from the South Bronx and its rows of attached, six-story multiple dwellings, tenements, and row-houses. Middle Village was dominated by one- and two-story buildings; mostly private dwellings with a small piece of property that had grass, trees, and bushes. Plenty of green, green, and more green as compared to the Bronx's concrete and asphalt, concrete and asphalt and more concrete and asphalt.

Its main thoroughfare through the business district was lined with one- and two-story storefronts, known to firefighters as taxpayers, not one of them vacant; all open for business.

Yeah, it was different from where Luke worked. A clean, thriving, middle-class enclave. Here there was very little poverty, hardly any crime. Rarely was there a fire. And here too, just about everybody was employed.

∗　　　∗　　　∗　　　∗

Rubin reached for the Plexiglas divider that isolated the Mayor's chauffer from the passenger compartment—the people in the back of the limousine—and slammed it shut, a certain insult to the driver. Malloy scowled at him, detesting his arrogance; and Steele shook his head in disgust, having experienced Rubin's irritating self-importance many times before.

At thirty, the conservatively dressed, handsome Malloy—no sideburns on this man—was the youngest member of the council. He was also a whiz kid, just like Rubin, but he had a contagious personality to go with it.

"Terry, why did you have to slam that?" asked the Mayor.

"Oh. Sorry, sir."

It was the norm for the Mayor to keep the divider closed, not wanting the drivers to overhear conversations going on in the back. On this trip, Mayor Dunlap had invited Commissioner James Steele and Councilmember Danny Malloy to ride with him to the funeral of Lt. White. And, of course, one did not turn down an invitation from the Mayor if they wanted to keep in his good graces.

"You look well, Danny. The council apparently agrees with you," said the Mayor, smiling approvingly. "And if I may say so, you have made yourself a popular figure there. That's very important when you're looking to get things done, or when you need a favor. As they say, one good deed deserves another."

Malloy sensed where Dunlap was heading. The smile left his face.

"It's noble of you to want an investigation into the death of that poor fireman, Lt. White. A very popular man himself. I hear he never used curse words. That's unusual for a man working in such a hazardous occupation."

"Yes, sir. I owe this favor to their unions. They were very helpful to me in getting elected," said Malloy. "They're very upset over his death. They swear it's the result of that arson-for-profit plague they have been telling me about."

When they were about midway across the Brooklyn Bridge, Dunlap directed their attention to the southern tip of Manhattan Island. "Look at the height of those towers. That future Trade Center never ceases to fascinate me. I'll want an office on the top floor of one of them when they're finished. An office with a panoramic view of the city."

"They certainly didn't take into account firefighting on the upper floors when they designed those monsters," complained Commissioner Steele.

"Danny, you can't expect to give them everything they want, when they want it," said Dunlap. "I need you to hold off on the investigation. As a matter of fact, I'd like you to forget it."

"But why, sir?" asked Malloy.

The Mayor saw the surprise and immediate hostility in Malloy's eyes.

"The fires are actually doing some good. They're clearing the South Bronx of people. That'll make it easier to rebuild when we get the federal money. You know, Danny, my South Bronx Revitalization program. And besides, a preliminary investigation found it was the work of a lone junkie seeking revenge. An isolated incident."

"Sir, that's not what the unions are telling me," said Malloy.

"As usual, Danny, the unions are overreacting. Let me assure you, contrary to what they are telling you, the vast majority of the fires are caused by careless vagrants. Not, as they call it, arson for profit."

"Sir, but I promised," said Malloy.

"Oh, in this business you learn that promises are not always kept," replied Dunlap, still speaking in a pleasant tone. "And besides, you've been pushing me to give them a two-year contract with seven percent each year. Isn't that enough to give them?"

"What are you saying, sir? You agree to that package?" asked Malloy, turning in his seat so as to face the Mayor.

"Yes," said Dunlap. "Seven and seven." Actually, the Mayor and his negotiating team had already decided to give the firefighters and police seven and seven, but had not announced it.

"I can't fight you on that, sir. That'll make them very happy, and will let them know that I am effective on their behalf," said Malloy.

"So then it's agreed, no investigation?" asked Dunlap.

"Yes. But please give me something I can hang my hat on with the investigation," Malloy requested.

"Terry. You're good at screwing our fireman. You come up with the answer," said the Mayor.

Commissioner Steele and Malloy gave Rubin dirty looks.

"Yes. Sure, sir," said Rubin, avoiding eye contact with the others. "I'll talk to the council president. We'll come up with something good."

"Oh my God, look at them all. I feel so proud of them," said the commissioner, when they turned into the block where the firemen were lining up in preparation for Luke's funeral Mass.

"There are thousands of them. This is my first," said Malloy. "Holy cow, I'm impressed. I'm jealous—a true brotherhood."

*   *   *   *

Outside St. Brendan's Roman Catholic Church, more than five thousand somber-faced firefighters stood smartly dressed in their blue uniforms and white gloves. They were lined up four rows deep for almost two blocks each way. It was an impressive sight by any standard.

They came from as far away as Los Angeles, these brothers in blue.

The brotherhood of firefighters is special. Like soldiers in battle, they are prepared to risk their lives for one another and for the people they serve. They operate as a team often under the most dangerous of conditions. They will take the greatest risks imaginable when performing their duties.

On the sidewalk outside St. Brendan's, hundreds of relatives, friends, and neighbors stood waiting to enter the church.

Immediately next to Dorothy White and her three children stood Mayor Nicholas Dunlap and his assistant, Terrence Rubin; Commissioner James Steele and his Chief of Department; Councilman Malloy; and the union leaders, including Chucky Boland. They all looked mournful, even the Mayor and his assistant.

"Look at that user," murmured Packy under his breath. The men from the Tin House did not appreciate seeing the Mayor. They regarded him as a hypocrite, as did many ghetto firefighters who had to deal with arson.

"As far as I'm concerned," said Bull, "this bastard killed Luke. Luke died because he failed to act against the arsonists. Am I right or am I right?"

"Of course. He'd plenty of time to act," agreed Mulligan.

Two male family members supported the grieving Dorothy, who was holding her daughter, Fiona. Her two young sons stared innocently. It was heartbreaking to look at them.

The men from the Tin House, who were serving as the honor guard, lined up on both sides of the steps outside the church entrance.

Then came the command from a loud, sharp, military-style voice: "Ten-hut." And more than five thousand firefighters snapped to attention.

The Department's Emerald Society Bagpipe Band, dressed in their Irish kilts, began playing a dirge. Only the drummers played. They rolled slowly on their drums, producing an eerie, haunting sound. Then came the command, "Hand salute," to which the many thousands of uniforms saluted sharply. The brothers in blue held their salute as the coffin was removed from the hose bed of Engine 85 by the pallbearers, which included Mulligan, Juan, Bull, Packy, Copper, and Jimbo. The bagpipers continued their drum roll as the men carried the coffin up the steps into the church. They were followed by Luke's family; the Mayor and his entourage; hundreds of firefighters; and then relatives and friends. The Mass lasted more than an hour. The church was filled to capacity, all honorable people paying homage to this fine man who gave of his life to save another.

The mother of the young girl Luke saved was also there. Her daughter was still in the hospital. "I feel like it's all my fault," said the sobbing woman to one of the members of the honor guard.

After the monsignor finished eulogizing Luke, he motioned to the Mayor. "We'd be privileged if the Honorable Mayor Dunlap would come to the pulpit."

Bull laughed an angry chortle under his breath. "The monsignor is as phony as the Mayor. I overheard him arranging with Rubin to call the Mayor up. And now look at the Mayor pretending as if it's spontaneous."

Dunlap, with his head tilted downward as though grieving, walked slowly to the altar.

The Mayor praised Luke as if he knew him, calling him "the bravest of the brave." He went on to address Luke's wife and children by their first names, and told them to be strong, and to be proud of Luke. "Your father is a true hero."

Many among Luke's family and the large number of friends present were moved by the Mayor's words. There was many a teary eye.

"Oh, how kind of him to say such nice things," one woman whispered.

Mulligan, Bull, Juan, and the rest of the pallbearers sat in the first row right in front of the Mayor. Often, during what Bull called a vote-getting eulogy, the Mayor looked at them.

"I see before me a sea of blue, New York's Bravest. These men I respect more than anyone else. Courageous men, who are prepared to risk their lives for complete strangers. And sometimes," he paused to look around at all the faces, "to sacrifice their lives. I know too the great danger they constantly face in the ghettos because of arson." He nodded his head, looking angrily out at the mourners. "And I am working hard with my Fire Commissioner James Steele," at whom he pointed, "and his top brass to resolve this arson crisis once and for all. It remains one of my most pressing priorities."

The bastard! What a nerve to get up there and lie to these people, thought Mulligan.

Then the Mayor faced Dorothy and her children, who sat just to the right of the pallbearers, and nodded his head. "Thank you! Thank you, Mrs. White." He spoke with feigned emotion. Then, with his arms extended out in front of him, he appealed to the mourners, "Fellow New Yorkers, please join with me in giving a standing ovation to Dorothy and her wonderful family." He paused, dipping his head, "In honor of a brave, hero husband and father, Lt. Luke White. Let them know that we love and support them, that we'll always be there for them."

As the church boomed with a thunderous applause that was directed as much at Luke's family as it was at Mayor Dunlap, which was the Mayor's intention, the thought rushed through Mulligan's mind: *Just like Bull said; Luke is dead because this creep refused to do anything about the arson.*

As much as these guys detested the Mayor; as much as they wanted to scream out in unison, all 5,000 of them: "We hate you, Mayor Dunlap. You're not a friend of the firefighters," they wouldn't do anything that would be disrespectful to Luke. And Dunlap knew that.

On cue, right after the service ended, the pallbearers rose from their seats to take their positions around the casket. They managed one more angry glance at the Mayor. It irked them when he placed himself beside Luke's wife and children. They looked away, except for Bull, who continued glaring at Dunlap, making him very uneasy.

Mulligan was fearful that Bull would explode. "Easy, Bull," he whispered, as he elbowed him. "Let's get Luke out front before you get in trouble."

"Yeah, let's do that," said Bull.

Looking straight ahead, they proceeded slowly, moving the coffin to the back of the church. While they were just inside the church entrance, lifting the coffin to their shoulders, out on the street the officer in charge was calling the men to attention. Again he ordered: "Hand salute."

The pallbearers proceeded down the steps with the coffin. Slowly and in step, they moved out into the street to the waiting fire truck. In one several-step, military-like maneuver, they placed the coffin up into the hose bed. Then they stepped back from the fire truck, snapped to attention, and presented a hand salute.

The bagpipers commenced playing "The Minstrel Boy," a tune that when played at a firefighter's funeral never failed to move many a person to tears. And that included Mulligan, Bull, Packy, and the Puerto Rican Tiger.

Dorothy wept uncontrollably, needing constant support from her family.

Mulligan's eyes remained glued to Luke's coffin as it moved slowly away on the fire truck. *So long, Luke. I'm going to miss you.*

A sad but impressive sight: thousands of firefighters lining the street saluting Luke, as his coffin passed slowly by them to the sound of the bagpipes.

After the men were dismissed, Mulligan, Juan, and Bull walked over to where Mayor Dunlap, with Terrence Rubin, Danny Malloy, and Commissioner Steele at his side, was conducting an impromptu press conference.

"I have to hear what he has to say," said Bull.

"We've been fighting the arson plague up in the South Bronx," said Dunlap, sounding a bit like an orator, "and in Brooklyn and Harlem too, since I became Mayor. And we can't forget the Lower East Side. Granted, it's been a tough battle. More like an ongoing war. But we are determined, and that's why we've made considerable progress. And it will remain one of my top priorities, until there is no longer an arson problem." He pointed to the fire commissioner. "My commissioner here is the heart and soul of this very effective anti-arson campaign."

"Man! Can he bullshit or can he bullshit?" said Juan.

"Mr. Mayor! Can you spell out just what is being done to stop the arson, or to at least get it under control?" asked a TV news reporter.

"The Bureau of Fire Investigation has been going all-out to stop it. That's why there's been so much progress. I have complete confidence in the Bureau."

Another reporter asked, "Then why are the firemen and their unions still demanding that you expand the Bureau of Fire Investigation? They say that's the only way the arson can be checked, or at least slowed down. Why do they not agree with you on the progress?"

"I cannot understand their gripe. But my deputy here, Terry Rubin, will be working closely with them on that."

Rubin nodded in agreement with the Mayor.

Another reporter asked, "Councilman Malloy. You are calling for an investigation into the matter of arson for profit. Specifically, to determine whether or not arson for profit exists and was it responsible for Lt. White's death. Is that right, sir?"

"Not at this time," stuttered Malloy, hanging his head in shame. The shocked union reps looked at him with raised eyebrows. Boland stomped the sidewalk, punched his hand, then walked off; his outrage noticed by everyone.

"Why, that whore," muttered Bull.

But the reporter pushed Malloy, who was now feeling the heat from the firefighters. "Didn't you promise the unions a full investigation?"

"Yes. Yes, I did." Malloy was troubled. "But, but that was before the results of a preliminary investigation found no sound evidence of arson for profit." He stole a quick, nervous glance at the union reps.

"And what does that mean, sir?" the reporter shot back.

Rubin cut in: "It was the work of a lone drug addict, getting revenge against the landlord. And that's all for now, on that matter."

That's when Bull had enough. "That's bullshit!" he said, not caring who heard him. When Rubin turned to see who it was, he was met by Bull's angry glare. He nodded his chin in Bull's direction as if challenging him. They locked eyes.

"Look at this arrogant scumbag. I'm going to knock him on his ass," said Bull, while observing the crowd to see if anyone was watching him. Bull used hand signals to invite Rubin to join him for a fistfight across the street by a bar. Rubin's complexion paled. He motioned over a chief fire officer, talked to him in an arrogant manner, while pointing over at Bull. The officer looked at Bull, nodded to Rubin, then walked briskly over to Bull.

"Hey, fireman," he pointed back at Rubin. "The Mayor's Deputy said you were threatening him with your fists."

"Oh my God," said Bull, clasping his hands as his face lit up, pretending to be shocked, which quickly turned to a feigned look of hurt. "Oh no, no, sir. I thought he was an old friend of mine. I wanted to know if he wanted to have a few beers with us. It's all a misunderstanding, I can assure you. I like—I mean I just love Mr. Rubin. He's a wonderful man. A great friend of the firefighters."

"I thought that was the case," replied the grinning officer. "Good day, gentlemen." The officer left to return to Rubin and the press conference.

"Who I'd like to knock on his fat ass," mumbled Bull out of the side of his mouth.

"Let's make it, my man," said Juan. "Before we get ourselves into some serious trouble. You dig what I'm saying?"

"Right you are, Juan! I heard enough of his bullshit," said Bull, loud enough to be heard by the media. "Think I'm going to puke."

Just about everybody at the press conference, including the Mayor, turned to see Bull shaking his head and glaring at Mayor Dunlap. The three firefighters turned and walked away.

Chapter 28

Already a month had passed since Luke's death and not a sign of Jose. Not been seen since Mulligan and he had punched it out. Since then, he and Molletti spent a lot of time searching for him, circulating his picture wherever they could. They sought help from the community, but the answer was always the same: nobody had seen him since Luke's death.

Yet there was sufficient evidence that he'd been in the area. After the brief pause in suspicious fires in the neighborhood following Luke's death, there was once again an upsurge in suspicious fires.

Finally they got a break. It was Jose's sister Linda who gave Ester the possible answer. Since childhood, Jose had been making himself look like famous people. He was a *master of disguises*, which Ester attested to: "He could be standing right next to you and you wouldn't know him." Of course, they still hadn't a clue as to his whereabouts.

∗   ∗   ∗   ∗

"I can't believe it," said Mulligan, grinding his teeth. "Accidental manslaughter? That's bullshit!"

"Well, that's how they're playing it down at City Hall. They're circulating the story that a stoned junkie started the fire that killed the fireman. And it was all an accident," said Molletti. "They're afraid the truth would blow the lid off this arson-for-profit thing."

"Sounds like there won't be justice. It's like if we want justice here, we'd have to take the law into our own hands," said Mulligan. "And I just don't think I could do that."

"That's why I'd prefer that his gang takes care of it. They'd certainly benefit from his demise," said Molletti. "So we have to put pressure on them. When we leave here we'll pay a visit to the El Tico." He put his hand on Mulligan's shoulder. "I hope you guys stick with me 'til we get this rat bastard? Or they get him."

"Of course. But what can we do? We're not cops. We can't arrest anybody. Not even this crazy bastard."

Molletti laughed. "No. That's not what I mean. Just be on the lookout for him. And if you see him, make sure you call me right away."

"You got it," said Mulligan.

"Good. Now let's get started."

Twenty minutes later they were watching Jose's hangout from the concealment of the fire-blackened interior of one of the burned-out, third-floor apartments where Ester had lived.

"Does your girlfriend still live here?" asked Molletti. He was genuinely concerned with her safety.

"No. They're down the block. Right over the bodega," said Mulligan. "They're hoping to move by the Concourse."

"They had some balls … well, whatever," Molletti laughed, "to stay here as long as they did."

Three hours into the stakeout and still no sign of Jose. All they had seen, besides a few shouting kids running up and down the block, was a stoned junkie; a gray-haired old man with a limp and a Ho Chi Minh goatee; and a nervous mailman who watched his back. He hurried through the few remaining buildings on the block that had legitimate tenants. Shortly afterwards the gray-haired old man reappeared and entered the building they were in.

"Look at this guy. He's got to be a wacko living here. He knows this place is going to be burned again and again. He'll probably leave here in a body bag," said Molletti, shrugging his shoulders. "Can't worry about everybody."

"Probably nobody to look out for the old bugger," said Mulligan. "But that's not my concern. Revenge for Luke is more in my line."

"We'll give it a couple minutes more," said Molletti.

"Why don't we leave now if we're going to stop at the El Tico? I'm on duty in an hour," said Mulligan.

Right over their heads stood the master of disguises, Jose, the gray-haired, old man with the limp, looking down at them through a good size hole in the floor. In his hands he held two ultra-fragile Molotov cocktails with their wicks aflame, ready to bombard them. Jose, with a deranged smile on his face, was going to put an end to these two *thorns-in-his-side*. He would burn them to a crisp. But before he could carry out his deadly deed, the two men walked out of the apartment on their way to the El Tico.

There will be another chance, thought Jose.

✳   ✳   ✳   ✳

"You guys won't be safe until he's gone," said Molletti.

"We have to shake these fuckers up," said Mulligan. "Do you have any more of those pictures?"

"Yes, I do," said Molletti. "Good thinking. We'll leave another one at the bar." From the backseat he retrieved a manila folder secured by a rubber band.

They parked the car across the street from the bar. Less than a hundred feet away stood Jose's former partners in crime, watching the duo as they headed to the El Tico. The three bad boys had been lying low, staying out of sight.

"These *bomberos* would never have known anything about us had it not been for that fucking cousin of yours." Miguel's patience was worn thin. He ordered Tito, "Find him and get rid of him."

Tito tapped a bulge under his shirt. "I carry this all the time anymore for that purpose, man. I will get him." Tito was determined.

Miguel laughed. "Now we are the fireman's friend."

There was no one in the bar but the bartender, and he paid them no heed as they entered. He just went on rubbing down the bar with a cloth. When they identified themselves as fire marshals, the bartender asked: "Is there a fire somewhere?" He didn't show any interest in them.

"That's not why we are here, mister," said Mulligan, sounding macho. "First, you can give us two ice-cold bottles of beer."

As the barman set up the beers, Mulligan asked, "You wouldn't happen to know a man named Jose Nieves, would you?" He showed him the picture of Jose starting the fire.

To their surprise, the Hispanic-accented man replied, "Yes. I know him. He's the guy they say killed the fireman."

Mulligan continued, "Have you seen him?" He sat on a stool and took a sip of his beer.

"No, man. Not since before that fire. He used to come here all the time. But he's not welcome here anymore."

"He's involved with one of those gangs that set all the fires around here. As a matter of fact, he, and his gang, are wanted for killing that fireman. We have seen them hanging out in here."

"No. There's no gang hanging around here. He did these things by himself. He was crazy, you know. A junkie." With a bit of sadness in his eyes, he said, "I hope you catch that *maricon*."

"We will," said Mulligan, feigning optimism. "The police expect to get him soon," Mulligan lied. "And when they do, they'll take down the whole gang. They're all wanted for his death, you know." He finished his beer. "Have a good day." He left the photo on the bar.

They started for the door, but stopped. "You know what," Molletti shouted back to the barman. "You know, he'll probably hang them all."

*   *   *   *

Packy saw the little toddler totter out onto the roadway. He had plenty of time to stop and let its mother come for it. But she didn't move her butt fast enough for Packy. When she finally did appear, she was stoned. She stumbled out from between two parked cars, and on seeing the pissed look on Packy's face, she cursed him out. *Why is she cursing me? Should be the other way around.*

He continued across 174th. They were returning to the Tin House from a building fire that was not suspicious. But right behind that fire, on the next street over, at the very same time, was a second-alarm fire that swept through two attached, wood-frame buildings. That fire was suspicious.

Inside the rig sat the regulars: Mulligan, Juan, Packy, Copper, Lt. Bannon, and Bull; their fire gear removed, and as usual their faces dirty and sweat-streaked.

From the cab Lt. Bannon called Mulligan. "Jackie! The dispatcher's got a message for you."

"What's that all about? Tell him go ahead," said Mulligan.

Over the radio the dispatcher gave him the following message: "Jackie! It's your buddy Jumping Johnny Carlson with good news. As of tomorrow morning, you're a lieutenant."

"All right!" shouted Mulligan.

"Where's he going?" Lt. Bannon asked over the cheers of the others.

"Downtown, First Division," replied the dispatcher.

"That's cool, Jackie baby. My main man is a boss," said Juan. "But we're gonna miss you around here."

"How the hell did he make lieutenant?" asked Copper.

"They picked his name out of a hat," said Packy.

"Lieu, will you do me a wee little favor?" asked Mulligan.

"Now what?" asked Lt. Bannon.

"Stop by Charlotte. I wanna tell somebody the good news."

"I wonder who that might be?" said Lt. Bannon.

*   *   *   *

Ester stepped out of Santana's carrying a bag of groceries, followed by the gray-haired old man with the Ho Chi Minh goatee. She stopped to listen to the musicians whaling on a bongo, maraca, conga drum, cowbell, and timbales. She watched with a smile as several couples danced to their rhythmic sounds. The old man limped on up Charlotte Street.

As Packy brought the rig to a stop by the bodega, Mulligan shoved open his door. Looking happier than a pig in shit, he jumped from the rig, shouting after Ester.

Except for Bull, the rest of the guys got out of the rig to listen to the music and watch the dancing. "Shut the windows. I don't want to hear that shit," he yelled, a curious look on his face.

"What the hell. You don't like anything about my people, do you?" said Juan.

"Whoa! I like you. And I like," he pointed to a young female dancer, "her ass. And to prove I do, tell her come over here and I'll kiss it, just to make you happy. How does that grab your *mountain oysters?*"

Before Juan could respond, Bull broke out laughing, leaped out of the rig, and started dancing.

As he hurried to Ester, Mulligan's helmet was knocked off his head by a pair of sneakers a kid was attempting to hang on a utility wire, but missed. Startled slightly, he didn't even bother to investigate where the sneakers came from. He heard the kid shout, "Sorry, fireman," and that was enough for him.

Stepping close to her, he mouthed in a soft voice, "I love you," then grasped her hands. "Come on, let's dance."

"You crazy, or what?" she said, while pulling him close to her. Cheek-to-cheek they danced, dirty face and all.

"Yes, crazy about you," he said.

*   *   *   *

Up on the north side of Boston Road, sitting in a battered, nondescript car wearing a gray-colored wig and Ho Chi Minh goatee, was the defiant Jose. "Hey, Chico!" he shouted.

Chico stood several yards from the car, sipping a soda while staring at the man, wondering who he was. He turned away.

"Don't you know who I am?" He laughed.

Recognizing the voice, Chico closed in on the car. "Jose, it's you, isn't it?" he asked, his voice turning emotional.

"Yes, amigo. It's me."

Chico glared at him, speaking angrily. "Why you look like an old man? You hiding, aren't you?"

"I just want to fool you," he said, removing the wig and goatee. "Why you giving me that dirty look for, my friend?" Jose continued.

"'Cause you killed my friend Mr. Luke," he answered and began weeping.

Jose's eyes saddened. Chico's friendship was so important to him.

Neither of them saw the man who was wearing a South American-style hemp Fedora who came from around the corner, walking briskly up behind Chico, with his eyes glued to Jose's. The man, whose face was covered with a woman's nylon, headed straight for the car, holding a .45-caliber pistol behind his back.

"The fire killed him, man. Not me," said Jose.

"But they say you started that fire," challenged Chico.

The man stopped, then brought the pistol to his front and with two hands aimed it at Jose, but Jose, a quick thinker, grabbed Chico by the collar and swung him in the line of fire. "Sorry, my friend!" At the same time he threw the car into drive, then pushing Chico towards the advancing gunman, floored the gas pedal. The screeching of the fast-spinning tires got everybody's attention. People turned in time to see the gunman shooting. When they heard the loud explosions of the gun firing, they scrambled for cover.

Jose heard the continuous *ping-pang* of the bullets hitting the car. Burning rubber, he sped recklessly through the intersection to the next light that was red, trying to avoid those head-shattering .45-caliber slugs. Through the rearview mirror he watched the gunman, who ran out into the street and kept firing after him. The last thing he saw before he was broadsided by a fast-moving car was his rear window disintegrating. Jose's body tossed around inside in car as it flipped over. The bang of the two cars colliding and the shattering of glass made a lot of noise, but the locals and firefighters down by Santana's didn't hear a thing. They were too busy listening to the music and watching the people dancing.

*   *   *   *

"Hey look! The fireman knows how to merengue. He's cool, man," said one of the kids.

"I got good news. Very good news," said Mulligan.

The delight in his eyes aroused Ester's curiosity.

"I got promoted! And I'm going to a slow firehouse. Does that make you happy?"

Choking up, she blurted out, "I'm so happy for you. And for myself. Now I don't have to worry so much." They continued dancing cheek-to-cheek.

"Good. Then how about doing something that would make me real happy?" he said.

"Uh-oh! What's that?" she asked.

"Marry me."

"Yeah, why not," she said, with a no-big-deal expression on her face. He felt like an ass. And when he was about to vent his anger, she laughed and put a lip-lock on him. "Of course I'll marry you. I would have married you back then if you had only asked."

Mulligan's friend in the band shouted, "Irish Jackie, we play a mambo for you. Okay?" They started to dance the mambo, but that ended with a blast of the air horn and a shout from Lt. Bannon. "Let's go, Jackie, me boy. We are on duty, you know."

"Be careful tonight," she shouted after him.

*   *   *   *

They had just gotten back on the road to the Tin House when the dispatcher sent them to investigate the auto accident and warned them that shots had been fired.

"Who's shooting who?" Mulligan wanted to know.

"Don't really give a shit, my man. As long as they ain't shooting at me," replied Juan.

Lt. Bannon had one finger on the siren button, another on the air horn button, making a hell of a racket all the way to the accident scene, hoping that the noise of an approaching emergency vehicle would chase the *shooter* away. As soon as they turned onto Boston, they were in the middle of the crash site. Engine 85 pulled in at the same time.

Quickly the firefighters took over, pushing the bystanders back to give the injured a little breathing room. Those who were helping the injured were let be. One man was using his belt as a tourniquet to stop the flow of blood from the leg of one of the casualties. Close by, a man sat on the street, moaning and rocking in place. A dazed-looking man sat in the back of the car; his face was bloodied.

Mulligan heard little Chico shouting, "Mr. Jackie! Mr. Jackie!" but didn't see him until he emerged from the crowd. As soon as he saw his face, he knew something was wrong. "What's the matter, Chico?" he asked.

The kid could hardly get his words out, he was so excited. "The-the-the man was shooting at him."

"Wait a minute!" Mulligan waved his hands to silence the kid. "Wait a minute. Who was shooting at who?"

"A man with the lady's stocking on his face. He-he-he had one of those straw hats. You know, that cool-looking hat."

"The Fedora, you mean?"

"Yes! Yes! But he's gone."

"Shooting at who?" asked Juan.

"Jose! That's who," he continued, shouting. "He killed Mr. Luke."

They were on the car like bees on honey, where they dropped to the ground as if doing push-ups to get a look inside the overturned car.

They saw Jose lying limp with the gray wig sloppily placed on his head. When Mulligan removed the wig, he found the underside of it covered with blood. So was the top of his misshapen head. He saw a large hole where he suspected the bullet exited.

"Ugh. What the fug?" he grunted, sounding like somebody about to get sick. "You know, he looks good dead."

Bull and Jimbo joined them.

"Who did what shooting?" asked Bull.

"I don't know, but look who got it," said Mulligan, kicking the roof of the overturned vehicle.

Bull again asked, "Who did it?"

"Don't know," said Mulligan, "other than that the guy used a nylon to cover his face and that he wore one of those tan-colored hemp Fedoras."

Bull asked Chico if he could remember anything else that might help the police.

"I think he was wearing a yellow shirt. But I don't know, I was so scared," said Chico.

"You sure he's dead?" asked Jimbo.

"With a head like that, he couldn't be anything else but dead. Ha, ha, ha," said Bull. "I'm so happy," he said nonchalantly.

"Amen," said Juan.

The quiet was broken. This time by the squeal of sirens converging from different directions.

"Brothers," called Jimbo, getting to his feet. "You know, with this guy dead," he looked them all in the eye with a pleased look, "our arson problems are over. There's nobody to start the fires."

"You got to be kidding," snapped Mulligan, with a chuckle. "The whole South Bronx is being burned. And if it does stop *around here*, that will be because there is nothing left to burn. Not because this scumbag is dead."

Jimbo disagreed with Mulligan, insisting the arson was over.

"And by the way," said Mulligan, getting their attention, "see that wig Jimbo's holding? That's how Jose continued to operate undetected. He disguised himself as a gray-haired old man. I saw him earlier."

The loud noise of the two arriving ambulances, with their sirens at full blast, made it difficult for Packy to hear the message coming in from the dispatcher. But he heard the key words, "Five-Nine," and "available for a building fire."

"Stand by, dispatch," Packy replied. "Lt. Bannon, are we available for a building fire?"

Raising one finger, Lt. Bannon shouted back, "One moment." He then put words in the attendant's mouth: "Hey pal, we have a fire to go to. You don't need us, right?"

"Nah. There's four of us."

"We're available," shouted Lt. Bannon. Then, with a wave of his hand, he shouted, "Let's go, Five-Nine! Think we got a job."

Packy smiled, as he advised the dispatcher of their availability.

"Okay, Five Nine! Respond to a phone alarm for box 2–7–4–3, a building fire on Charlotte and Jennings Street. Take Engine 85 with you."

Packy jumped into the driver's seat, hitting the siren to clear the area of pedestrians. Straight ahead down Boston Road towards their firehouse, he saw a huge column of smoke.

"Hey, Lieu, looks like there's a fire right by our firehouse. Guess we're going to have to miss that one."

"Yeah. We got our own right here," said Lt. Bannon, pointing down towards Jennings Street.

All heads turned in the direction of the corner of Charlotte Street and Jennings, where Santana's would be, where another column of smoke rolled up into the sky.

"Check it out, man," said Mulligan. He put his tools back on the rig.

"Yeah, we'll check that out." Lt. Bannon pointed to the smoke back by the firehouse. "Oh boy! Looks like it's going to be one of those nights."

As much as they wanted the arson fires to stop, they still got charged up when they knew they had a job. They started yelling to each other, readying themselves for the hell they were about to enter.

"As Luke would say, 'Let's go kick the red devil's ass,'" shouted Mulligan.

A speeding police car pulled up, coming to a halt right next to Mulligan's seat. The doors flung open with two gun-toting cops jumping out. "Where are you guys going? We need information, man," one of them said.

"We got a fire. Gotta go, man. The dead guy set the fire where the fireman was killed," said Mulligan, leaning out the side window, pointing to the upturned car. He shouted a description of the shooter as the rig moved away.

Ladder 59 sped off, leaving the two cops open-mouthed, proceeding down Wilkins Avenue to Jennings Street, where it would cut across to Charlotte.

They heard one of the cops shout, "Detectives will want to talk to you guys."

Again the rig was hit by several missiles. A bottle shattered on Lt. Bannon's side window. He flinched, looked out the side window, then calmly shook his head. There were several more thumps on the rig.

"I thought the police caught the bottle throwers," shouted Mulligan. "Must be their replacements."

Lt. Bannon didn't even report the incident to the dispatcher. He knew it would be a waste of time.

When Ladder 59 pulled into Jennings Street, a fast-spreading fire awaited them on the corner of Charlotte and Jennings. Flames and heavy smoke were rolling upward from every visible window of the top three apartments—one above the other—on the front left side of the building that was home to Ester and her girlfriend, Carmen, and Santana's bodega. Until that moment, every apartment had a tenant. Fire was burning through the roof.

Even though most of the tenants were already out of the building or at work, several people were still escaping down the fire escape.

Hardly noticed by the men of Ladder 59 as they pulled into the block were the four defiant-looking men who crossed the street in front of them, heading away from the fire. One of them wore a hemp Fedora and a yellowish shirt, fitting

Chico's description of the gunman who shot Jose. There was a fourth man with them, a young man not seen before.

Mulligan did a double-take. "That's the hat," he shouted. "The guy who did the shooting. They're the guys Molletti took the picture of standing outside the El Tico—Jose's partners." *Now I know what Molletti meant when he said, 'Let his gang mates take care of him instead of us.'* He didn't recognize the fourth man. He was younger, perhaps Jose's replacement.

Now everybody turned to get a look at them. But they were too late. All they saw were the backs of the strutting-cool culprits.

"Look! Over towards Miniford," shouted Lt. Bannon. He caught a glimpse of another fire; rolling smoke clouds soaring up from the back of an apartment building. "That makes number three. I better call it in. Fifty-Nine to Bronx. You better send another full assignment for a separate building fire at Charlotte Street and Miniford Place."

Fifty-Nine stopped just beyond Santana's. "Let's go, Irish Tigers," shouted Lt. Bannon.

Mulligan yelled back, "Good man, Lieu. I like that. Just for Luke."

They exited the rig together: Mulligan, Juan, Lt. Bannon, Bull, Packy, and Copper. They jogged toward the building, passing Engine 85 that was stretching a hose line. Some of the people in the street were helping them with the stretch.

"Here we go again," Mulligan yelled to Jimbo. "Do you still think our arson problem is over?"

"I guess I was wrong this time thinking that the arson ended with Jose." Jimbo continued, "I guess the burning will continue as long our City's leaders remain sitting with their thumbs up their asses."

Mulligan ran to the underside of the fire escape to release the drop ladder. The rest of Ladder 59 started into the courtyard.

EPILOGUE

In 1977, ten years after the arson-for-profit blitz began in earnest in the South Bronx, New York City finally gave the Bureau of Fire Investigation the manpower it needed to deal with the arson problem. Unfortunately, by then the Charlotte Street area, as well as many other large areas of the Bronx, Brooklyn, and Manhattan, were already gutted, gone, literally burned to the ground.

The damage was done; or as some would say, the areas to be rehabilitated were now cleared. Streets that were once teeming with people, jammed with six-story tenements and multiple dwellings, were completely deserted. They were now devoid of people and housing.

The destruction of the South Bronx and the relocation of hundreds of thousands of people were complete.

ABOUT THE AUTHOR

John Finucane retired as a lieutenant in the New York City Fire Department. Cited several times for bravery, he was granted membership in the Department's Honor Legion. He was writer, editor, and publisher of the *American Irish News-letter* for more than twenty years, and was also the founder and chairperson of the Advocates for a 9-11 Fallen Heroes Memorial (2002–2005).

Made in the USA
Middletown, DE
08 December 2020